A STRING OF SHOOTINGS. A list of victims. A wealth of suspects. And it all hinges on one dead man …

It's been a year since ex-NYPD detectives (and former enemies) Joe Serpe and Bob Healy teamed up to solve the murder of a retarded young man who worked at Joe's company and prevented the Russian Mafia from infiltrating the home heating oil business on Long Island. Now partners in an oil business of their own, Serpe and Healy are faced with an even more heinous series of crimes: Five oil truck drivers have been robbed and shot to death, their lifeless bodies left to bleed out on the cold and loveless suburban streets.

But the killer should have chosen his victims more wisely. The fourth victim, Rusty Monaco, was another retired NYPD detective—one who once saved Joe Serpe's life while they were both still on the job—and Serpe won't let that debt die with Rusty.

As Serpe and Healy dig into the murders of the five Long Island oil truck drivers, they descend through several rings of hell, a hell that isn't just confined to the Long Island suburbs. Following a trail littered with the bodies of the guilty and innocent alike, they investigate leads from a crime-ridden Indian reservation to a Brooklyn housing project, from a day-old homicide to a nearly forgotten murder that happened in the wake of 9/11. There are reams of evidence, but none of it seems to hang together. What possible connection can there be between a firebrand African-American preacher from Brooklyn and the murders of oil truck drivers in Suffolk County? How is the owner of a failing auto body shop connected? Are Serpe and Healy too busy looking at the wrong suspects that they miss the most obvious suspect of all?

The Fourth Victim is a tale of greed, blackmail, corruption, vengeance, racism, fear, and what righteous men do in the face of a world gone wrong.

Also by Tony Spinosa

Hose Monkey

THE
FOU4RTH
VICTIM

Published by
BLEAK HOUSE BOOKS
a division of Big Earth Publishing
923 Williamson St.
Madison, WI 53703
www.bleakhousebooks.com

Library of Congress Cataloging-In-Publication Data has been applied for

12 11 10 09 08   1 2 3 4 5 6 7 8 9 10

ISBN 13: 978-1-60648-009-0 (Trade Cloth)
ISBN 13: 978-1-60648-010-6 (Trade Paper)
ISBN 13: 978-1-60648-011-3 (Evidence Collection)

TONY SPINOSA

THE FOU4RTH VICTIM

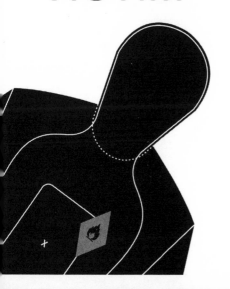

Bleak House Books
Madison, Wisconsin

ACKNOWLEDGMENTS

I would like to thank my first readers and listeners Peter, Megan, Ken, and Ellen. I would also like to thank Bob Gloria and everyone else at Bell Oil, Inc. None of this would have been possible or worth it without Rosanne, Kaitlin, and Dylan.

For Meredith, Jesse, Bradley, Jeremy, and Laura

And now the sparrows warring in the eaves,
The curd-pale moon, the white stars in the sky,
And the loud chaunting of the unquiet leaves,
Are shaken with earth's old and weary cry.

—W. B. Yeats "The Sorrow of Love"

[Canadians]

TUESDAY, JANUARY 4TH, 2005

At his best, Rusty Monaco was a miserable, self-absorbed prick and tonight he was paying even less attention than usual to the world outside his head. That was saying something given that it was raining like a son of a bitch and that the night had swallowed whole any last traces of daylight. If he'd been the type of man to notice, the transition from day to night would have taken him by surprise. It snuck up on a man; at one stop the sun was out and by the time he got his truck to the next drop, it was like the sun had never shined. It was light, then it wasn't, and the dark was always mournful. But Rusty Monaco wasn't the type of man to notice.

Even when he was on the job, he never gave the quality of light much thought. Rusty's two years on the truck, the two years since he'd put in his papers, hadn't much changed him. He lived at face value. Everything was, according to Monaco, as is. You look beneath the surface and you find more surface. Beneath that, only bullshit. That attitude had served him well on the streets. Yet even he would have been forced to admit that spending so much time alone on the truck allowed a man to sometimes see things that maybe he'd forgotten or things he never knew existed. Not tonight. Tonight he was blind with distraction.

Monaco had a lot on his mind other than the wet, the cold, the dark. He was oblivious to his normal misgivings about doing deliveries at night, about the fact that he had two more to go after this next one. Shit, he didn't even care that the stops were in Wyandanch. Usually, he'd swap out his Wyandanch and Wheatley Heights deliveries regardless of the extra driving involved. The other drivers at Armor Oil, Inc. were only too happy to trade in their pain-in-the-balls north shore stops—backing down long driveways, hundred foot uphill hose pulls, my-shit-don't-stink customers—for a little time with the Canadians.

Canadians, that was copspeak for niggers. Monaco knew several other colorful code words for African-Americans, but they all meant the same thing. Twenty-three years on the job in the city had given him his fill of Canadians, thank you very much. First in uniform and then as a detective, no matter where the NYPD stuck him, it was always jungleland.

"The eggplants are ruinin' this city," he remembered his training officer saying. "Fucking animals, the lot of 'em."

Nothing in Rusty Monaco's experience had done a thing to disabuse him from that point of view. After more than two decades in the shit, his own assessment wasn't nearly so pleasant. Soon none of it would matter, as the envelope of signed closing documents on the seat next to him attested. His condo in Plantation City was singing the siren's song, but currently the growl and rumble of the truck and the noise of his own thoughts made it impossible for Rusty to hear it. Finally, he turned the International left off Nicholls onto Buchanan.

"Ah, fuck!" he groaned, the darkness and rain refusing to be ignored any longer.

Squinting his eyes as he slowly rolled the truck down the block, Monaco looked through the sheets of rain for an address, any address, so he could establish odd and even sides of the street. He was a third of the way down Buchanan Avenue before he found a numbered house.

"Niggers," he said. "No pride."

The delivery would be on the driver's side of the street. Although that was of no consequence, he was about to discover something that was.

"Shit!" He slammed his fist into the steering wheel. "A dead fuckin' end."

He pressed down hard on the brake pedal and clutch, the truck lurching to a stop. The rig swayed slightly as seven hundred gallons of home heating oil sloshed around in the tank behind him. Not only was Buchanan Avenue a dead end, it was a dead end with no turn around. Monaco cursed himself for his unfamiliarity with the area. The other Armor drivers would have known to back down the street. In good weather, in daylight, he might back the rig up to Nicholls, swing her around, and come down the block ass end first, but with shitty visibility and parked cars lining both sides of the street, that wasn't an option now. Already two thirds of the way down the block, he was committed. He let his foot off the brake, put the International in first gear, and eased up on the clutch.

It just gets better and better, Monaco thought, pulling up to the last house on the left side of the block. He checked the ticket. The address was right. Unfortunately, the house was utterly dark, but not just *no-one's-home* dark. It was *the-bank-has-foreclosed-on-this-shitbox-and-they-can't-give-it-away* dark. Still, he had to get out of the truck and try to make the delivery. You got paid per delivery, not per attempt. He didn't like it, but that's how the system worked. One way or the other, he'd been banging his head against the system his whole life. He popped out the parking brake, stepped on the clutch, flipped on the PTO, released the clutch, grabbed the delivery ticket, and climbed down out of the cab.

It was colder out than he remembered, his breath throwing out huge plumes of vapor before him. At least the rain had let up some, but the thin sheet of water on the asphalt felt slick beneath the soles of his boots. If the temperature dropped another degree or two, it would be a holiday on ice. Nothing like driving a thirty foot long, thirty ton rig on icy roads. Every red light became an adventure.

He took the stoop steps two at a time. There were jagged remnants of a bulb in the porch light fixture and two moot copper wires sticking through a hole where a doorbell should have been. He rapped his knuckles on the front door, peeling paint flecking off like dandruff.

"Armor Fuel," he said, feeling foolish for even bothering. He didn't bother trying a second time and rushed back to the warmth of the cab. He never quite made it, slipping on the last step and sprawling face first out into the street. Before Rusty could push himself back up, he felt something colder than the air and very hard being pressed into the back of his head. "Fuckin' nig—"

He never did finish the thought or make those last deliveries.

[Fifty-first Gallon]

WEDNESDAY, JANUARY 5TH, 2005—MORNING

Joe Serpe stood atop the tank of his old green Mack, guiding the six foot long fill manifold through the open hatch. When he heard the mouth of the manifold clank against the bottom of the aluminum tank, he eased the manifold handle forward and the pump squealed slowly to life. Joe knew the routine; the first fifty gallons of the three thousand to be loaded would fairly trickle out, the meter click, click, clicking like the second hand on a watch. Then the oil would gush out of the pipe against the bottom of the tank with such force that it would lift the top of the manifold six inches above the rim of the hatch. He had seen rookie drivers panic the first time they loaded their rigs by themselves, when, seemingly with a a will of its own, the manifold reared up that way.

Serpe didn't need to look behind him to know the sun was coming up. He could feel it warming his back and see its rays reflected in the fine, red-dyed mist spraying out of the open hatch. As he kneeled to look into the abyss of the tank to make sure the manifold was still seated right, he caught a full on whiff of #2 home heating oil. Some people's mornings smelled like fresh roasted coffee and frying bacon. His smelled like a high school chemistry experiment. His entire life smelled of it, though he rarely noticed. He spent even less time worrying about what these fumes and his truck's diesel exhaust were doing to his lungs. It didn't pay for a man to focus on those kinds of things.

Although he had loaded the tugboat—his nickname for the green Mack—this way six days a week for years now, the process was still a revelation to him. Just lately he'd become fixated with the fifty-first gallon, with the transition from trickle to gush. It was that transition, the moment when things went from control to chaos, the moment when things slipped away that fascinated Joe Serpe. If only he could learn the secret of that transition, he thought, he might comprehend how he had lost Marla. For as sure as the sun was coming up at his back, she had slipped slowly away from him. He knew the signs. He had heard the clicking of the meter, but still he had been unable to stop her from leaving. No one knew loss better than Joe Serpe. No one.

Over the past decade, he had lost everyone and everything of value in his life. Once a legendary NYPD narcotics detective, Serpe had gotten jammed up covering for his partner and best friend Ralphy Abruzzi. Not only was Joe forced to leave the job in disgrace, but he had to testify as a prosecution witness in open court. Ralphy, godfather to Joe's son, ate buckshot for breakfast the weekend before his sentencing hearing. After the suicide, the few cop friends Joe had left, abandoned him. Although it was Ralph who had the coke habit, who stole and extorted money, who eventually sold information and protection to dealers, it was Joe Serpe who was to be punished.

The media frenzy surrounding the trial and the fallout from the suicide cost Serpe more than a few friends. The stress destroyed his already fractured marriage; his wife and son fleeing to Florida before the ink was dry on the divorce decree. Joe didn't mind losing his wife so much, but the distance—emotional and geographical—between him and his boy was pure hell. While the distance in miles remained constant, the emotional distance grew so that they barely spoke.

None of it—the trial, the suicide, the divorce, the estrangement—hit Joe nearly as hard as the death of his fireman brother on September 11, 2001. Vinny was crushed by debris as the first tower collapsed. That was the final blow. On that day, Joe Serpe's world grew so small that it would have fit inside a paper cup. God, Joe thought, had a funny way of showing his boundless love for humankind. That day he handed the Almighty Mindfucker his pink slip and began his slide into the bottle.

So no, no one had to school Joe Serpe on the subtleties of the signs of loss: the emptiness, the nagging questions, the long sleepless nights. Very few men had lost as much or fallen quite as far and lived to tell about it. Even fewer had picked themselves back up and rebuilt their lives. But to rebuild his life, Joe had been forced to come to an uneasy understanding with loss.

As he noticed the rising pink foam near the lip of the hatch, Joe gazed quickly at the meter to his left. With fifty gallons to go, he eased back gently on the loading handle to slow the pumping: …2956…69…76…89…96…97…98…3000. Silence. Serpe hit the red cut-off button and lifted up the spring-loaded manifold so that its mouth rested only inches above the surface of the oil in the tugboat's tank. This permitted whatever oil was left in the pipeline to drizzle out into the tank. When it was down to a spit, he lifted the manifold up to shoulder height, hooked a capture bucket onto the end of the pipe, and folded back the loading arm to clear room for the truck that would follow the tugboat into the loading rack.

Climbing down off the loading platform and disconnecting the grounding plug from the chassis of his truck, Serpe realized he had learned nothing, that there were no lessons to be learned from the fifty-first gallon. Marla was gone. Deep down he knew that even if he comprehended the mechanics of her leaving, he couldn't have stopped it.

He removed the wheel chock, got into the tugboat and drove the fifty feet or so to the checkout booth. Out of the truck again and inside the booth, Joe waved his magnetic loading card at the scanner and the printer spit out his bill of lading. Still thinking about Marla, it took him a minute to see the notice posted on the wall above the printer. Even then it didn't quite register.

WARNING:
ALL C.O.D. OIL DRIVERS BEWARE
FOURTH DRIVER ROBBED AND MURDERED
MEETING 7PM TONIGHT AT ST. PATRICK'S GYM
SUFFOLK P.D. REPS TO ATTEND

Only when Serpe saw the second notice, the one about the wake for Rusty Monaco, did it hit home. He mouthed the dead man's name and hung his head. There was history between Monaco and Serpe, a debt that now could never be repaid.

★   ★   ★   ★

The trucks were all out and the phones had slowed down, so Bob Healy finally had a chance to breathe. He sat down at his desk with a fresh cup of coffee, a buttered roll, and a copy of *Newsday*. He still hadn't gotten quite used to the five o'clock alarm and life in a trailer in an oil yard. He'd been coming into the office for a few months now, quoting prices, answering phones, taking stops, laying out delivery routes, but he wasn't liking it much. The yard was either dusty or muddy depending on the weather. It stank of diesel fumes in the morning when the trucks warmed up and of heating oil the rest of the time. And when they used certain runways at nearby MacArthur Airport, it smelled of spent jet fuel. The trailer itself was a dump; too hot in summer and an icebox in winter. Besides all that, it was paradise.

Like he had told Joe in the hospital after Serpe had been shot, retired cops were good at only two things: owning bars or working security. Joe didn't disagree. The plan was that the two of them would open a bar together someday, but Joe Serpe knew the oil business. He had learned it the hard way; starting on the bottom rung as a hose monkey, then driving Sunday, holiday, and night shifts. He knew how to make money at it. So the two of them had compromised. They pooled their resources to buy back Mayday Fuel from the government who had seized it from a Russian mob's front company. They put aside a set amount of money each week out of the profits toward the purchase of a bar. Two years, that was the plan. Two years and then Healy could get out from behind the dispatcher's desk and get behind the bar.

Healy sipped the coffee and made a sour face. Christ, he thought, even the coffee was beginning to taste like fucking heating oil. He flipped the paper over from the sports section to the front page, saw the headlines, and nearly shit.

[The French Connection]

Bob Healy heard the throaty growl of the tugboat before it even turned off Hawkins onto Union. He held up his right wrist, checking his watch against the reality of the night. It wasn't as late as it seemed, only 5:15, but John and Anthony had brought in the other two trucks over an hour ago and cashed out. That was Joe's new rule. Until the cops caught the skell killing the COD drivers, he didn't want his trucks out on the street after dark. A life, anybody's life, was too precious to be pissed away for an extra forty or fifty bucks. Anybody's life, of course, except Joe's.

He didn't feel the rules applied to him. He had once been supercop, Joe "the Snake" Serpe, doing buy and bust operations in the worst parts of New York City. He could smell trouble coming and felt sure he could handle anything. If Colombian drug gangs didn't scare him, he wasn't going to be intimidated by some cowardly piece of shit who hid in dark corners killing hard working men. Although Joe had lost his carry privileges when he had his troubles, he always kept the Glock Healy had given him tucked in his waistband.

Healy didn't talk right away when his partner came hobbling through the office door. First, he let Joe put down his map and metal ticket box, let him exhale and wash up. Only after Joe emerged from the trailer's coffin-sized bathroom, his limp more pronounced after a full day on the truck, did Healy speak.

"The leg hurting?" Bob asked.

Like a motherfucker. "It aches a little all the time, but it just gets weak after twenty-three stops."

"So, you heard about Rusty Monaco, huh?"

"I heard."

"I knew him," Healy said.

"You did?"

"Yeah."

Joe shook his head. "Internal Affairs detective knows you, that can't be a good sign."

"I knew *you.*"

"Yeah, and you ruined my career."

"That was your loyalty to Ralph Abruzzi that did that, remember? I just came around with the broom and dust pan to sweep up what was left."

They let that hang in the air between them like a balloon filled with poison gas. This was the first time since Joe had been in the hospital recovering from his leg wound that the subject had come up. Although now friends and partners, they both took great pains to avoid the details surrounding Joe's dismissal and disgrace. Neither one of them could claim innocence in this area.

"Fair enough," Serpe said, diffusing the tension. "So what was your beef with Monaco?"

"You mean besides the fact that he was a miserable son of a bitch?"

"Not for nothing, Healy, but half the NYPD are miserable fucks. So yeah, besides that."

"First five or six times it was for excessive force. He tended to be a little too enthusiastic with his fists. Then the last time it was that rooftop thing in Brooklyn. You know, when the black kid allegedly waved a pistol at him and the kid wound up impaled on the courtyard fence twenty stories below. If that incident didn't happen right after Nine/ Eleven, it would've been a major scandal."

"Did he murder the kid, do you think?" Joe asked.

"We couldn't prove it. Doesn't mean he didn't do it. And let's just say that in the wake of the terror attack, the department didn't have much enthusiasm for hanging a cop, any cop, even one like Rusty Monaco, out to dry."

"But do *you* think he did it?"

"Rusty Monaco was a piece of shit and a disgrace to the shield."

"Don't pull your punches or anything, Bob. Tell me how you really feel about him."

"Why are you so interested, huh? Were you two buddies or something?"

Serpe shook his head yes. "Or something. I knew the man, too."

"And what'd you think of him?"

"That he was a violent, miserable, racist prick, but—"

"But! Are you kidding me? You're not seriously going to defend this guy to me, are you? It was miraculous that he didn't end up in prison, never mind lose his pension. He was an asshole."

"No doubt, but an asshole who saved my life."

☆　　☆　　☆　　☆

Albie Jimenez was breathing easy. He had gotten his green card a year ago and his Hazmat license two months after that. Finally, he had been able to stop living in that shadow world in which most of his friends were forced to exist. Life on Long Island was strange enough for a man from Tehuacan, Mexico without having to loiter in front of the 7/Eleven on Horse Block Road with a hundred and fifty other Mexicans and Salvadorans waiting to be chosen like cattle at auction.

Those days were in Albie's past. Now he kept his eyes only ahead. Soon he'd have the cash to send for his wife and son. He even had a binder on a two bedroom house on Westwood Avenue in Brentwood. It needed some work, but he wasn't afraid of work. Life was good and it would get better as soon as the authorities caught that *cono* who was killing his fellow drivers. Not that Albie was too worried. He did his deliveries far away from the *myates*, in towns where his own skin was darkest.

He turned his Ford right off Indian Head Road onto Old Northport Road, past the driving range and into the heart of the industrial area between Commack and Kings Park.

A little bit before the gates of the masonry supply yard, he spotted a car parked in the road at an odd angle. There was a woman lying between the side of the car and the shoulder of the road. Albie skidded the Ford to a stop, put on his flashers, and hopped out of the cab.

"Hey, lady," he called, reaching for his cell phone. "Lady, you okay?"

Then something disrupted his world. There was a thunderous ringing, but it sounded as if it was coming from inside his head. Except for the pounding of his own heart and the whoosh of his breaths, the ringing was all he could hear. The asphalt came to life, rolling like black waves beneath his boots. He nearly steadied himself against the asphalt tide, but in the end he just could not keep his balance and he tumbled face first into the solid surf. Then, when he was down, things got quiet and dark, impossibly dark.

☆　☆　☆　☆

"He saved your life, huh? How'd he manage that?" Healy asked.

"It was eighty-nine and me and Ralphy and Monaco were assigned to a federally funded task force aimed at clearing drugs out of city housing projects."

"Yeah, like that was ever gonna happen. You could blow up everyone of those projects and they'd be selling drugs outta the rubble."

"Wasn't my idea."

"What happened?"

"Ralphy and me got a tip that Papa Doc Willingham's crew was running a major crack distribution center out in one of the apartment houses in Bath Beach across the little bridge from Coney Island. I forget the name of the project, but you know the one. It's where they shot that sniper scene in *The French Connection*."

"Yeah," Healy said, his face lighting up, "the ones by the elevated subway over there by Dewey High School."

"Right. So the thing is we got this information, but we're supposed to run everything up the chain of command before we take any action. It was a total cluster fuck because by the time any info got up to the top of the chain, it was worthless. Big drug operators aren't stupid. They're moving their shit around all the time to protect their assets from the cops and competitors. And there were other problems too. Not only was our chain of command long, but it was leaky too. Anything we knew tended to get known by anyone who was a target. Even when we could manage to keep intelligence in house, the feds always insisted we do a full on assault. It was like trying to catch someone by surprise with the Third Army behind you. Spotters saw us coming from the next neighborhood over."

"So you decided, what, that you were going outside the chain of command?"

"Something like that, yeah, but it was just me and Ralphy who wanted to go in. Monaco was put on the task force by his captain to dump his problem child on somebody else's doorstep. This was after one of those incidents you were talking about, so Monaco was just doing time, you know, trying to keep his nose clean until his next assignment. But he was on duty with us that night and knew the layout of those buildings better than we did. I'll spare you the details of how we got inside and got passed the spotters. It's the kind of stuff that would just piss you off."

"Okay, I'll take your word for it," Healy said.

"Anyway, we grab the last spotter in the stairwell and we persuade him that it's in his best interests to help us. He was easy to convince. So we step into the hallway and it's completely quiet. We get to the door and the spotter gives the password and we think we're in. The door pulls back and the minute it does, I know it's wrong. Before I can even blink, all hell breaks loose. Ralphy got our shotgun and hears something to his left and wheels around that way. I step out to push the spotter out of the line of fire, but a shotgun blast comes out of the apartment and hits him square in the chest. He falls back taking me with him, so I'm down with this guy's body on me and my gun hand is pinned to the floor. Ralphy's screaming 'NYPD, don't move!' at whoever he thinks is coming down the hall. I'm trying to free myself and this fat fuck charges out of the apartment with a sawed-off in his hands.

"Monaco can't fire because the hall is so dark and Ralphy's just a few feet away on the opposite side of the big man. If he misses, he'd hit Ralphy. He can't even fire a warning shot because the hallway's all concrete and tile. A bullet might ricochet anywhere. Meanwhile the fat man bends over me and puts the shotgun so close to my face I can feel the residual heat from the first shot. I squeezed my eyes shut and started praying. There's a second blast. Its heat registers even before the concussion. My ears are ringing like crazy and there's Monaco all over the big bastard. Ralphy comes over and puts the cocksucker down with the butt of his shotgun. In the end it was all bullshit. There was no stash in the apartment. We'd been set up."

"Wait a second, Joe. I read all of your jackets. I've gone over everyone of your cases. Fact is, I probably know your cases better than you do and I never saw anything about this."

"That's right, you didn't. Officially, it never happened."

"Forget it. I'm not even going to ask."

"Okay, but the fact is that Rusty Monaco, nasty prick that he was, is the reason I still got this head on this neck. I owe him for that."

"Yeah, but how much?"

★　★　★　★

He held the dead man's driver's license up to the flashlight.

"Not your lucky day, Jimenez...Alberto, you stupid fuck. How much did he have on him?"

"Twenty-two seventy-eight. He was a busy little amigo."

"Yeah, meanwhile all he had in his wallet was four bucks. He was really living the American dream. Stupid moron. Come on, let's wrap him up."

They rolled the body onto the blue plastic tarp, neatly tucking in the edges.

"He's like a little burrito."

"Very funny, asshole. D'you get rid of—"

"Don't worry about her. She's not gonna say nothing."

"You sure?"

"Yeah, I gave her a sample of what would happen if she opened her mouth."

"Okay, then let's finish up with Alberto over here and get going."

☆　☆　☆　☆

Serpe didn't answer Healy's question, but they both knew he was going to take Monaco's murder on his shoulders. That's what made Serpe the man he was and what made Healy admire him even as he built the case against Joe that would end his police career. Healy hadn't been a sentimental type or the kind of man to lose sleep over putting other cops away. Healy was a man who believed in right and wrong, good and evil; one type of good, all sorts of evil. And to mask evil with a badge or hide it behind a priest's collar was plain wrong. It was that granite conviction that gave him the strength to withstand the withering criticism and abuse he received at the hands of other cops during his twenty plus years in the Internal Affairs Bureau.

Soon after putting in his papers and settling into retirement with his wife Mary, the bottom dropped out of the assumptions by which he had lived his life and that rock solid foundation crumbled. He and Mary had long ago agreed that she would put up with whatever she had to until Bob left the job, but after that, the time was hers. Problem was, the time wasn't hers to bargain with. Within a year, she was dead of pancreatic cancer.

For months after Mary's death, he'd been haunted, haunted by the anger in her eyes, by the silent accusation that he had somehow cheated her out of her due. He was haunted by the thought that Mary had paid his karmic bill for all the lives he'd help destroy. The faces of dirty cops came to Bob Healy in his sleep, especially the ones that had, like Ralphy Abruzzi, eaten their guns instead of facing the fallout from their crimes. Bob Healy questioned everything about his beliefs and for the first time in his life he found little solace in the church. So it was no small irony that Joe Serpe had been the man to help him find his way back and why, in spite of how he felt about the late Rusty Monaco, that he would help Serpe find the killer.

"You're going after this guy, huh?" Healy asked, threading the thick chain through both sides of the yard gate.

"You have to ask?" Serpe hooked the heavy lock through the end links of the chain and snapped it shut.

"Stupid question. I know."

"Where you headed?" Joe tugged hard on the chain.

"I'm gonna grab a bite and then head over to that meeting at St. Pat's. You?"

"Heading home and then maybe I'll drop by Lugo's to hear if the drivers have any ideas about what's really going on."

"Okay. See ya in the morning."

"Yeah."

Healy sat in his car a minute, watching his partner's taillights fade in the distance. Rusty Monaco might have been a worthless piece of shit, but, Healy thought, it would be good to feel like a cop again.

☆　☆　☆　☆

"Where the fuck are we gonna put him?"

"Shit! I didn't really think about that. Let me see."

"Now's a little late to start thinking about it, don't you think?"

"What the fuck else you want me to do, asshole? We can't leave him here."

"We can unscrew the brace that holds the hatch to the top of the tank and throw him in there."

"You must be a fucking rocket scientist. If we throw him in there, then how the fuck are we supposed to get him out of the tank when we get where we're going? We'd have to jump in there after him and I ain't diving into no fucking tank fulla heating oil. Besides, it sorta defeats the purpose if the cops can figure out Speedy Gonzales's body's been moved."

"We can put him in the cab with us."

"Yeah, that'll work great, especially if the cops pull us over. 'Sorry officer, never mind the dead wetback in the tarp. He's just sleeping.'"

"Then what the fuck are we gonna do?"

"I'm thinking… Okay, I got it. Help me lift him up on top of the tank. We'll wedge him in there between the rail and the hatch."

*   *   *   *

Joe Serpe was a tough motherfucker. Ask anyone who knew him or cut too closely across his path. And he was a smart guy in that feral kind of way, but he wasn't much of a deep thinker. Deep thinking and cop work didn't go together like hand in glove. Oil delivery and deep thinking was even less well-suited. But since Marla came and went, he had changed.

He now dreaded the part of the day between the end of work and sleep. Earlier in the day he had the business to worry about. At night he was too exhausted to beat himself up. This is when the guilt got to him. It wasn't guilt over losing her exactly. Guilt over loss, Joe Serpe had long ago learned, was a colossal waste of time. No it wasn't that. It was that he had ruined her.

He needed to get out of the house before the walls closed in.

*   *   *   *

They pulled Albie Jimenez's truck over to the prearranged spot by where they'd left their car. After their earlier missteps, things had gone smoothly. They hadn't been stopped on their journey south and east across Suffolk. No one had even seemed to notice them. It's not like oil trucks were a rare winter sight on Long Island. Now all that remained was for them to retrieve the body from the top of the tank and dump it.

"Here, take the flash and get up there. I'll follow you up."
"Fuck!"
"What is it?"
"Jesus Christ!"
"What the fuck is it?"
"You better get up here, man."
"I'm right behind you. What the—"
"He ain't here."
"I can see that, shithead, but where the fuck did he go?"

"Fuck if I know."

"Dead men don't fly. He *was* dead, right?"

"I think so."

"What do you mean, you think so?"

"I mean, I think so. We smashed his head up pretty good. He wasn't moving or nothing."

"Did you check his pulse?"

"Did you?"

"Do I look like a fucking doctor?"

"Do *I*?"

"Nah, you're right, he was dead."

"Maybe he fell off. We hit some pretty good pot holes."

"Fuck!"

"Yeah, come on, let's wipe the truck down and get the fuck outta here."

[Poospatuck Creek]

WEDNESDAY JANUARY 5TH, 2005—EVENING

Located only a mile or two from the big fuel depot in Holtsville and in close proximity to most of the oil companies in central Suffolk, Lugo's Bar was a natural hangout for the area's oil drivers. Joe Serpe didn't go to Lugo's much anymore. It had once been his home away from home; the place where he'd troll for women whose desperation and loneliness was exceeded only by his own. He thought meeting Marla would put an end to all that. Now he wasn't so sure. Even with Marla gone, Joe didn't think he had it in him to go back.

These days Serpe only went to Lugo's with Healy and their drivers after a rough shift or to celebrate a good week. Delivering oil was a tough job with a lot of downside, no perks, and even fewer guarantees. Medical benefits consisted of prayer and the first aid kit on your truck. Needless to say, company loyalty was in short supply in the oil business. So when a boss had the chance to reward his drivers with little things—an extra fifty bucks here and there, a free dinner, drinks, tickets to a ballgame—he was smart to take advantage of it. Serpe had learned to be generous to his employees from Frank Randazzo, the former owner of Mayday Fuel. Joe had learned everything he knew about the business from Frank. It was Randazzo who gave Joe a job and threw him a lifeline when no one else would touch him. More than anyone else, he had helped salvage Joe's life after the loss of his job, family, and brother. Unfortunately, Frank was unable to save himself.

Frank had gotten mixed up with the Mafiya—the Russian Mob—and had been blackmailed into selling off Mayday to a front company. If it had just stopped there, with the extortion, Frank might still be alive and Joe Serpe's world might have been a very different place. But it hadn't stopped there, not at all. A retarded kid who worked for Mayday as a hose monkey—a laborer who pulled the oil hose from the truck to the house and back again—had sneaked into the oil yard one night and witnessed illegal truck transfers of black market oil. The Russians caught and murdered the kid. It was Joe Serpe who found the kid's battered body at the bottom of a tank and Joe who, in the end, found his killers. Frank, guilt ridden over his role in the hose monkey's death, tried to hang himself. He botched the job, lingering for months in a coma before finally succumbing. Though it had all happened less than a year before, it seemed to Serpe several lifetimes ago.

The thing was that Joe felt pretty naked at the moment, walking into Lugo's without Healy or his guys along for company. There were still some drivers around, but it was close to that time when the oil men headed home and the night crowd filtered in. Serpe spotted four drivers from SafetyNet Oil at one corner of the big square bar. They had a wall of empty tall boys in front of them and were laughing it up pretty good. Didn't seem like they were too broken up over Rusty Monaco's murder or too worried about meeting a similar fate.

"Gentlemen," said Joe.

They nodded hello, raising their beers in salute.

"Another round here," Joe said to the barman, gesturing at the empties.

The drivers groaned and grumbled, making noises about having to get home. Two of them actually got up and left.

Stan Brock shook his head. "Newly—fuckin'—weds! Jesus Christ, they'll learn, right Joe?"

"For their sakes, I hope so," Joe agreed.

Brock was a rough motherfucker with a gravelly voice and the scarred face of a boxer with more heart than skill and more balls than brains. His face didn't lie. He had been the kind of middle weight opposing managers liked to throw against their fighters because his hands were slow and his chin was hard. Still, he'd kicked more ass than all the men in Lugo's combined. Serpe knew it. So did everyone else in the place. Hard as he was, Brock was a good guy and a lifer. When they buried him, there'd be a hose and nozzle sticking out of the coffin.

"I'm outta here too," said Paulie Falcone, shaking Joe's hand and slapping Brock on the shoulder. "Some other time, Joe, okay?"

"No problem."

"I guess that just leaves me and you," Stan said, patting the stool next to him. "Park yourself."

Joe sat. The bartender, who'd already uncapped five bottles of Coors, scowled at Serpe and the newly vacated seats. "Try not to cry about it, pal. I'll take care of it."

"Don't mind him," Brock said loud enough for the barman to hear, "his pussy's sore." That got a laugh from everybody but the bartender. "So what's shakin', Joe? I don't see you around here so much no more."

"Busy trying to keep my head above the shit."

"Wrong business if you don't like shit in your nostrils."

"Tell me about it, Stan. Much harder to run a business than it looked from the other end of the hose."

"Never wanted to be the boss of anything in my life. Tough enough being the boss of me."

"I hear that."

Brock turned to face Serpe. "So what are you really doin' here?"

Joe thought about being coy with Stan, but decided that would be a waste of time. He knew the ex-pug was smarter than he appeared. On the job he had learned that brains and wisdom came in all kinds of packages and that stupidity often came in the gift wrapped boxes. So he answered Stan straight:

"Rusty Monaco."

"Asshole."

"I see you knew him."

"Enough to not wanna know him better."

"Aren't you being a little harsh on the dearly departed?"

"May he rest in peace." Brock crossed himself. "What's the interest?"

"We were on the job together a little bit and I owed him."

"Seems somebody took care of the debt for you," Stan said.

"Wasn't that kind of debt."

"Money's easier."

"Only time it is," Joe said. "I'm taking a little unofficial look into the murders, so anything you know or hear about them…"

Brock knocked down his beer in a swig, stood up and shook Serpe's hand.

"Thanks for the beer, Joe. Somebody's gotta catch this motherfucker. Drivers are nervous out there and nervous people do stupid things. All we need is for some panicked driver to shoot a customer or some guy walking up to a truck to ask directions. We'd all be fucked."

"Yeah."

"If you find this guy before the cops, you call me first. I ain't hit the heavy bag in alotta years."

Joe watched Brock amble out of the bar. When Brock disappeared, Serpe turned to ponder the three opened bottles of Coors. The barman seemed to be pondering the same thing.

★   ★   ★   ★

Bob Healy moved through the gym at St. Pat's in a bit of a daze. He'd met his wife at a CYO dance back in Brooklyn about a million years ago. He could almost feel his arms assuming the shape of Mary's young body, feel her wayward hairs brushing against his cheek as they slow danced. He thought he smelled the grassy scent of her perfume and, putting his fingers to his lips, imagined the bittersweetness of her sweat when he kissed her softly on her freckled neck. Even the squeaks of his shoes on the gym floor and the sight of the retracted basketball backboard brought Mary back to him. But when he saw the man standing at the podium, the reverie was over.

In his late forties, Suffolk County PD Detective Lieutenant Timothy

Hoskins was a hulking man with a jowly red-face and a cruel sloppy mouth. His irises were the vacant blue of a sled dog's and his lazy left eye only heightened the effect. His brown suit jacket was shiny at the elbows and it had probably fit him once, ten years and thirty pounds ago. But it wasn't Hoskins' looks or ill fitting clothes that bothered Healy. It was the man's black heart.

Last year, when the hose monkey was killed at the oil yard, Hoskins had been the lead detective. By nature, detectives get very territorial about their cases and don't often appreciate unsolicited "help" from civilians. They appreciate it even less from ex-cops. And when those ex-cops are an Internal Affairs detective and a disgraced legend who drives an oil truck, they really get surly. It didn't much help that Hoskins was related to Ralphy Abruzzi's wife. Hoskins had made their lives miserable. And given that they had publicly embarrassed Hoskins by breaking the case, his attitude toward them wasn't likely to have mellowed in the intervening months.

Healy thought about leaving, but decided he'd find a seat far away from the little stage under the retracted basket. He wasn't so much interested in what Hoskins had to say as he was in the chatter in the crowd. He knew Hoskins was unlikely to share any useful information about the homicides or the progress of the investigations. No doubt he would say something completely generic. *The investigations are moving ahead and we are following every potential lead.* Bob also knew what advice Hoskins was likely to give: *Don't deliver after dark. Don't send your drivers out alone. If you have to do deliveries after dark, have a car follow your trucks. Don't encourage any unlicensed person to carry a firearm. Blah, blah, blah...* It was the kind of advice that would have been more helpful three murders ago, but cops are necessarily reactive and were seldom out in front of the wave. When they were, they usually drowned.

Some white-toothed local politician got up before Hoskins and did five minutes on everything from property taxes to school budgets. He managed to squeeze in a few seconds on the murders, reminding the assembled crowd that none had taken place in his district. Yeah, like he had anything to do with that. Two people—his assistant and the parish priest—applauded when he turned the mike over to Hoskins. Hoskins got as far as his title and name when a uniform stepped up to him and whispered in his ear.

"You'll have to excuse me, gentlemen," he said, looking equal parts relieved and dejected. "Officer Dimeola here will help you. Goodnight."

With that, Hoskins jumped down off the stage and broke into a trot. A murmur went up in the gym, but Healy was too busy making his way to his car to notice.

★ ★ ★ ★

Something Stan Brock said was eating at Joe. Not everyone in the business *would* be equally effected if a panicky driver shot an innocent bystander. In fact, the impact of the killings had been completely lopsided. All the murder victims had been COD drivers.

What the layman didn't understand was that the oil business was really two businesses. There were COD—cash on delivery—companies like Mayday Fuel and there were big, full service companies like Gastrol and Mehan. The COD companies were non-union, operated smaller fleets, and catered to a lower income clintele. The full service outfits delivered oil too, but they offered a wide range of services and options to the customers. But as far as the murders went, there was one fundemental difference: COD drivers carried cash, often a lot of cash, and full service drivers didn't.

It wasn't a state secret. The killer knew it. And since the news media had gotten hold of the story, everyone knew it. Then why, Joe wondered, was he so irked by what Stan had said? If you were going to commit murder for money, you might as well get more than what was in a man's wallet. Maybe that was it, the logic of it that bothered him. In Serpe's experience, murder wasn't logical. He'd known crackheads to kill for pocket change. But whatever it was that was bothering him, it would have to wait.

"A penny for your thoughts," a woman cooed in his ear. Her voice was familiar, but not as familiar as it once had been.

"Hey Kath, have a seat. Here," Joe said, handing her a bottle of Coors.

THE FOU4RTH VICTIM **25**

Kathleen Cummings was blond, built, blue-eyed and, in Lugo's low lighting and loud music, it was easy to think her a catch. In the light of day, however, she was less than the sum of her parts. And as Joe discovered when they had dated, together they were even less than that. It wasn't so much that Kath had begun to fray as unravel. Nor was it so much about her looks. She was still hot by any standard. Twice divorced, Kath was the pin-up girl for bitter pills; bitter pills washed down with inevitable disappointment.

"Thanks for the brew, Joe. I heard you were married."

"Living with someone." He didn't feel like explaining about the break-up.

"To look at you, it don't seem she makes you happy."

Joe's cell vibrated in his front pocket. He made a phone of his pinky and thumb and excused himself. He walked to the back exit, pulling the cell out of his pocket.

"Yeah."

"I need you to get over here." It was Healy.

"Where's here?"

"In Mastic."

"What the fuck are you doing in—"

"Just get over here!"

"Where are you exactly?"

Healy gave the location. Joe knew the spot from when he used to drive the route for Frank.

"I'll be there in fifteen minutes. So you wanna give me a hint?"

"There's been another murder."

Serpe clicked the phone shut and headed back through Lugo's to his car parked out front. Kathleen was waiting for him just inside the back door. She didn't bother with chit chat, threading herself through his arms and kissing him hard on the mouth. He knew that no matter how he responded, he was bound to give her, if not what she wanted, then what she expected. He pulled back.

"There are guys in here that've given their left nuts to fuck me."

"You'll have to show me your collection sometime," he said, and pushed past her.

*   *   *   *

Poor and white, Mastic was the kind of place where people who fell through the cracks landed; the kind of place where cars on cinder blocks were considered lawn sculpture and pit bulls lap dogs. But no place on Long Island is ever completely safe from the real estate speculators, not even Mastic. Yet it would be quite a while before the speculators worked their way over to the area of Mastic where Bob Healy was pacing a rut in the ruined asphalt. Then when he spotted Serpe's car, he motioned madly for his partner to pull quickly over to the side of the road. Joe tucked his car half into the tall reeds just behind Healy's car.

"What's up?" Joe asked, stepping out of the car.

"Look over there," Healy said, pointing at the small fleet of Suffolk County Police vehicles parked along the south bank of Poospatuck Creek. Just across the way, on the north bank, was the Poospatuck Indian Reservation. The Shinnecock were the Long Island tribe everyone knew about. The Poospatuck were a tiny, impoverished tribe confined to fifty ugly acres of double-wide trailers along the Forge River. The major activities on the rez were selling tax free cigarettes and crime. "You see the oil truck out there?"

"Yeah. Green and white Ford L8000...looks like an Epsilon Energy truck. What would an Epsilon truck be doing way the fuck out here? They're strictly a North Shore outfit and don't deliver this far east. I don't see an ambulance or the ME's wagon. I thought you said there was another homicide."

"Trust me, partner, there was another homicide," Healy said.

"I don't know. Maybe one of their drivers got lost or something."

"Follow me."

About five feet past the front end of his car, Healy turned into the tall reeds. Serpe trailed a few yards behind.

"I can smell the oil from here," Joe said

When Healy was sure Serpe had caught up, he popped on his flashlight and aimed it at the ground near Serpe's feet.

"Holy shit!" Joe jumped back at the sight of Albie Jimenez's body laying face-up and still half covered by the blue plastic tarp.

"See what I mean about that other murder?"

"It'd be hard not to. How'd you find him?"

"Dumb luck. I followed the cops here, but I wanted to stay far enough back so they wouldn't notice me. When I came to take a leak, I nearly fell over the poor bastard."

Serpe got down on his hands and knees, grabbing the flashlight out of his partner's hand. "I don't know him, but he's wearing their uniform and he smells like home heating oil. Alberto," Joe read the name stitched into the green Epsilon coveralls. "Somebody made mashed potatoes outta his skull. The other four victims were shot, right?"

"Nine mills, either in the chest or the back of the head. At least that's what it said in the paper. They musta dumped the body here, ditched the truck over there, and split."

"I don't like it."

"Doesn't fit, huh?"

"None of it does. I guess we gotta go tell the cops," Joe said, getting to his feet.

"Not so fast, Joe. I think maybe we better just phone this one in anonymously."

"Why?"

"Because Tim Hoskins is the lead detective."

"Fuck!"

"Yeah," Healy seconded, "fuck."

[Zeus]

Friday, January 7th, 2005—Before Sunrise

They sat across the desk from each other, sipping their 7/Eleven coffees and reading the paper. A grainy photo of Alberto Jimenez was on the front page of *Newsday*, but there were scant details about the latest victim or the methods used by the newly dubbed Oilman Murderer. Some hotshot at the copy desk was probably jerking off over having come up with that one. It wasn't as catchy as Zodiac or Son of Sam nor were the victims teenage girls or prostitutes. Still, nothing gets the news media's juices flowing like a serial killer. Healy put his paper down.

"Anything about the anonymous phone call?"

"Nope."

"I see you're not dressed for delivering oil. Nice suit, Joe."

"Marla picked it out."

"I haven't wanted to ask, but—"

"It's okay," Joe said, his expression belying his words. "She's living back home with her folks. She lost her job."

"That sucks. Is she getting help?"

"Yeah, but it's not helping. This Post-traumatic shit doesn't go away overnight. I've been reading about it on the internet. Christ, Bob, she's a fucking psychologist and still it doesn't mean a thing. Those Russian motherfuckers ruined her. Getting involved with me ruined her."

Healy didn't say a word. Joe was punishing himself over Marla the same way he had punished himself over Mary. He understood that it was worse for Joe. Marla was still alive and slipping further and further out of Joe's reach. And the ugly truth was, Serpe was right. If Marla hadn't gotten involved with him, the Russians couldn't have used her as leverage.

"Do you know how many times they threatened to kill her that night? That sick fuck Pavel stuck his hand inside her and made her lick his fingers off while he held a knife to her throat, he beat her, held a gun to her head. For chrissakes, Bob, they made her watch a guy being hacked to pieces with a chainsaw. A fucking chainsaw!" Joe bit his fist in frustration. "By the time she moved out, she wouldn't let me touch her. She'd wake up screaming. She was scared all the time. And there wasn't a thing I could do about it. Not a fucking thing!"

"But there is something you can do about this!" Healy said, slapping his hand against the front page of the paper. "You're the one with the debt here, partner, not me. Try and remember that. So what's the plan?"

"I'm going to start casting the big net, asking around all the companies who lost a driver. Maybe there's a link the cops aren't seeing. With Hoskins catching the cases, that wouldn't surprise me. Then I'm going to pay a call to the Monacos."

"And me?"

"You get the easy part."

"I'm gonna love this." Healy rolled his eyes." I can tell already."

"You're gonna call your little brother George the ADA and get all the info on the homicides that they're not printing in the papers."

"Oh, is that all? Should I also sprout wings and fly like an angel? That would be easier."

"The wings are optional."

"Fuck you."

"While you're at it, call your homies at IAB and get a hold of Monaco's jacket."

"That I can do. It won't be easy, but—"

The phone rang and Healy answered, "Mayday Fuel, good morning."
When he turned back around, Joe Serpe was gone.

☆   ☆   ☆   ☆

While most drivers got along, the owners of COD oil companies
weren't exactly part of a tight knit community. These were small operations run by fiercely competitive men who'd chop their own profit mar-
gines down to nothing to steal a customer from the next guy. So while
Serpe had engendered a lot of good will when he was a driver and by
clearing the Russian mob out of the COD oil business, not many of his
fellow owners were apt to roll out the red carpet when he came calling.

Baseline Energy on Long Island Avenue in Holtsville had been the
first company to lose a driver back in late November. It was the first cold
week of the heating season and Steve Reggio was doing night deliveries so customers wouldn't get caught short on Thanksgiving. The cops
found his body alongside his truck on a dead end block in Hagerman
where it bordered North Bellport. He'd taken two bullets to the chest
and one to the back of the head. They figure the killer got away with
about twenty-five hundred bucks in cash.

Baseline Energy was a profitable company. Unlike Joe and Bob's
dusty yard, Baseline's was blacktop paved and their offices were housed
in a neat little concrete bunker. Their eight trucks were all newer than
Mayday's ragtag fleet of four. Many of the trucks were just rolling out of
the yard on their way to load when Serpe pulled up. He waited for the
trucks to leave before heading into the office.

There were two women—mother and daughter, he figured—answering the phones when Joe stepped inside the office door. The mom was
in her fifties and trying way too hard to hide her age with a raven black
dye job, skin-tight clothes, and a layer of makeup so thick it could've
been peeled off like a rubber mask. She wasn't unattractive, but Joe
thought all the hedging just made her look older. The daughter was
maybe twenty, came by her black hair naturally, and had everything else
her mom aspired to.

"Can I help you?" Mom asked, putting down the phone.

"Is Jimmy in?"

"Who's asking?"

"I'm Joe Serpe from Mayday Fuel."

"Oh yeah, you're the guy that killed the Russians last year, right? I read all about that in the paper. Good riddance, but it was a shame about that retarded kid."

"Yeah, he was a good kid." Joe took the opening. "Shame about Stevie. I knew him a little bit from the terminal and Lugo's. A real sweetheart and a good looking boy."

The daughter blanched. The phones started ringing again, but both mother and daughter ignored them. Finally, the mother shouted for her daughter to pick up.

"I'm Marie, Jimmy's wife," said the mom, offering her hand to Joe. "You have to forgive Toni, that's my girl, she and Stevie..."

"I understand."

"I hope they string that cocksucker up—Pardon my French—when they find him. But the kids were engaged and when they got married, Jimmy was gonna make him a partner. Now..."

Both mother and daughter had tears streaming down their faces and no one was answering the phones.

"I'm sorry. That's why I'm here."

Now suspicion crept into the eyes of mother and daughter along with pain and grief. Marie stood up and came around the desk like a mother lion ready to protect her young. Joe put his hands up, palms forward.

"Listen, ladies, I'm not here to cause you any pain or anything or to try and take advantage of your grief."

"Then why are—"

"If you read that stuff about the Russians last year, then maybe you know that me and my partner used to be NYPD detectives; pretty good ones, at that."

The daughter unclenched her body, but the mother wasn't letting down her guard just yet. "So what's that got to do with anything?" she asked.

"You know they found another dead driver last night."

"I heard it on the news this morning, yeah."

"That's five of us, Marie. Two in the last few days. Rusty Monaco, the fourth victim, I used to be on the job with him and I guess when he was killed… I mean, how many more of us are gonna have to get killed before the cops find this guy?"

Marie relaxed, finally. "Can I get you a cup of coffee?"

"Sure. Milk, no sugar."

"I'm kinda glad, I guess, that someone else is gonna look into this. That detective who came and talked to us was kinda an asshole," she said, replacing the pot.

"Big, red-faced guy with a funky eye, named Hoskins?"

"Yeah, him," she said, handing Joe the Baseline Energy mug. "Toni, answer the phones while I talk in the office with Mr. Serpe."

☆   ☆   ☆   ☆

Bob Healy assumed getting hold of Rusty Monaco's records, though not strictly kosher or legal, would be easily done. He still had a lot of friends with juice inside NYPD IAB and anything that might help catch a cop killer—even if that cop was a mutt like Monaco—was probably doable. Skip Rodriguez, Healy's former partner, promised to give him a call when the copies were ready to be picked up. That meant a trip into Brooklyn and a few drinks at Cloudy Dan's bar—on Bob Healy's tab, of course—with Skip. Although Rodriguez was a bit of a cutthroat, Bob missed him and looked forward to hanging out at Cloudy Dan's.

Dealing with Suffolk County Assistant District Attorney George Healy was a very different kettle of sharks. Several years younger than his brother and more ambitious by half, George had risen to the head of the Major Crimes Unit and prosecuted most of the headline cases, such as they were, in the county. When that East Hampton billionaire got clubbed to death by his wife and her handyman lover, it was George's case. And when the cops finally brought in the Oilman Murderer, it would no doubt be George's case to try. It wouldn't help Bob's cause that his brother hated Joe Serpe and resented him for his interference in the Russian mob case nearly as much as Hoskins did.

"Major Crimes Unit, ADA Healy," George said, distracted. "Please hold a second."

Bob heard his brother cover the phone with his hand.

"Hey, little brother."

George hated when Bob called him that. "What is it?"

"Late breakfast?"

"Sure," he said, trying to get Bob off the phone. "Where?"

"What are you in the mood for?"

"A month's vacation in Tuscany."

"Sorry. How about the diner in Hauppauge in forty minutes."

"I'll be there."

★　★　★　★

Joe Serpe had worn the same grave look of concern on his face for nearly thirty minutes, interrupting his trance with the occasional *I see* or *time heals*. He'd gotten all the useful information out of Marie Mazzone in about five minutes, but he hadn't wanted to upset her anymore than she already was. Now, however, she had moved way beyond the murder to complaints about her husband's inattentiveness. So when the office door swung back, Serpe almost clicked up his heels. That was until he saw the look on Jimmy Mazzone's face.

"What the fuck you doin' sniffin' around my business?"

"He was just asking about Stevie," Marie jumped to Serpe's defense, which pissed Jimmy off even more.

"Did I ask you? Get out there and answer the fuckin' phones."

Marie didn't argue. She got up, nodded so long to Serpe, and brushed by her sneering husband.

"So now that your lawyer's gone, you wanna answer my—"

"Your wife was right. I came by to ask about Steve Reggio's murder. Fact is, I came in to talk to you. Ask your daughter."

"I don't have to ask my daughter shit. Now get outta here. Stevie's dead and ain't nothin' gonna change that. You just worry about your own shop and let me worry about me and mine."

"Whatever you say, Jimmy."

Serpe got up and walked past Mazzone into the front office. "Bye ladies. Again, I'm sorry for your loss."

Joe didn't linger. He thought Jimmy's level of belligerence was a little over the top, but he'd worry about that later. For now, he had other owners to piss off.

☆ ☆ ☆ ☆

The diner called attention to itself like a fake twenty carat diamond ring. Beneath the flash and glitz, it was nothing more than a luncheonette. George Healy was already in the lobby, pacing the terrazo and checking his watch, when his brother came in.

"You're late," George said.

"I'm five minutes early."

"Like I said, you're late."

"And mom always thought I was the crazy one. Come on, let's sit."

Bob Healy was careful not to say anything about the purpose of this meeting until they had ordered their food.

"A half a melon, dry toast, and green tea! Christ, George, you an assitant district attorney or a model?"

"Very funny, big brother," he said as the waitress walked away. "And by the way, the answer is no."

"The answer to what?"

"Come on, Bob, don't play dumb with me. It doesn't suit you. A fifth driver was killed last night and you're partnered up with the hero of the oil business, Joe 'the Snake' Serpe."

"Okay, you got me, so—"

"There's no so here, brother. The only reason I even agreed to this meeting was to tell you that this is the first and last conversation we're ever going to have about these homicides. When the Suffolk PD catches this guy—and they will catch him—I'll be the one to prosecute the case. I can't be seen to have given out any information to—"

"You sound pretty confident, little brother. I figure they'll catch him eventually too, if he doesn't die of old age or run out of drivers first. You know who the lead detective is, huh?"

"Hoskins," George mumbled, frowning.

"Bingo! The same prick who would be tripping over his own shoe laces while the Russian mob murdered women and children and took over the COD oil business. Yeah, him."

"That's outta my hands, Bob, and you know it. Even if I agreed with everything you just said, I couldn't help you with this."

Bob Healy stood up and threw a twenty dollar bill on the table.

"Where are you going?" George asked.

"Back to work. I just lost my appetite."

☆   ☆   ☆   ☆

Serpe was on his way to his third stop of the day, Five Star Fuel, but he couldn't get the second stop out of his head. Panther Oil was out of business. An ancient cab-over Ford with a for sale sign in its dirty front window sat out by the empty, gated yard collecting dust and very little interest. Joe knew it had been a small operation, but hadn't realized that Cameron Wilkes, the second victim, was running a one man show. Most everyone knew and liked Wilkes, one of the few African-American owner/drivers in the business. For fifteen years he drove for other companies before taking the leap this past September. They found him dead in Wyandanch in the first week of December. Fifteen hard years for three months of independence. Joe wondered if it was worth it.

Five Star was a one star operation run by Tommy Breen, a man as popular as a bad case of the crabs. His drivers were all head cases and nasty to boot. His equipment was worse. Five Star had a raggedy six truck fleet that was kept running with duct tape and prayers. Oil trucks carry hazardous material, but Five Star's trucks were themselves hazardous. They were all scavenged rebuilds whose parts had seen better days during the first Reagan administration. And Breen's idea of fleet maintainance included the use of retreaded rubber on front tires, which was strictly forbidden by law. He was also known to run his trucks with heating oil—essentially diesel fuel—which was also completely illegal. Yet, Five Star seemed never to get anymore grief from the IRS, Department of Transportaion, or New York State Department of Environmental Protection than any of the other COD operators.

Joe knew several other owners who had, to no apparent effect, dropped dimes on Five Star to rat out Breen's practices. It was a bit cowardly, but sort of SOP in the business whenever someone bent the rules, by which they all had to live. Though it was never talked about directly, everyone knew and understood. It was kind of like old time baseball, when there were unwritten laws about when pitchers could throw at batters. There was no hot dogging or home run trots in old time baseball. And in the COD oil business, people knew how far they could bend the rules.

Five Star's office was a run down shack in a dirty, pitted yard. Next to the office, a burly hispanic guy in filthy coveralls was doing a rear brake job on '77 Mack with a dented tank, mismatched fenders, and balding tires. As Serpe approached him, the man slid his torso under the rear axle.

"Nice rig," Joe said to the mechanic's legs.

"You think so, jefe?" a voice echoed from under the truck. "I think you are blind or a liar, no?"

"Maybe both. Breen around?"

"You his amigo?"

"If I was, I'd be the only one," Serpe said.

The mechanic slid out from under the truck and stood up, wiping his stubbled face with a greasy blue rag. He wasn't more than five foot nine, but he was big through the chest and shoulders. He had the telltale cold stare—both blank and threatening—of someone who'd survived a long bid. When he shoved back his sleeves and peeled off his blue latex gloves, the tats confirmed what Joe already guessed.

"What you want with Tommy?"

"To talk."

"Talk to me first."

"You his secretary?"

"You a comedian?"

"You got a name?"

"Yeah." Silence.

"Me too."

"You smell like five-o, so where's your tin at?"

"And you stink like a shitbird, but I'm not a cop anymore and you're not inside, so let's start over. I'm Joe Serpe from Mayday Fuel." Serpe stuck out his hand.

If the name meant something to the mechanic, he didn't show it. "They call me Zeus." He shook Serpe's hand.

"Hands of steel," Joe said, taking back his hand. "Is Tommy around?"

"Out on his truck."

"Did you know the driver that was killed?"

"Dave? I knew him. Asshole. What about him?"

"Nice way to talk about the dead."

"I talk about him to his face worse when he was alive. Dying don't get you no extra points. Besides, Dave's no different from the rest of these fuckeeng drivers." Zeus' English got worse and his accent got more pronounced as he grew more agitated. "They can all get killed." He spit for emphasis.

"What about Breen?"

Zeus stepped forward, the cold stare on his face replaced by an angry, more overtly threatening glare. "You shut your mouth about Tim. The man, he save my fuckeeng life."

Before Zeus could take another step, Serpe stuck the muzzle end of his Glock under the mechanic's chin.

"Listen to me, Zeus. I'm not a cop no more, but don't for one fuckin' second think I won't blow your worthless brains through the top of your fuckin' head. I'm not here to bust your boss' balls or cause him grief. I just wanna talk to him. When I put this away," Joe said, pressing the Glock a little harder into the fleshy area between Zeus' chin and adam's apple, "I'm gonna give you a card to give to him and I'm gonna give you a card to keep. Tell him to call me. You gimme me a call if you want extra work, because to keep these pieces of shit trucks on the road, you must be a magical fuckin' mechanic. Shake your head yes and step back."

The mechanic shook his head and stepped back. Serpe tucked the gun away and handed Zeus two refrigerator magnets shaped like oil trucks with Mayday's name and phone numbers printed on the tank.

"These ain't no cards."

"I own an oil company, Zeus. What the fuck do I need business cards for?"

"I see your point."

"Go finish your brake job and maybe the next time we meet, we can leave the macho bullshit out of it."

The mechanic didn't say anything. He stuffed the magnets in his pocket and walked back toward the jacked up Mack. Serpe watched him until his body disappeared under the truck.

[Fu Manchu]

Skip Rodriguez wasn't sitting where he was supposed to be nor was he anywhere to be found inside Cloudy Dan's bar in Red Hook. Even after the new rules about rotating officers in and out of IAB were established in the 90s, it was uncomfortable for regular cops to hang with their IAB brothers and sisters. Cloudy Dan's, once the exclusive hangout of the toughest, most crooked longshoremen on the planet, had become IAB's ironic little joke. It was sort of their home away from home and away from other cops. And it was the place where Bob Healy and Skip Rodriguez used to meet to conduct their business away from prying eyes and curious ears.

Sitting in the red vinyl booth where he and Skip always met, was a rail thin, dark- skinned black chick, drinking a Diet Coke and trying to force down a bowlful of Cloudy Dan's famously awful chili. Healy gave her a lot of credit for even trying. The joke was that the local rats fed the chili to their pet roaches under the table. Bob Healy sat at the bar, ordered a Jack and Coke, and sipped while he waited for Skip to show.

Twenty minutes later, when he was gnawing on ice cubes and had left messages on both Rodriguez's cell and land line, he got up to leave.

He was shaking his head in disgust and cursing under his breath as he stepped through Cloudy Dan's front door and walked back out into the bright, but heatless, Brooklyn sun. He was so pissed off that he didn't hear the footsteps coming up behind him. He started at the touch of an unexpected hand on his arm. Jumping back, he slid his hand under his coat for his old off-duty piece. When he recognized his potential attacker as the chili eating black chick from Cloudy Dan's, he relaxed and flushed red with embarrassment.

"Detective Healy?" she asked, ignoring his red face.

"Who's asking?"

She flipped open an ID case and showed him a shiny detective's shield. "Raiza Hines, IAB."

"Razor, as in blade?"

"Raiza as in R-a-i-z-a, but you can call me Blades. Everybody else does." She held her hand out to Healy. Her grip was firm. Her fingers were elegant, long, and tapered to perfectly done nails finished in a glossy blue. "Captain Rodriguez sent me to see you."

"And what did Skip say about me?"

"That you were old school and the best."

"Uh oh," Healy said, letting go of her hand. "That's trouble, Blades."

"What is?"

"First, that Skip sent you instead of coming himself. Second, that he's blowing smoke up both our asses." She didn't react to the language. Bob liked that. "Did he give you anything to bring to me."

"A message and instructions that I was to help you anyway I could. He also says he's cleared me for all the overtime and time away from the bureau I need to do what I gotta do on this. Is he trying to fuck me up?" she asked, frowning.

"Not that I would put it past Skip to try and get ahead by screwing up someone else's career, but I don't think so. He's putting you on an island to test you. If nothing comes of your working with me, then there's no fallout and he knows he can trust you. But if we come up with a score, then—"

"—he'll take the credit."

"Smart woman. I think we're gonna get along. Come on back in the bar and give me that message."

★　★　★　★

Armor Oil was located on Reddington Street in Bay Shore, very far south and west from Joe and Bob's yard in Ronkonkoma and from the big terminal in Holtsville. They loaded their trucks at a smaller terminal operated by Mann Brothers, the largest privately owned, full service company on Long Island. Mann loaded COD company trucks for a four to six cent a gallon premium above the rack price at the Holtsville terminal. The outfits that loaded at Mann Brothers weighed speed and convenience against the added cost. There were no long lines at the smaller terminals and that allowed an owner to get his trucks in and out fast and to do many more stops. Armor's location and their loading practices accounted for the fact that Joe had never run across Rusty Monaco during his years on the road. It also meant that Joe knew nothing about their operations.

Armor's yard was paved with concrete and there was one late 90s GMC cab-over —their spare truck, Joe figured—parked in a far corner. Their office, like Mayday's, was a trailer propped up on blocks. Joe went up the flimsy stairs, knocked, and went in without waiting for permission.

A heavyset man with sleepy eyes and a slackjaw was watching satellite porn on a wide screen TV mounted to the near wall. He sat with his boots up on a desk and leaned back in his chair as far as it would go. There was an open bottle of Corona in his hand and a half-smoked Camel turning itself to ash at the edge of the desk. It was gang bang central on the screen with so many intertwined arms and legs that it looked like a bowlful of spaghetti.

"What can I do for you?" the big man asked, eyes fixed on the screen.

"Is the owner around?"

"No soliciting. Go read the sign on the door."

"I'm not selling anything."

"Everybody's selling something, bud."

"How profound."

He ignored Joe's wit. "I don't know how the fuck they manage this shit with all them bodies. How do they do that?"

"Computers."

"Either grab yourself a beer and sit down or get the fuck out," the big man pointed at the mini fridge under the window.

Joe grabbed a beer and sat just in time to hear five women fake orgasms in unison.

"So that's what it sounds like. I'm used to hearing 'em fake it one at a time," he said, clicking off the TV and swivelling the chair around to face Joe. "I'm Bill Eiserman and I own this lovely establishment. What can I do for you?"

"I'm Joe Serpe from Mayday Fuel."

"The guy that whacked the Russians, right? Good for them cock-suckers. This business is hard enough without organized crime getting involved. Am I right?" He clinked bottles with Serpe.

"You don't seem very broken up about Rusty Monaco."

Eiserman wiped the jolly look off his face, put his beer down on the desk, and rubbed his chin thoughtfully before speaking. "Look, I got a business to run. I'm paying for the guy's funeral. What the fuck else do you want, that I should cry for him? I'm not happy he's dead. I don't wish it on anybody to die like that, alone in the cold and the rain, but he was a nasty pain in the balls. I mean, he wouldn't do stops in black areas, for chrissakes. But he would trade stops with the other drivers and did all the ones they hated. Worked out, I guess. The thing of it is, he was leaving soon anyway."

"Monaco?"

"That's who we're dicussing, right? He was headed to Florida. He bought a condo in Plantation City. Beautiful place. Showed me pictures. Nicer than the place I got for my folks in Boca."

Finally something, Joe thought. He didn't know what to make of it, but at least it was something.

"How'd he afford that?" Serpe asked.

"He bought moldy bread. How the hell should I know? He's got a nice pension, right? He did okay here. I don't ask my drivers about shit I wouldn't want them to ask me about."

"Fair enough."

Serpe and Eiserman talked for another ten minutes, but nothing the big man had to say revealed anything of interest or meaning. Eiserman took Joe's numbers and promised to call if he remembered any relevant information.

"Do me a favor," he said, just as Serpe was leaving, "take these." He handed Joe several index cards. "They're longtime customers, but they're so far east of my territory that it kills me to have to get to them. I'll call them and tell them to use you from now on."

"Why?"

"It's good for you, it's good for me. I know you'll take care of them and I won't have to schlep my trucks out of the way."

"You don't know me at all."

"I know you plenty, don't worry. I know you'll do the right thing."

"How?"

"Because if you're worried about who killed a cocksucker like Rusty Monaco, I know you'll treat people right."

Serpe closed the office door behind him without saying another word. It was tough to dispute Eiserman's street logic and Joe wasn't going to try.

☆   ☆   ☆   ☆

Raiza Hines sat back down in the unofficial official booth of NYPD IAB as Healy went to the bar to get their drinks. As he waited, he looked back at Raiza, taking her measure. She seemed a cool customer, determined, not crazy ambitious like Skip Rodriguez. Skip had gotten pretty far, but he liked Raiza's chances of getting further up the food chain.

"Vodka rocks, lime," he said putting her glass down on the table and then sat himself opposite her with his beer in hand. "So, what's the message from your fearless leader?"

"The food in that Indian restaurant is too hot for takeout. You're better off eating it there," Raiza said, shaking her head at her boss' childish code. "You know what he's talking about?"

"Blades, I think the question is, do you?"

"Monaco, Russell T. Born Elmhurst General Hospital, September ninth, Nineteen-sixty. Graduated NYPD Academy Class nineteen-eighty. Retired September twenty-fourth, Two thousand and three. Rank, Detective third… Should I continue?"

"Very good. I take it that since he was a recent victim of violence that his jacket's too hot to touch."

For the first time since they met, Detective Hines smiled at Healy. "Before."

"Before!" Healy coughed up a little beer. "That means someone was grousing around in his files before he was killed."

"Indeed there was and now there's an access block on almost all his files."

"I take it it's not IAB's doing."

"Please put that in the form of a question," she tweaked.

"Smart, pretty, a sense of humor. Skip better watch his back and cover his ass."

"No comment."

"Rusty Monaco was a piece of shit, but he was two years retired. The brass must have breathed a big sigh of relief when he put in his papers. Why would they be rooting around now, I wonder?"

"I suspect that's what my boss wants me to help you find out."

"Skip's always had a nose for a big score."

Healy handed Blades a Mayday refrigerator magnet and a napkin with his cell and home numbers scrawled out.

"Classy stuff. I think the NYPD should start using magnets and napkins too."

"Come on, finish your drink detective, we've got work to do."

✷   ✷   ✷   ✷

Turning right at the Smithtown Bull statue and off Main Street onto St. Johnland heading up into Kings Park, Serpe smiled, shaking his head in disbelief. Even now, as he recalled the unlikely set of circumstances surrounding the transformation of two bitter enemies into partners and friends, he couldn't quite believe it.

It had been late in the afternoon last Valentine's Day; a raw, miserable Saturday when Serpe got an urgent call from Frank Randazzo's mom. She was the dispatcher back then and told Joe there was one more stop to be done, one that couldn't be put off until Monday. It was already dark out, Joe remembered, but just as he pulled over to write up the delivery ticket, it began to snow like a bastard. Worse still, he had to about-face over the LIE and head all the way back north into Kings Park. Maybe that was why the name Healy made no impact on him as wrote the ticket.

Twenty minutes later, as he began to make the delivery, it hadn't yet dawned on Joe that the man he was rescuing from a frozen weekend and a wall full of burst pipes was the same man who had meticulously built the cases against him and Ralphy Abruzzi. Only after Healy walked up behind Joe while he was pumping the last of the two hundred gallons and uttered a few words of thanks at his back, was Serpe's memory sufficently shaken. But it wasn't until Joe went to collect the money and saw the family pictures through the glass storm door that he knew for sure. "Motherfucker, it's him," Joe said. And when Healy came to the door he said, "Fuck if it isn't Joe 'the Snake' Serpe." Not exactly the stuff friendships are made of.

Who knows? Maybe if the hose monkey hadn't been murdered that same night or if Healy—long guilt-ridden over evidence he had kept from Serpe about the case against him—hadn't showed up at the kid's funeral service to talk to Joe, they would have stayed enemies forever. In a weird way, Joe and Bob owed Tim Hoskins a thank you, because when the detective showed up at the funeral too, he made himself their common enemy. As the old proverb goes: The enemy of my enemy is my friend. Generally, Joe tried not to focus on the past. Loss had taught him to look ahead, but he guessed it was sort of inevitable that he should think about Healy as he drove into Kings Park, taking the same route he had on that miserable, snowy Valentine's Day.

Serpe knew even less about Epsilon Energy than he had known about Armor Oil. He had seen their trucks on the road every now and again, but there were only a very few areas where Mayday and Epsilon territories overlapped. Epsilon rarely ventured south of the LIE to make stops nor did they deliver east of Setauket. Like Armor, Epsilon didn't load at the big Holtsville terminal. They filled up their trucks at a tiny satellite terminal by the Long Island Railroad station in Kings Park. The one tank terminal was owned by a consortium of full service companies who used the location to refill their trucks that were too far north to drive back and forth to Holtsville. As Epsilon's yard was located very near the terminal and Healy's home, it was probably the one oil company in Suffolk County Bob was more familiar with than Joe. Oddly enough, Healy's house was Mayday Fuel's only remaining stop in King's Park. In a push to maximize profits and limit costs, Joe and Bob had given up most of their North Shore stops west of St. James in order to develop their routes further south and east. Good thing for them Frank Randazzo hadn't had that same idea the year before.

Epsilon Energy, it turned out, didn't even have a yard of its own. The company parked its trucks in the back of a body shop across the road from the Kings Park Fire Department. When Joe went inside the shop to ask about where he could find Epsilon's offices, he was greeted by a young woman who couldn't have been more than a year or two out of her teens. She was cute, on the heavy side, but had a great smile.

"What can I do for you, mister?"

"I see Epsilon Energy parks their trucks here."

That knocked the greatness right out of her smile and she began nervously combing back the right side of her long blond hair. Serpe couldn't help but notice the splint on her index finger.

"What happened to your hand?" Joe asked.

She hesitated as if not understanding the question. "Oh, this," she said finally, letting go of her hair and looking at her hand. "Can you believe it, I slammed it in my car door?"

Serpe didn't, but he acted as if he did. "Amazing the clutzy things we do to ourselves, right? So about Epsilon…"

"What about 'em?"

"Shame about their driver getting killed."

"I don't know their drivers and I don't know anything about what happened."

"You knew he was murdered, didn't you?"

"I guess, but look, I'm not even here when they come to pick up their trucks or nothing and I'm almost always gone when they get back."

"But not always?"

"What?"

"You're here sometimes when their trucks come back in," Joe pressed.

"I guess."

"Where'd you hear about Alberto getting killed?"

"The paper."

"I thought you said you didn't know their drivers."

She didn't say anything, but fumbled through the top drawer of her desk and came out with a refrigerator magnet shaped like a tanker truck. "Here's how to get in touch with Epsilon," she said, handing the magnet to Joe. Her hand was shaking more than just a little bit.

"Thanks. You play much poker?"

"What? I don't get—"

Just then, the side door that led from the shop to the office swung open. A thirty-something biker type in coveralls and paint spray strolled in. He had a few days worth of black stubble on his cheeks, a badass Fu Manchu mustache on his lip, goggles on his forehead, and a respirator mask slung around his neck. He shot a quick look at Serpe and took a much longer one at the blond behind the desk. His expression made it plain that he didn't much like Joe's being there, but that he liked the blond's harried and confused demeanor even less.

"Anything the matter?"

"No, this guy was just asking about how to get in touch with the oil company."

Fu Manchu was skeptical. "Then why you look so upset?"

"That's my fault," Joe said. "I was talking about their driver getting murdered and I guess it kinda upset the young woman. I'm very sorry about that, miss. I didn't mean to upset you."

"That's okay, mister." Her smile returned, but it now had a twitchy quality to it.

"They just pay the owner of the property to park their two trucks here. We got no connection to them at all," Fu Manchu said to Joe, his tone making it clear that the discussion was at end.

"Well, thanks for the help," Serpe said, waving the magnet at the blond and the tough guy. "Again, I'm sorry for upsetting you."

"Have a good day," she said.

"Yeah," Fu Manchu agreed, and when the door closed behind Joe added, "have a great fucking day, asshole."

When Serpe got back into his car, he considered staking out the place. He might have been off the job for seven years, but wasn't so far gone that he couldn't spot amateurs or catch the telltale odor of guilt. And the stink of guilt in that office easily overwhelmed the paint and body filler fumes. Guilt over what, was the question. Serpe dialed the number on the magnet and pulled away from the curb.

[Preferences]

FRIDAY, JANUARY 7TH, 2005—EVENING

They started their evening as they had started their morning, seated across the office desk from each other in the Mayday trailer. They both looked a little worse for wear, but the day seemed to have played out tougher for Joe Serpe. He still felt awful about what had happened to Cameron Wilkes. The image of the dead man's truck sitting out in front of the abandoned yard was stuck in his head nor was his mood much improved when he got in touch with the owner of Epsilon Energy. It seemed the dead driver, Albie, the man called him, had gotten murdered before he got to realize his American dream.

"Albie had a wife and boy he was saving to bring up from Mexico," the owner said. "Also had put a binder down on a house in Brentwood. Fucking pity. Great guy and the hardest working driver I ever had. Woulda sold him the company someday too. I'm moving down to North Carolina with the wife in a few years. This isn't a business for old men."

No it wasn't. It didn't burn you out like cop work, but it was pretty rough on your body if not on your soul. Serpe sat and listened as Healy explained about how he had gotten back to the office in time to cash the drivers out and set things up for Saturday, their busy day. He listened with a little more interest when Healy described his meeting with Raiza Hines.

"She cute?"

"I tell you that someone else's been sniffing around about Rusty Monaco even before he was killed, that all computer access to his files has been blocked, and that's what you're gonna ask me: Is she cute? Yeah, Joe, she's cute and twenty years younger than me and black."

"Racist!"

"Fuck you, Serpe!"

"All right, forget her for now. Any idea why the cops are curious about a guy who's been off the job for two years, a guy they were happy to see go?"

"Thing is, Joe, we can't even be sure it *is* the cops looking at Monaco. Weird, huh?"

"Worth looking into."

"That's what Blades is doing."

"Blades? Getting kinda cozy there, aren't you Bob?"

"Drop it."

"It's dropped. So your prick brother's not going to help."

"Nope. Says he's probably gonna prosecute the case when it comes in, so…"

"I guess I can't blame him."

"You can blame him, but it isn't gonna do us any good. So you said something about a body shop…"

"You know the one right across from the Kings Park Fire Department by Indian Head Road?" Joe asked.

"I live about a mile away from it and my church is around the corner. Yeah, I know it: Noonan's Collision."

"They're guilty about something in there, but I'm not sure it's got anything to do with the dead drivers. I mean it's a fucking body shop, right? And they had a shitload of Hondas, Toyotas, and Escalades in their lot."

"Chopshop maybe, stolen parts you're thinking? You know any totally clean body shops?"

"What I know is that my being in there asking questions spooked the shit out of the blond and that the biker guy made me for a cop. I don't think I should go back there. Might raise a red flag."

"Which means I should go?"

"First maybe you should bring a box of donuts over to the fire house and make nice so you can sit across the street and see what's what."

"I know how to make nice with the neighbors. Don't worry. I'll be on it first thing in the morning."

"Good," Joe said, flipping through the tickets for Saturday delivery. "Looks like I'm gonna have to drive tomorrow. Busy day."

"Busy is good."

"After my brother died, busy is all I lived for."

"Tell me about it. After Mary died I used to go nuts looking for ways to fill up my days with something other than *General Hospital*. I looked for anything to occupy my thoughts."

They sat silently for a moment, both together and apart, remembering where their lives had been only several months ago. Men find it easy to drink and bullshit together, but silence is the real test of friendship between men.

"So," Healy said, "how about the other oil companies?"

"I didn't learn anything except about other people's grief at Baseline. The business died with Cameron Wilkes, so there was nobody to talk to there. The guy who owned Armor didn't seem too bent outta shape about Monaco, but who the fuck would be? I'll talk to Tim Breen from Five Star next week or maybe I'll go looking for him at Lugo's tomorrow after work. And as far as Epsilon goes... That guy was looking for a way out even before this happened to his driver."

Bob Healy stood and stretched. "I'm going home, partner. Long day. You sure you can manage tomorrow without me?"

"No problem. I'll have one of the guys load my truck. I'll take stops, route the trucks and then I'll go out. I'll have the calls forwarded to my cell and dispatch from the truck."

"Sounds good. Where you headed now?"

"Monaco's wake."

"That sucks."

"I don't know. As popular as he was, it might just be me and him."

★　　★　　★　　★

The wake was in some funeral parlor in Massapequa on Sunrise Highway somewhere. He was pretty sure he'd find his way, but the truth was that Serpe wasn't in any fucking rush to get there. Fearless as a cop, or at least able to control his fears better than most, he dreaded the idea of running into any guys he'd known from the job. It was always awkward and never turned out good for Joe. In the end, they could never understand his testifying against his partner. To them, he was worse than a man like Healy. Sure they would consider Healy a rat, but his was a career decision. In their eyes, what Joe did by giving up his brother cop that way, was not only inexplicable, but unforgiveable. So Serpe had given up trying to explain that blind loyalty sometimes comes with a heavy price.

Joe parked in the nearly empty lot behind the funeral home and breathed a sigh of relief. He'd already had a rough day and thought he deserved a break. He should have known better than to think that bad times earn you anything good. Just as he was passing by one of the few other cars in the lot, the driver's side door swung open behind him and smacked hard into the back of his bad leg.

The ironic part about it was that the bullet that had shattered Serpe's femur and nicked his femoral artery might have been fired by a dead man. When the cops burst in on the Russians, bullets were spraying everywhere. Joe had never wanted to know if the bullet was part of the spray or if it came from that sick fuck Pavel's handgun. Pavel—the man who had tormented Marla—died that night too, so he really didn't see the point.

None of that mattered now as Joe collapsed face first in a heap on the cold blacktop. His leg had healed as well as it was ever going to heal and could pretty much take the daily stresses delivering oil put on it, but any direct hit like the one he'd just got, put him right down.

"What's a matter, fuck face, you fall down and go boom?" It was Detective Hoskins. "Here, let me help you up, scum bag." He grabbed

Serpe by the back of his coat and yanked him up so that Joe's body-weight sat right atop his bad leg. "You look like your're hurtin', Snake. Let me fix that." He kicked Serpe square in the solar plexus with the toe of his shoe and Serpe went down gasping for breath.

Hoskins just stood over him patiently waiting for Serpe to try and get up. But a patient temperment wasn't a description that fit Tim Hoskins, so he got on his knees next to Serpe and put his lips almost against Joe's left ear. His breath smelled of old beer, fresh garlic, and hatred. "Listen to me, you cowardly-cunt-rat-cheese-eatin'-bastard. You already embarrassed me once with what you did with the Russians. Once is too much, but there's nothin' I can do about it now. But I hear you been askin' around about these murders. That's right, asshole, somebody ratted you out instead of the other way around. How's it feel to get the dime dropped on you?"

"Drop dead."

Hoskins laughed and the air got colder. "Stop sticking your nose in my shit. Stop it now! Stop it now or I'll get into the oil driver murderin' business my own fuckin' self. Understand?"

"Fuck you!" Serpe coughed.

"Fuck me, huh?" He kicked Serpe in the ribs and then did it again. "Fuck me, huh?"

"You deaf or just ugly?"

He kicked him again.

The headlights of a car swept across the lot.

"Fuck me, huh?"

"Get that hearing aid fixed, motherfucker."

Hoskins reared his leg back.

"Hey!" a woman screamed. "What are you doing? Leave him alone. I'm dialing nine-one-one right now." She waved her open and lit up cell phone at Hoskins.

"Remember, cocksucker, you been warned." Hoskins got in his car and tore out of the lot, tires squealing as he went.

"You okay?" the woman asked, helping pull Joe up in a sitting position.

"I've been better. Thanks," he said, getting to his feet and brushing himself off.

"Who was that guy?"

"An incompetent, frightened little prick."

"Whatever."

With his feet firmly under him, Serpe took a closer look at his rescuer. She was, he guessed, about thirty with a pretty, but hard face. Her brown hair was cut short and her eyes were pennies with some of the shine worn off. She was about five foot five, curvy, but thick through the neck and body. She wore a black leather coat over a plain black dress and black, low-heeled shoes.

"Joe Serpe." He shook her hand. "I'm here for Rusty's wake."

She took his hand. "Georgine Monaco. Rusty's little sister. You a cop?"

"Used to be, Georgine."

"Call me Gigi, G-i-g-i, like two soldiers. Everybody calls me that."

"Your brother saved my life once, Gigi."

She laughed. "Probably the only good thing he ever done. He was a prick, my big bro. Easy to tell with this overwhelming outpouring of love. Look at this parking lot. I buried cats where more people showed. So, d'you like my brother?"

"Not really. He was a hard guy to like, but I owe him. I also own an oil company now, so I got my reasons for coming."

"Thanks for coming, no matter why." She wrapped her arm in his and walked Joe into the home.

In front of five rows of empty wooden folding chairs, the closed coffin lay in the chapel's smallest viewing room. There was a uniformed honor guard from the NYPD standing a bored vigil along the walls. They outnumbered the rest of the attendees even if you included Rusty Monaco's body in the count. A funeral director strolled laps around the room.

"I guess you were right about the cat burials," Joe said.

"What does it matter anyhow? Rusty ain't counting heads. Come on, let's get a prime seat before all the good ones are taken."

"You're pretty funny."

"Comin' outta our family, I had to be." She wasn't smiling now and before Joe could ask another question, Gigi walked up to the coffin, knelt, and crossed herself. She moved her lips and crossed herself again before touching her bent fingers to her mouth.

"Go say something," she said, pushing Serpe's arm, "even if it's thanks."

It wasn't Serpe's style, but he did it anyway. He said a quick thanks and sat back down. They sat there quietly for a few minutes, Joe studying Gigi's hard face. No tears. No cracks. Not much of anything washed across it.

"You guys keep in touch?" Joe broke the silence.

"Not really. There wasn't a whole lotta love in our house, not from my folks and not between us kids. Rusty kinda looked after me when I was little, so I guess I owe him too."

"So you didn't know about him moving to the condo in Plantation City, I guess."

Now Gigi showed more on her face than she had since coming to Joe's aid in the parking lot. And what she showed wavered between skepticism and total disbelief.

"Get the fuck outta here! My brother didn't have two nickels to rub together his whole life. What he didn't blow on the ponies and pussy, his bitch wife soaked him for a few years back in the divorce. Not that she didn't deserve it for putting up with his shit for so long. Christ, Joe, the only time I ever heard from Rusty was when he needed a stake from me. Why you think he was driving a oil truck for ten bucks a stop? No offense."

"None taken. Still, the condo is a fact. Maybe he borrowed the money from a friend."

"Yeah, right! How many friends you see here? Even if he coulda found someone who didn't find him a miserable bastard, no one woulda lent Rusty a dime. Would you?"

"No."

"And he saved your life, right?"

Joe conceded her point. He looked around and noticed that the honor guard was gone. A priest came in, made a little speech about Russell's service to his community, said a few prayers, and then beat a quick path out of the place.

"I'm heading out," he said.

"Wait, I'll go with you."

As he offered his hand, Gigi asked if he didn't want to go get a drink or something to eat. Joe felt as awkward as a teenager. He kind of liked her style and he had certainly been with women a lot less attractive than her, but he was still connected to Marla.

"I don't think so," he said, and started making excuses about his early morning.

"I don't wanna fuck ya, for chrissakes, I just wanna have a drink with you."

"I'm hurt."

"I like men when I'm in the mood for 'em and if that wasn't my brother's carcass in there, I could probably work up the mood for you. But on the whole, I think you and me have the same preferences…if you catch my meaning."

"I do. Okay, one drink."

[Omerta]

SATURDAY, JANUARY 8TH, 2005

The temperature was warmer than had been predicted and as the sun rose it seemed ready to preview its spring muscles. The firetrucks were parked on the concrete outside their bay doors. The guys at the firehouse were thrilled to interrupt their washing and waxing to make a new friend. No one asks questions of a man bearing donuts and coffee. And there was an added bonus; a Suffolk cop from the 4th precinct. His white and blue unit was already parked in the house's side lot when Healy pulled in.

As he bullshitted with the guys from the house and the cop, Healy kept an eye on the doings across the street. At 7:00, a guy pulled into the body shop's lot and parked his gray Acura in a corner spot. He was in his fifties and walked with the stooped grace of a man who had done the same hard job for many years. To Bob it seemed there was a sort of resignation in the man's stride. Dressed in the now familiar green coveralls of Epsilon Energy, he carried a metal ticket box and his Hagstrom maps in one hand, a tall cup of 7/Eleven coffee in the other. 7/Eleven coffee: the oil man's breakfast of choice. When he disappeared around the back of the body shop, Healy excused himself from his new pals and walked across the street.

The Epsilon guy was just getting into the cab of a 2000 Mack cab-over with a 3000 gallon tank. The truck was cleaner than any oil truck Healy had ever seen and it started right up without the grumble and coughs of Mayday's aging fleet.

"Nice, clean truck," he called up to the cab.

"You want buy it?" the driver shouted over the din of the diesel.

"You the owner?"

"Couldn't sell it to you if I wasn't."

The man stepped down from the cab, approaching Healy cautiously. It didn't escape Healy's notice that the guy's right hand was tucked out of sight.

"You might not want to let me think you've got an unregistered firearm there behind your back," Bob said, pointing.

"I don't give a shit what you think, but if it makes you feel better, it's registered," he said, showing Bob the blue finish on the short-barrel .38. "Funny thing, you know. I've owned Epsilon for about fifteen years, another oil outfit for ten before that, and not once has anybody come up to talk to me about how clean I keep my equipment at seven in the morning."

"I see your point." Healy held his hands up in surrender. "I just wanted to say I was sorry to hear about your driver, Albie."

The man put the .38 at his side. "Sorry about the gun, but I'm a little nervous these days."

"You've got cause. I'm Bob Healy from Mayday Fuel. You talked to my partner on the phone yester—"

"Joe Serpe. Seemed like a nice enough guy."

"I'll tell him you say so. I live in town and, like I said, I just wanted to come over and express my condolensces."

The man rushed back to the truck, put the revolver away, and came back to Healy with his right hand extended. "Jack Peterson. Again, sorry about the gun."

"No problem." Bob shook his hand. "You talked to Joe so you understand that we're looking into what's been going on with these murders. We both knew the fourth victim from the job."

"Good. The asshole the Suffolk PD's got in charge didn't exactly inspire my confidence. Didn't strike me as a man who could find his own dick to piss with."

"Hoskins is an asshole, but that doesn't mean you shouldn't cooperate with him."

"There wasn't much I could tell him anyway. Albie was a great guy. Had no enemies that I knew of, not that I knew many of his amigos. We deliver only on the North Shore, so I didn't figure anything like this was gonna happen to him. I mean, all of my stops are in good areas and all my customers are good people."

"You mean white people."

"You wanna put it like that, okay, yeah, white people. I got nothing against nobody, but look for yourself where these murders happened. C'mon, you think a Jewish doctor from Commack and the guy that owns the Italian restaurant from Smithtown are killing these drivers? You know how many times some crackhead nigger stuck a gun in my face when I was delivering down in Bay Shore in the eighties?"

"Not much fun getting a gun stuck in your face, no matter who's doing it."

"Sorry again about the gun."

"I'm not judging you, Jack. I just wanna stop the killing."

"Okay."

"One question about Albie. You said he was paying to bring his family up from Mexico, that he put money down on a house, and that you were looking to sell him the business. That's a big nut to carry for an oil man, any oil man, even for a hard working one. You sure he wasn't going down the South Shore or out east doing some deliveries for cash? They did find him in Mastic."

"Look, even if I didn't trust Albie—which I did—I'm a meticulous person. What, you think only my trucks are clean? Look at my coveralls, for goodness sake; clean like new. From the day I started as an owner, I've been a hard-on about paperwork. I made my guys keep mileage logs. I check the odometers every night. I keep records of every gallon of number two oil bought, pumped, and spilled and of every gallon of diesel used to run the trucks. Since the cops impounded Albie's truck, that's the most time that rig has spent out of my sight since I bought her. Whoever buys my equipment from me will know everything about it. So if Albie was running side jobs and stealing my oil to do it, he was either a magician or a criminal genius."

"Fair enough," Healy said. "I guess you better get on the road. Glad we met and, again, too bad about Albie."

"No sweat." Peterson turned to go back to his truck.

"Jack," Healy called after him.

"What?"

"I'm looking to get my daughter's fender fixed. Noonan's Collision any good?"

"Used to be before the father moved to Ft. Myers last year. Now his kid runs it."

"What's wrong with the kid?"

"Take a look inside the shop. I gotta go." With that, Jack Peterson closed the cab door, put the Mack in gear, and rumbled by.

When the truck was gone, Healy walked around front and took a look through the glass of the shop doors. The reasons behind Peterson's less than ringing endorsement of the body shop were painfully evident. Loose tools, uncovered paint cans, body filler cans were all over the place. The tape job on the Subaru in one of the bays was careless and uneven. Very sloppy.

"Can I help you?"

Healy turned to face the heavyset blond Serpe had described to him the night before. The splint on her hand was hard to miss even with it down at her side.

"Yes, hi, I was just talking to the oil guy and he recommended you guys to fix my kid's Honda. Dented fender."

She flashed the smile Joe had mentioned. "No problem."

"I don't know about that. We've got a five hundred dollar deductable."

"Like I said, no problem. We'll just bury it in the estimate."

Nice, Healy thought, offering to commit insurance fraud before your first cup of coffee of the day. They exchanged pleasantries while she opened the shop, turned off the alarm, and flipped over the OPEN sign.

"Almost seven-thirty on a Saturday morning. Must be a busy day. I'm surprised you guys don't get in earlier."

"Yeah, I know, but the boss lives out east and—"

"The Hamptons?" Healy cut her off.

She laughed. "The Hamptons, that's pretty funny. Nah, Mastic. Hammer ain't a Hamptons kinda guy."

"Hammer?"

"Hank Noonan. His dad owns the place."

"When will he be in?"

"Before nine," she said.

"Thanks. I'll be back."

☆   ☆   ☆   ☆

Her tiny silhouette was backlit by the early morning sun. She was sitting on the hood of his car as he came around the side of the town house. There was a big sports bag on the ground at her feet. She looked so small and pale; her hair limp and dull. Some of the life had been bleached out of her. But when she smiled at him, he thought he recognized a trace of the woman he'd fallen in love with. He was slow to approach her, reminding himself to look closely, to make certain he was seeing her and not the her he wanted to see. It was no use.

"Hi," she said, tears in her eyes.

"Going somewhere?"

"Away, yeah."

"Where?"

"Just away."

"You need some money?"

She hesitated. He took all the money he had out of his wallet plus the fifty dollars he used as a bank and folded it into her hand.

"If you need more, call me," he said. "If you don't wanna call me, call Bob. If you need me, I'll come get you."

"I know."

"You sure you won't tell me where—"

"Shhh." Marla put her index finger across his lips and then wedged herself into his arms. "Just let met go, Joe."

"Okay."

"You know I miss this smell sometimes, the way it stays on your work clothes even after you wash them."

"Heating oil?"

"Crazy, right? But I do."

"Crazy."

"It's Saturday morning, you've gotta go," she said, gently pushing him away.

"I love you."

"I know you do. I've gotta go."

He stood and watched her disappearing around the corner of the town house. As she went, Joe searched for signs of the fifty-first gallon in her gait.

☆   ☆   ☆   ☆

Bob Healy was pretty used to the Blue Wall of Silence. He'd banged his head against it for over twenty years. Cops didn't give up other cops; that was the myth. Yeah, and the Mafia had *omerta*, their code of silence. The reality was a lot less romantic. Healy had never made a big case without the cooperation of other cops and one look at the state of the American Mafia revealed that the RICO statutes were a lot more persuasive than *omerta*. What Bob Healy didn't expect to find was a conspiracy of silence amongst the owners of body shops, but that's pretty much what he'd run into.

He had gone all the way from Kings Park, to Commack, to Smithtown, to St. James, twelve shops in all, and he couldn't find anyone willing to talk to him about Noonan's Collision. He guessed it made sense. With all the insurance fraud and stolen parts floating around, these guys weren't anxious to open themselves up to investigation or retaliation. That said, Healy was losing patience. And as any one of the cops he had targeted during his career could testify, that wasn't a good thing.

He walked into Pete's Towing and Collison on Middle County Road in St. James and asked the guy at the counter for Pete. A bald, wiry man in his forties, wearing a ripe tomato red sweater—the name Pete embroidered in blue above his heart—stepped out of the office.

"I'm Pete. Can I help you?"

"I don't know, maybe. I was gonna bring my kid's car here to get the fender fixed and repainted because I heard good things about your shop, but I was having a brew at TGI Friday's at the mall and met this guy named Hank from Noonan's in Kings Park."

Pete's skin turned as red as his sweater. "Yeah, and what'd he say?"

"Said you guys did shabby work, bought used parts and charged for new, and that—"

"Fuck him!" The veins throbbed in Pete's skinny neck. "Noonan, the dad, he was a good guy, but the kid's an asshole. We don't ever buy used parts. People hear that, they don't come back. We've been here for twenty years and we got good accounts with every car company and supplier on the island. That schmuck Noonan's so fucked he can't even buy sandpaper on credit."

"What do you mean?"

"They're on credit hold with all their suppliers. He's burnt so many bridges that the local Honda dealerships won't even sell him parts for cash. He's gotta go all the way down the South Shore for cash parts from Honda."

"Amazing."

"Yeah. I don't know how he fucked up that business, but he did. Noonan's was a great shop for years. Great rep, lotsa cash walking through the door, but I guess you do sloppy work, start cutting corners and word gets around…"

Healy stopped himself from rolling his eyes. Now that he found somebody to finally talk about Noonan's, he couldn't get him to shut up.

"This your business card?" he finally said.

"That's it."

"Thanks, Pete. You've been a great help."

☆　☆　☆　☆

"One hundred gallons, right?"

"That's what you ordered, Mrs. Perchico. That's what I put in."

"Yeah, but the last few times the oil went so quick."

"Until today, it's been pretty cold out. Oil goes faster in the cold unless you lower your thermostat."

"You're not shorting me oil, are you?"

"If I was, I wouldn't tell you Mrs. Perchico, would I? But no, I'm not shorting you oil."

"I know companies they do that sometimes, short their customers. They take advantage of old people."

"Some do. I don't. I hope to get old myself someday."

"Okay, you're a good boy. Here," the old woman said, slipping a solitary quarter into Joe's oil-dirty palm. "Go get yourself a cup of coffee."

"Thanks very much, Mrs. Perchico. Happy New Year."

Joe Serpe turned and went down the front steps before the door closed at his back. Normally, Mrs. Perchico's routine made him want to stick needles in his eyes. She had been a Mayday customer for all the years Joe had driven for Frank and had stayed on after he and Healy bought back the company. In all that time, Joe must have made fifty deliveries to her house and every single time—regardless of per gallon price or season—she complained about the oil going too fast and asked if she was being shorted. And for his patience, Joe was always rewarded with a twenty-five cent tip for coffee. Good thing he wasn't a Starbucks man. But today, nothing, not even bullets could get through the numbness.

After all these years of driving, Serpe had never quite gotten used to the people aspect of oil delivery. On the street, as a detective, he saw the worst people at their worst; people at their most selfish, most violent, most desperate; people who were barely people anymore. Because the stakes were so high or maybe because the adrenaline rush was so intense, Serpe never quite saw his narcotics work in terms of routine. In oil, it was all about routine, his interactions with customers were the same, always; voices on the phone, faces through doors, quarters in palms.

His invisibility was one aspect of the job he would never understand but had come to accept. Almost from the first, he noticed that no one noticed him. People paid far more attention to their mailboxes than their mailmen. That's how he thought about it. He loved to tell Marla the stories of what people had done in front of him. To this day, women would come to the door half naked, some more than half, hand him the cash for the delivery and point out where the oil fill was on the side of the house. He had stood at the door and watched people smoke crack, shoot heroin, smack their kids, their wives, their pets. To his customers, he was as invisible as the water main or electric or cable wires. If he ran into Mrs. Perchico in the supermarket, she wouldn't recognize him. But Joe didn't sweat it anymore. It was just another part of the job, like dirty hands and smelly clothes.

He climbed back up into the tugboat's cab, put the quarter tip in the ashtray, and looked at the next delivery ticket. He didn't really see what it said. Maybe invisibility was contagious.

☆　☆　☆　☆

Normally, Healy wouldn't've been thrilled to see that the Suffolk cop from breakfast was back at the firehouse after lunch. He didn't know about the rest of Kings Park, but it did seem to have the best protected firehouse on Long Island. Healy decided to put the cop to work, if not for the county, then for him and Joe.

"Jeff, right?" Healy asked, walking up to the cop.

"Right."

Jeff was young, a real muscle-head who liked wearing his uniform shirt tight and spent as much time out of his unit posing as doing anything else. Healy knew the type. Out here they could survive their twenty years. In the city they tended to get chewed up and spit out.

Healy walked up to him conspiratorially. "Listen, Jeff, a piece of advice."

"What?" The kid squeezed a lot of the wrong kind of attitude into that one syllable.

"You know what I used to do for a living?"

"How would I know and why would I care?"

"I was a detective."

"Yeah. Macy's or Sears?"

"That's funny. No, NYPD."

"How was Traffic Control in the city?"

"You missed your calling, kid." Healy called him that purposefully.

"No, but close. Internal Affairs."

The kid tried to look completely unaffected, but mentioning IA gets a rise out of every cop, civilians too. While the young cop didn't exactly blanch, a little of the piss went out of him.

"There some message here for me?" He stuck his chest out in an act of physical defiance.

"You know any of the Suffolk County DAs?"

"Some."

"My last name's Healy. Healy, like George Healy."

Now came the blanching, and the kid got that panicky look even innocent people get when they're not sure what they've gotten caught up in.

"I didn't do nothing," said the cop.

Christ, Healy thought, how many times had he heard people say those same words in just the same tone and how few times was it true?

"Calm down, Jeff. I really am doing you a favor. What I want to tell you is that I think this firehouse, cozy as it is, could use a little less protecting than the rest of Kings Park. Better I tell you than some other citizen calling into the Fourth Precinct. You don't wanna have your supervising sergeant start watching you. That's how bad things start."

"I hear you. Thanks."

"No problem." Healy slapped the kid on the back and gave him a big smile. He had him right where he wanted him. "Listen, Jeff, could you do me a favor..."

[Confetti]

For the first time in a long time, Healy wasn't there when Serpe got back to the yard. It was odd not having him around. You get used to people in spite of yourself, Joe thought, and all the loss in the world can't teach you how to undo that. He had cashed out John and Anthony, paid them for the week, watched a little TV, checked and rechecked the tank valves on the trucks, swept the office floor, and then ran out of ways to avoid going home. He was about to lock up the office and close the yard gates when Healy pulled up. Joe looked out the trailer window, then sat in the quiet office listening to the car door slam, the crunch of his partner's footsteps, the chuffing of Healy's soles against the steps, the creak of the door.

"I caught you. Good," Healy said.

"So, anything?"

"Everything maybe."

"How so?"

"I think your instincts were right. There's something going on in that body shop."

"Yeah, but what?"

"I like somebody in the shop for Jimenez."

"That's a helluva a leap there, Bob."

Healy explained about the body shop's being on credit stop and how Noonan lived in Mastic.

"It's a long way from not being able to buy fenders from Honda to homicide," Joe said.

"Maybe, but maybe not. Noonan lives five blocks from where we found the body."

"How do you know that?"

"A Suffolk cop ran some tag numbers and sheets for me when I was at the firehouse."

"And you got him to do this how?"

"I said pretty please."

"You threatened him?"

"Something like that. Hank Noonan's been in the system since he was a kid, drugs mostly, some other petty shit. Probably drove his old man crazy. But he's got a real hard case working for him, a guy named William Burns. He has an up close and personal knowledge of the New York State Department of Corrections. Among other things, he did a long bid for assault with a deadly weapon."

"You got a name and address on the blond?" Joe asked.

"Sure. Debbie Hanlon. Lives right over here in Farmingville."

"I wonder what she does with her Saturday nights."

"You're thinking we should find out, huh?"

"I am," Joe said. "You think we should bring your brother into this or—I can't believe I'm saying this—Hoskins?"

"Hoskins, huh? You know, now that you mention the prick, was he at the wake?"

"He was there, all right. I got the bruises to prove it. But that's another story. I met Monaco's sister too. First, let's figure this shit out."

"Before I talk to my brother, let's talk to the girl. Shake her up a little and see what falls out of the tree. If what's going on at Noonan's isn't related to the murders, I can always get word of it to someone in the Suffolk PD without involving George."

Joe looked at the clock. "Okay, let's get something to eat and give

Debbie Hanlon time to get home."

☆   ☆   ☆   ☆

The red Civic two-door pulled onto the cracked blacktop at 47 Tulip Avenue at a little after 7:30. A motion sensitive floodlight popped
on and made it that much easier for Serpe and Healy, parked across the
street, to watch Debbie Hanlon. The blond pushed open the driver's
side door with her leg and got out of the car carrying a large drink and
a bag of KFC. She hip-checked the door shut and took a slow stroll
around the car. She put the bag down on the welcome mat, fished the
mail out of the box without looking at it and tucked it under her arm.
She fumbled with the the front door key before finally getting the door
open, picked up the chicken, and went inside the empty little house.

They waited until she got inside and had a chance to relax. They
wanted to throw a scare into her, but not push her to do something
stupid or dangerous. They wanted to knock her off balance, not run
her over. The fact was that detectives, even good ones , were sometimes
wrong about their hunches. They were on a fishing expedition and
couldn't afford to have it go wrong.

Bob Healy knocked firmly but politely, shield in hand, Joe Serpe
over his right shoulder. Although you are supposed to turn in your
shield when you retire, detectives often suffered convenient lapses of
memory when the time came. Healy had suffered such a lapse. Joe
Serpe hadn't gotten the chance. He had been forced to hand his gun
and shield over on the day he was arrested. The man he handed them
to was Detective Bob Healy. Looking back, that was only a small irony
in the scheme of things.

The door pulled back. There was recognition and resignation in
her face.

"Come on in," is all she said.

There were no questions, no protests, no hysterics. It didn't matter
to her that the shield was wrong or that one man didn't seem to have
one. The defeat was immediate and apparent in Debbie Hanlon's suddenly mournful brown eyes. Both ex-cops knew the look. She was inti-
mate with defeat. She expected it. And now that it had come, she was,

if not happy, then relieved. She turned and walked through her small, darkened house into the kitchen and slumped into a chair at the table. The strong smell of fried chicken filled up the whole house, but Debbie seemed to have lost her appetite and swept the food into the garbage.

She pointed at Serpe. "Billy figured you for a cop right away."

"That was Burns with the moustache?" Joe asked. "Where was Noonan?"

"In the back office. There's an office behind the shop." Now she looked up at Healy. "I'm surprised at you. You seemed nice."

"I am nice."

"No, you're a cop."

Healy changed subjects. "Your house?"

"My mom's. She moved down south last year."

"Listen, Debbie," Joe said, "we're not here to give you grief."

"You'd have to take a number to do that anyway."

"Aren't you a little young to be so bitter?" Healy said.

"I didn't know you had to be of age."

"But you have such a beautiful smile."

"I guess I shoulda been a clown then."

Joe pointed to his chest indicating that he wanted to question Debbie for the next few minutes.

"Like I said, we're not here to cause you trouble," Joe said.

"Why do cops always say that? It's stupid."

"We're here about the murder."

"What murder?" she asked, her expression unchanging.

"Alberto Jimenez, the driver from Epsilon Energy."

"I told you I did't know nothing about that."

"Why say that when we know you do?"

"Because it's the truth."

"Come on, Debbie. We know the shop's in trouble, that you guys are on credit hold with all your suppliers. We know that Hank's been in trouble with the law and that Billy's done hard time."

"So what? That don't equal killing nobody."

"Look, it's not hard to figure. Hank's cash poor and desperate. Billy comes to him and says he's got a way to fix that in the short run. With all these oil drivers getting killed, what's one more robbery? Maybe they didn't mean to kill Albie and things just got outta hand. Maybe the guy put up more of a fight than they expected. We understand how it can happen. It happens that way a lot. If that's what happened, you need to tell us so we can tell the DA."

"I don't know what you're talking about," she said, nervously combing her hair back as she had at the shop. "I got nothing to say to you guys."

"This is an unofficial visit, Debbie." It was Healy's turn again. "Next time it won't be. You talk to us now and we can protect you, keep you completely out of it. Maybe you can save Hank and Billy a few years inside. Frankly, I don't give a shit about them, but I do about you."

"You sound like every guy I was ever with before I sucked his cock. They all care about you until they come. Then afterwards I turn back into the fat girl. So get outta here. I got nothing to say to you."

Joe grabbed her broken finger away from her hair. "We didn't do this to you, Debbie. Remember that."

"I told you, I slammed it—"

"—in a car door. Yeah right."

"Get out!"

"Debbie," Joe said, squeezing her finger a bit, "I don't know which one of them you're hot for or which one broke your finger, but they've killed before and they'll kill again to protect themselves. If you're not gonna talk to us, be smart, don't go to them and tell them we were here. Bob, give her a card."

Healy handed her one of his old cards from the job, his home and cell numbers written on the back. "Call me, Debbie, anytime," he said. "I'd like to be able to do something for you."

"Why don't you just ask me for a blow job. It'd be easier." She ripped the card to pieces and threw them in the air like confetti.

"That was dumb, Debbie, and that scares me," Healy said, giving her another card. "You're not dumb. Let us help you. And watch what you say to these guys. My partner's right. Once you start killing, you might as well keep going."

She didn't say anything, but she didn't rip up the card either, slipping it into her back pocket.

Serpe made it a point to smoke his tires as he pulled away from the curb. They wanted to show Debbie Hanlon that the cops couldn't get away from her fast enough. They'd gone fast, but not very far. Serpe eased up behind Healy's car parked two blocks away on Ridgewood.

"How long you think it took her to get on the phone?" Healy asked.

"What's the world record?"

"I don't know, but I think she just set it."

"We better get back over there. Don't forget to park down the block on the opposite side of the street. Shut your headlights off and let the car roll to a stop."

"You know, Joe, most of the time it doesn't bother me, you're treating me like I wasn't a real cop. But remember, I was good enough to put people away who knew all the rules and all the angles. I was good enough to get you and your partner. Try and keep that in mind the next time we're working on something like this together," he said, sliding out of the car and leaving that balloon of poison gas in his place.

Serpe didn't know what to say, but even if he had, it was too late. Healy was in his own car and gone. What Joe did know was that the time was fast approaching when him and Bob Healy were going to have to have that talk they'd both been avoiding for months. You could float that balloon of poison gas only so many times before someone took a pin to it.

☆　☆　☆　☆

It didn't take long for the push they gave Debbie Hanlon to rebound. A little before 9:00, a fully pimped out Ford F-150 with a low rider suspension sped down Tulip and came to a stop in front of number 47. If the array of neon chassis lights, lime green and purple paint job weren't quite conspicuous enough, the earth rattling thump thump thumping of electronic bass that pounded out of the pickup's cab was guaranteed to get everyone's attention. The bass was so overwhelming, it completely swallowed up the throaty rumble of a Harley from the next block over. When the Ford's driver killed the ignition, Serpe's teeth were still vibrating.

The driver got out of the cab and looked around with distracted eyes that didn't seem to notice Joe sitting in his dark car a bit further up the block. Hank Noonan was a runty looking white boy dangling a cigarette from his lips and ill-fitting jeans from his hips. He wore a flat-billed Yankee's cap with the NY logo skewed to the left of the hat and a silver satin jacket, NOONAN'S COLLISION stitched in red across the back. He ambled over to the blond's front door with a gait that was part gangsta, part gangster, but mostly ridiculous. Serpe waited until Noonan went inside before calling Healy.

"Guess that's Noonan, huh?" Healy asked.

"Gotta be."

"What a clown. When you figure Burns to show?"

Before Healy even finished his question, Joe got the sick feeling in his belly that, unlike his hunches, was never wrong.

"What does Burns drive?" Serpe was screaming into the phone, but couldn't help himself. "What does Burns drive?"

"What are you shouting—"

"What does Burns drive?"

"An old Harley chopper, why?"

Serpe was out of his car and running across the street, .9mm in his right hand. Seeing this, Healy was out of his car too, weapon drawn, running to the house. Serpe was at the end of the driveway when a rapid succession of six or seven flashes lit up the front bay window. Each flash came with a loud bang. Joe froze for a second, just long enough for Healy to catch up and for darkness to settle back over the inside of the house.

"Fuck." Joe whispered. "Take the house."

Serpe, tucking the Glock into the pocket of his leather jacket, headed for the fence to the backyard. Before getting wounded, he'd have been able to put his hands on the cross bar and vault it. Now he was forced to slowly scale the four foot high cyclone fence and make sure to land on his good leg. Over the fence, between the house on one side and an overgrown hedge on the other, it was hard to see more than five feet ahead. But he heard a rapid thudding of footsteps and the distinctive groan and chinking of cyclone fencing as it strained against the weight of someone slamming against it.

Pulling the gun out of his pocket as he went, Serpe took off toward the back fence. His toe snagged on a hedge root and he went sprawling, the gravel chewing up the clenched fingers of his gun hand and the palm of his other. As he fell, there was a flash, a bang, something hissed and whistled over his head. Serpe rolled quickly to his right, pressing himself as tightly to the outside wall of the house as he could. There was a second flash, a bang, and the gravel spit up at him. His mouth was dry and his heart was pounding out of his chest.

There was no third flash. The fence groaned again and, as Serpe rolled over, he could just make out Billy Burns straddling the top of the six foot tall backyard fence. As Burns swung his other leg over the fence, Serpe made a desperate run at him. He missed, but the force with which Joe hit the fence sent Burns flying. He hit the concrete patio in the adjoining backyard with a nasty thud and something snapped; more likely a bone than branch.

Burns screamed in pain and ran, cursing loudly as he went. Serpe tried to climb the fence to go after him, but the blood on his hands made it slow going. Just as Serpe finally got to the top of the fence, Burns' Harley roared to life and this time there was no thumping bassline to dampen the rumble. By the time Serpe had one leg over the fence, Burns was gone. When he got down off the fence, he found an old Army issue Browning .45. He left it where Burns had tossed it and limped through the open backdoor of the house.

Walking through the kitchen, he saw Bob Healy at the opposite end of the hallway that connected the kitchen and the living room. Healy was kneeling over Noonan, pressing a blood soaked bath towel down hard on the man's chest. Debbie Hanlon's lifeless body, arms straight out in front of her like Superman in mid-flight, lay in the hallway between them. There was a dark splotch almost dead center between her shoulder blades, one on her lower back, and a nasty little red crater in the back of her head. Her pretty blond hair wasn't so pretty or so blond anymore. There was a big pool of blood beneath her. Serpe didn't want to think about what those .45 slugs had done to her on the way out.

"He's still alive," Healy said breathlessly. "Call the cops."

Even before Joe dialed 9-1-1 on his cell phone, he could hear sirens filling up the night. He walked over to Debbie Hanlon and retrieved Healy's card from her back pocket. Odds were, she wasn't going to have used it anyway. Now it was a sure bet.

[The Brain God Gave Me]

SUNDAY, JANUARY 9TH, 2005—EARLY MORNING

There were the four of them in the office in Hauppauge: Hoskins, Serpe, Bob and George Healy. They all looked like shit, but Serpe and Bob Healy were in the sorriest shape. Neither one had slept more than ten minutes and both had endured several hours of police interrogation. Serpe's hands were caked with his own blood, his face scratched and dirty, his pants and jacket ripped, bloodied, and filthy. Bob Healy had almost as much of Hank Noonan's blood on his clothes as Noonan had left in his body when the EMTs showed up. Worse for them both was the guilt over Debbie Hanlon. Sooner or later they'd go home and shower, put on fresh clothing, and get bandaged up, but they understood that they would never be wholly clean again.

George Healy laid the phone back in its cradle. "That was the DA who just got off the phone with the police commissioner. You just can't imagine how pleased they both are with this mess. And guess whose job it is to clean it all up and make it smell sweet and look nice and pretty for the media?" He didn't wait for an answer. "That's right. It's mine. Now what the fuck am I supposed to—"

The phone interrupted George before his tirade got going in earnest. Just as he picked up the phone, the fax machine behind his desk began chittering away. George spun his chair around and scooped up the fax as soon as the transmission was complete.

He thanked the person on the other end of the line and hung up.

"Well, well, gentlemen, it's our lucky day. Noonan's dead. He started bleeding again and crapped out on the operating table at Stony Brook."

"How's that make us lucky?" Hoskins asked.

"Deathbed confession, right?" Serpe said, pointing to the fax in George's hand.

"That's right. The little scumbag gave the three of you a going away present just before his shredded artery blew its patch. He dictated a statement to a Detective Braun," George read off the fax. "The statement was witnessed by a doctor and two nurses and was signed by Noonan."

"What's it say?" Bob Healy wanted to know.

"It says that you and Serpe were right, but for the wrong reasons."

"Huh?"

"It wasn't about the body shop's cash flow, at least not directly. Here," George said, handing the fax over to his brother. "It seems that Burns knew some bikers who were raising cash to bring in loads of high quality marijuana from Canada. The minimum buy-in stake was five grand in cash, but Burns only had a grand. Debbie Hanlon put in two grand, but Noonan had nothing. He was in debt up to his eyeballs and the business wasn't his to sell. So Burns came up with the plan to rob one of the Epsilon drivers at the end of a busy day. Noonan said the papers gave Burns the idea because they listed how much money was taken from the other dead drivers. They had the girl blow Jimenez while they checked out his route for the day and then set a trap for him. Noonan says it was Burns that beat Jimenez to death and who broke the girl's finger to warn her about keeping her mouth shut. They thought that by leaving the truck and body over by the Poospatuck Reservation that it would get blamed on the tribe."

"What a bunch of rocket scientists," Hoskins said. "Jesus, if these guys had half a brain, we'd be in trouble."

"Yeah, that's why my brother and Serpe figured it out in three days and you had your thumb stuck so far up your ass you were gagging on it."

Hoskins' jaw clenched. "I had five fucking homicide investigations to deal with at once and the press breathing down my neck. Sorry, I don't have time to play Sherlock Holmes. I was checking leads. I woulda gotten to these guys soon enough."

George Healy slammed his palm down on his desk. "Soon enough! When was that gonna be? Don't lower my opinion of you beyond where it is now."

"What about tonight—I mean, last night?" Joe asked.

"Apparently, the girl got spooked," George said. "She called Noonan, who, like the total jerk-off that he was, called Burns. Burns figured to cut his losses and killed both of them. My guess is he was probably gonna do it eventually. Noonan and the girl were the only two witnesses against him and he had the cash to buy into the marijuna deal. He didn't need to split his take. If you two hadn't been lurking around, he would've gotten away with it too."

Hoskins scowled, but kept his mouth shut.

"Cops picked Burns up?" Bob asked.

"Not yet, but they will."

"Where do we go from here?" Serpe was curious.

"We," George said, "aren't going anywhere. My brother is going to hand over Noonan's statement to Detective Hoskins who is going to read it until he can recite it word for word. He's also going home to get showered and shaved and dressed in a suit that doesn't look like it fit him when he used to hang out with Travolta and the Bee Gees. And he's gonna be back here for a ten o'clock news conference. And during that news conference, he's apt to say that he had suspected the crew at Noonan's all along and that he was about to break the case when Burns took things into his own hands. He's also going to say that he's investigating the possibility that these suspects were involved with the other killings."

"But that's bullshit," Bob said.

"Yeah, we know that, big brother, but Detective Hoskins is going to say it in any case. It'll keep the press off our asses for a few days until it's clear to them that the first four cases were unrelated to the Jimenez homicide. By then…" George Healy turned and glared at Hoskins. "What the fuck are you still doing here? You have the statement. Make sure you're back up here at nine-thirty so we can go over your story."

Hoskins hesitated, opened his mouth to say something, but thought better of it. He left without farewells. When he was gone, both Joe and Bob stood to follow.

"Where do you think you're going?" George said. "Sit down!"

They sat.

"Not you, Serpe. You can wait for my brother downstairs or go home or do whatever it is you do when you're not getting my brother into trouble."

Joe got up, left, and didn't look back. George paced until he heard the elevator ring and the doors slide shut.

"What the fuck are you playing at, Bob? You could've gotten yourself killed tonight."

"But I didn't."

"Brilliant argument."

"It'll do."

"No, it won't," George said, taking a plastic evidence bag out of his pocket and tossing it on his desk.

"What's that?"

"It's a favor."

"Are we doing riddles now, little brother?"

"You tell me."

"That's almost funny, George."

"You think?" He picked the evidence bag up and tossed it to Bob. "It's a piece of an NYPD business card that one of the techs found at the scene. He told me about it before he logged it in and I asked him not to. I guess you and Serpe didn't get all the pieces when you cleaned up after yourselves. What did you do, flush the other pieces down the can? You realize what I'm doing could cost me my job, right? Was the card yours or Serpe's."

"Mine."

"So you were both in the house before and after the homicides."

"What makes you think that?"

"The brain God gave me and almost twenty years doing this job."

"We were there before the murders," Bob admitted.

"So you went in impersonating cops and... Come on, tell me. I'm already in up to my nipples. If I'm gonna get fucked, I might as well know why."

"Both Joe and I knew there was something wrong going on in that shop, but we couldn't be sure if it was connected to Jimenez's murder. We also knew the girl would probably be the weak link. She seemed like a good kid, but in over her head. We figured to throw a scare into her and..."

"The ploy worked."

"A little too well. It—no, we got her killed."

"Noonan got her killed. He called Burns, not the girl."

"Somehow that's not making me feel much better."

"Go home and get some sleep."

"Okay."

"Just one more thing," George said, reaching into his desk. "Here's your two weapons. Funny thing, though."

"What's that?"

"In all your time on the job, I never knew you to carry two pieces."

"I'm getting more insecure as I get older," Bob said, a sad smile on his face.

"I figured. I know you're way too smart to let a guy like Joe Serpe carry a weapon registered to you."

"Way too smart."

"Yeah, Bob, that's what I used to think."

"Me, too, little brother. Me too."

[Iago]

Thursday, January 13th, 2005—Morning

Bob Healy ignored the phone and threw his empty coffee cup at the TV screen.

"Come look at this shit!" he screamed to Serpe. "Five days later and they're still going. Now they got Debbie's mom on camera, collapsing in front of the funeral home. Look at the poor woman. These media whores have no shame."

"Shame? No one has shame anymore, or haven't you noticed?" Joe said, clicking off the TV. "Come on, answer the phones. We got a business to run."

Serpe had long ago learned how to ignore the press. For years after the Abruzzi trial and Ralphy's subsequent suicide, Joe stopped reading the papers, listening to news radio, or watching TV news. He blamed the media—not without some justification—for blowing up his marriage. TV reporters at his front door became as much a fixture as the statue of the Virgin Mary on his lawn. Reporters followed his wife to work and his son to school. As he once told Healy, "If you think all news is bad news, it's worse when it's about you." But Bob Healy was a news junky and could not look away.

Although the murders of Debbie Hanlon and Hank Noonan and their connection to the oil driver killings was not quite a grand slam like the Amy Fisher/Joey Buttafuoco debacle had been, the local media were doing a major circle jerk over the story. And they would keep at it until the next best thing came along. With Iraq War fatigue in full swing and no one wanting to read yet another story about suicide bombers at the fruit market or hear about one more of our own killed by a roadside bomb, a nice local story of murder and betrayal was just what the doctor ordered. So the TV and radio stations and papers had given the story the full Shakespeare-Ringling Brothers treatment.

With leaps of faith and fiction, but few facts, they had woven the relationship between Hanlon, Noonan, and Burns into a love triangle with wheels. Poor Debbie had been cast as Long Island's low rent Desdemona and Burns as Iago on a Harley. Noonan, a buffoon his whole life, had, in death, been miraculously transformed and thrust into the roles of both Cassio and Othello. None of the casting nor the mechanics quite fit, but the press never let the facts get in the way of a good story. They had long since traded in their honor for entertainment value. Perhaps the most egregious bit of miscasting was their portrayal of Detective Tim Hoskins as a real life Sherlock Holmes. Highly placed, unnamed sources inside the Suffolk County PD had let it be known that Hoskins was up for a medal. And Alberto Jimenez, the only really tragic figure in this whole mess, was forgotten by Monday morning, his memory washed away like the blood off the pavement of Old Northport Road.

"Still…" Healy growled.

"Let it go until the TV movie comes out."

"It's eating at me, Joe. It's eating at me."

That was another thing Healy was unaccustomed to; the guilt. Joe knew all about the guilt. First with Ralphy and then with Marla, he'd had to learn how to bear that cross. With Debbie, he had a few rough days, but he'd come around.

"Look, partner, remember what you told me your brother said. Burns would have killed the girl and Noonan soon enough. He wasn't gonna split his profits with them and they were the only ones who could've fingered him for Jimenez. We gave her a chance to save herself and she fucked up by calling Noonan. I know it's harsh, but if she had just come clean with us…"

"We didn't go to save her."

"That's true," Joe said. "But we threw her a line and she didn't take it."

"Maybe she didn't know how."

"Maybe. You gotta face it, Bob, there's plenty of guilt in this life we deserve to carry. There's no need to go looking for extra weight."

"Sounds nice, but I don't think it's going to help me sleep."

"Sleep. I gave that up a long time ago."

★   ★   ★   ★

With the weather having turned cold and snow in the forecast for the weekend, Serpe and his drivers were as busy as they'd been in weeks. Healy couldn't answer the phones fast enough. So when his cell buzzed in his jacket pocket, Serpe just assumed it was Healy calling with another stop.

The weird thing about people and weather was that sub-zero temperatures didn't seem to panic them much, but the mention of snow sent them into oil-buying hysteria. Of course, folks had it exactly wrong. Snow didn't burn oil. Low temperatures did. It was like that stupid bread and milk phenomenon. The weatherman predicts a Nor'easter or a hurricane and people who haven't touched a slice of white bread or had a glass of milk in thirty years, rush out to the supermarket for milk and white bread. Joe Serpe wasn't complaining nor was he feeling bad about it. Oilmen were pretty low on the totem pole of businessmen who profited from people's stupidity.

Serpe pulled to the curb and answered the phone.

"Hello," he barked over the noise of the engine.

"Joe…Is that Joe Serpe?" It was a woman's voice.

"This is Joe."

"Hey," her voice brightened, "it's Georgine Monaco."

"Hey yourself. What can I do for you Gigi?"

"You busy tonight?"

He was surprised to hear himself say, "Not that I know of. Why?"

"Let me buy you dinner."

"Okay."

"Come by my apartment around eight. I got something to show you."

"Sounds good."

She gave him her address and hung up. The phone buzzed again before he could get it back in his pocket. This time, it *was* Healy calling with another stop.

★ ★ ★ ★

Now that the phones had finally slowed down, Bob Healy took full advantage of the opportunity to torture himself. He clicked from news channel to news channel, hoping to catch a still shot of Debbie Hanlon or footage from the funeral. What he got instead was footage of Noonan's tearless father, a *my-son-had-it-coming* expression pulled across his hard face, yakking at a row of microphones. He could see the man's lips moving, but the father's words were drowned out by Healy's own disgust. The elder Noonan seemed more upset that his son had ruined the business than by his murder.

The phone rang again and Healy thanked God for it, aloud. He turned his back to the screen and picked up.

"Mayday Fuel, how can—"

"Detective Healy?"

"Not any more."

"It's me, Detective Hines."

"Blades?"

"Your memory works good for an old man."

"Very funny. What's up?"

"The D-O-I."

"The what?"

"The Department of Investigation."

"What about it, huh?" Healy asked.

"I'll give you two guesses who put the lockdown on Rusty Monaco's files."

"What would the New York City Department of Investigation want with a retired detective's files?" Healy said. "Strange how that retired detective turned up dead."

"Funny how I was thinking that same thing."

"You know what they say about great minds."

"Yeah, that they don't believe in coincidences," she said.

"Blades…"

"What?"

"Do we know what DOI was looking at?"

"I'm working on that now. I got some friends over there."

"IAB detectives have no friends."

"You may be old, Healy, but I didn't think you was blind."

"What's that supposed to mean?"

"My friends over there are *special* friends, if you hear what I'm saying."

"Blades, I think you and my business partner would get along. The first thing he asked me about you was if you were cute."

"And what did you say?"

He ignored the question. "Let me know when you get something."

Healy put down the phone and turned back to the TV.

[Walking Around Money]

THURSDAY, JANUARY 13TH, 2005—EVENING

Gigi Monaco lived in a cramped basement apartment on a generic block of ranches and split-ranches in Islip. The most interesting thing about the area was the street names. That wasn't saying a whole lot as the streets were named for other towns on Long Island. Although Joe Serpe wasn't sure what was on the agenda for the evening, he brought two bottles of red wine and some Costco flowers. Gigi smiled at the flowers, kissed him nervously on the cheek, and asked him in.

She looked pretty, prettier than she had looked the other night. She had taken real care with her makeup, softening the cut of her jaw and highlighting her cheekbones. She was dressed in a tight white sweater, a black leather sash that emphasized her breasts and ample curves, and black slacks over high heeled black pumps. In spite of the dress up, she seemed very uncomfortable in her own skin and couldn't manage to stay in one place for more than a few seconds at a time. Up and down, moving around the apartment, she chatted about this and that, everything and nothing. A few glasses of wine didn't slow her down at all.

At first, Joe chalked it up to sexual tension. He was a little nervous himself and given Gigi's stated preferences, it was possible that she regretted inviting him over in the first place. But that's not what it felt like to Serpe. No, there was something bothering her and he didn't think it was worry over the prospect of their sleeping together.

"What's going on, Gigi?" he asked, hooking his hand around her bicep to slow her down.

"What do you mean?"

"Come on. You're flying around this place like crazy. You mentioned something on the phone about wanting to show me—"

"Wait here a second," she said, slipping out of his grasp.

Gigi Monaco walked past the tiny eat-in kitchen, disappearing through a flimsy folding door. She re-emerged carrying two plastic grocery bags and plopped them down on the little roundtop kitchen table. She was breathing very heavily, more from nerves than exertion, Joe thought, and a thin bead of sweat on her upper lip was clearly visible under the cool blue flourescent light of the ceiling fixture.

She took a deep breath and then spilled the contents of the bags out onto the table. When she was done, she tossed the empty bags aside, and made a sweeping gesture with her arms like a TV gameshow hostess showing eager contestants the prizes they might win. As she did so, her left forearm knocked a few neatly banded stacks of hundred dollar bills off the top of the pile onto the floor.

It wasn't the first time Joe Serpe had seen that much cash in one place. In fact, as piles of cash went, this was a pretty small one. As a hotshot narcotics detective in the age of cocaine, Joe had found as much as five million dollars in cash during a bust. It was all carefully stacked in cardboard boxes in a closet in Washington Heights. He'd never taken a dime of the money he'd seized. The same could not be said of his late partner, Ralph Abruzzi.

"Well, at least now I know who's paying for dinner," Joe said.

Gigi laughed joylessly, loudly, and too long. She just needed to get it out somehow. When she was done, Joe asked about the money.

"I got a call from Rusty's lawyer to come for the reading of the will. When I went, Rusty's bitch ex-wife and their kid, and some older guy named Finn McCauly were there. McCauly said he was—"

"—a detective like your brother, right?"

"You know him?"

"Everyone knows Finnbar fucking McCauly. Guy should've been off the job a hundred years ago, but he's like an NYPD institution. He must've been one of your brother's partners somewhere along the way."

"Yeah, that's what he said. Anyways, the whole thing took like five minutes. The bitch got nothing. Their kid got Rusty's personal cop shit and an insurance policy my brother bought when he was on the job. I got a few grand from Rusty's bank account and that Finn guy got an envelope."

"An envelope?" Joe was curious.

"Yeah. When the lawyer handed it to him, McCauly left without a word."

"How about that condo I told you about?"

"It wasn't included in the will, not unless that envelope McCauly got had something to do with it."

"I guess that's possible. But what about this money?" Joe asked, fanning a stack of hundreds like a deck of cards.

"The lawyer asked me to hang around until the others left. When he was sure they were gone, he handed me a white envelope. When I asked what was going on, he just said that Rusty had left specific instructions that I be given that envelope if he died. Outside in my car, I opened it up and there was a note from Rusty apologizing for being a crappy brother. At the bottom there was an address and a key scotch-taped to the paper."

"Where was the address?"

"This self-storage place on Hempstead Turnpike in Plainview. There was nothing inside the unit except for a big garbage bag with those two plastic bags inside of it," she said, nodding at the discarded supermarket bags.

"Did you count it?"

"A hundred and twenty five grand...give or take," she said.

"Most people would be thrilled to have this fall in their laps, but you're scared, Gigi. Why?"

"Like I told you before, my brother didn't have nothing to his name. That means this is somebody else's money."

"Everybody's money starts out as someone else's."

"Maybe so, but what if that someone else should come looking for it? I don't need no bullseye painted on my ass."

Serpe thought about arguing the point, but Joe knew better than most that cops can have very sticky fingers. It wasn't difficult for him to believe that a bitter prick like Rusty Monaco could have used his shield to create a little unofficial retirement fund. Joe didn't think it was the time to discuss that possibility with Gigi.

"You're smart to be wary."

"That night when you told me about the condo," she said, gulping her wine, "I guess I didn't really believe you. I mean, you're a nice guy and all, but I don't know you. I figured you just got it wrong about Rusty having money to buy real estate."

"So, what are you gonna do with the money?"

"I don't know. I was maybe thinking of giving it to you," she said, pouring herself another glass of wine.

"You just said you don't know me."

"Who the fuck else am I gonna trust? I got no family to speak of, no friends I'd trust with all that money. What should I do, call up my ex and ask her to keep a hundred grand under her mattress for me? Besides, you said you owed Rusty."

"Maybe that was just bullshit."

"Nah. That was the truth. So," she said, "you gonna take it, the money, I mean?"

"I'll think about it over dinner. And if I decide the answer is yes, I'll hold it for you, but I won't take it. In the meantime, give me that lawyer's name and address. I think I need to have a talk with him."

She grabbed her bag, got her wallet, and dug out a business card. She handed it to Serpe. He read the name aloud. "Brian W. Stanfill, Esquire."

"Esquire my left tit. He's a slimy storefront bastard, Joe. Watch yourself with him."

"So, what kinda food are you in the mood for?"

"I should be asking you that. I'm treating."

"Steak."

"Cool. But what should I do with the money while we're gone?" she asked.

"Leave it there. Maybe someone will take it and solve your problem."

☆　☆　☆　☆

Joe Serpe rolled quietly out of bed and headed into Gigi's bathroom. As he showered, he half-hoped she would get up and follow him in. The sex had been good, very good, but disconnected from passion, even lust. They had used each other by mutual consent; Joe to exorcise a ghost and Gigi… Serpe wasn't sure what she'd gotten out of it. If it was merely comfort, then, he supposed, that was enough.

Gigi didn't stir. Serpe dried himself off, collected his clothes, and got dressed in the kitchen. When he was done, he put the money back into the two white plastic grocery bags, and left. He tied the bags up and put them in the trunk of his car. He thought about putting them in the front seat, but realized he'd have a hell of a time trying to explain that much walking around money to any cop who might stop him.

As he pulled away from the curb, Joe got an uncomfortable feeling. Maybe Gigi was right. Maybe the money was someone else's or maybe there was somebody out there who knew about it and thought maybe he deserved it more than Monaco's sister. In any case, he decided he'd be paying more attention to his rearview mirror than he usually did.

[Target of Convenience]

Serpe was already in and had mapped out the routes for the day by the time Bob Healy strolled into the office.

"I'm glad you're here," Healy said. "I got something to tell you."

"I doubt it's as big as what I've got to tell *you*."

"Nothing like a pissing contest first thing in the morning to get your blood going, huh?"

"Fine," Joe said, reaching into his pocket. "Heads or tails?"

"Tails."

"I knew you were gonna pick tails. You've gotta be contrary."

"Flip it and shut up."

Serpe flicked his thumb and the quarter jumped. Healy swiped it out of the air with his right hand, smacked the coin down on the back of his left hand, and lifted his right palm.

"Tails, it is," he said, showing it to Serpe. "But I'm feeling generous today, so you go ahead."

"Okay. Don't use truck number four for any reason at all for the next few days."

"That's your big news, huh, that number four is out of service?"

"No. The reason it's out of service is the big news."

"And that reason would be…"

"There's a hundred and twenty-five thousand dollars in the tank."

"Get the fuck out—" Healy stopped himself when he saw the expression on Serpe's face. "Holy shit! You're not kidding, are you?"

"No. Let me ask you something about Rusty Monaco. From what you said, I take it that you investigated the shit out of him."

"More than any other cop with the possible exception of you," Healy said.

"Talk about a dubious fucking honor, but let's forget that for now. Was Monaco a thief?"

"We never investigated him for—"

"That's not what I'm asking you, Bob. Was Monaco a thief?"

"I don't think so, no. In his way, he was like you."

"Jesus, partner, you're just making my day."

"What I mean is, I never got the feeling he was on the job to line his pockets. Don't get me wrong, as far as I'm concerned, he should have never made it out of the academy. He might've beaten the shit outta somebody for putting too much sugar in his coffee, especially if they were black, but he wouldn't have taken the coffee for free."

"I thought you were gonna say that. Problem is, for a guy who didn't take stuff on the arm, he died owning a condo in Florida that neither of us could afford and he left his sister a hundred and twenty five grand. Better yet, neither the money nor the condo was in the will," Serpe said, noticing a grin on Healy's face. "What are you smiling at?"

"Nothing, except that maybe what I've got to tell you has something to do with what you just told me. Blades—Detective Hines called me. Seems that the people who put the access block on Monaco's NYPD files work for the city DOI."

"What would the Department of Investigation want with a retired detective?"

"That's the same question that popped into my head when she told me. She says she's got friends inside DOI, so maybe she'll get back to me today. Somehow, I get the impression that Monaco having a

THE FOU4RTH VICTIM **99**

hundred and a quarter large and the DOI blocking access to his files are not unconnected."

"You're a suspicious bastard."

"Just my nature, but I never let my suspicions get ahead of the facts," Healy said. "I got pretty far by following the evidence where it took me, not by where I thought it should go."

"One thing, though, before we get too wrapped up in this. I was thinking last night that the money and the condo are all very interesting, but that's not why Monaco was killed. He was robbed and murdered because he drove an oil truck down the wrong dark street in the wrong neighborhood on the wrong night, not because he owned a condo he couldn't swing or had a bag full of cash."

"Maybe."

"What do you mean, *maybe*?" Serpe asked.

"I mean maybe. You weren't the only one doing some thinking last night. After I spoke with Blades, I tried to get some things straight in my head. Look, Alberto Jimenez was killed because he had cash in his pocket and he was a target of convenience, but his murder wasn't directly connected to the other four, not really."

"Yeah, okay, I'm with you so far."

"I was thinking that maybe the other four murders were connected, but not in the obvious ways. Sure, on the surface they all seem like robberies where the perpetrator killed the victims so there'd be no witnesses. But I got this crazy idea in my head that maybe they were homicides first and—"

"—robberies second," Serpe said.

"Right. That there was only one intended target and that the other robberies and homicides were window dressing done just to throw off the cops."

"Like that sniper asshole from a few years back who killed the guy through the diner window in Commack and who shot that kid in the fast food joint in order to set up another murder. That's a pretty big leap there, partner. What happened to following the evidence?"

"I said it was a possible, that we should keep it in mind, not that I was sure about it. Besides, you'd have to be some sick calculating bastard to kill three innocent men just to kill a fourth."

"Sick, yeah, or desperate. After the shit I saw in narcotics, Bob, I have no trouble believing that desperation could drive a person to do anything. How far someone will go can be a function of how desperate they are, but let's follow your prescription and follow the evidence where it goes."

"Sounds nice," Healy agreed, "but until we get the Suffolk PD reports on the homicides, we won't have much evidence to follow."

"Leave that to me," Serpe said. "I think I've got an idea how to lay our hands on 'em."

"This I gotta see."

"Forget that for now. You know Finnbar McCauly?"

"I was in Internal Affairs, not shipwrecked with Gilligan and the Skipper, for chrissakes. Everyone in the department knew McCauly. Why you want to know that?"

"He was at the reading of Monaco's will. I guess they musta been partners once."

"A very important once."

Serpe screwed up his face. "You just lost me."

"When that black kid took the tumble off the roof in Brooklyn, McCauly was Monaco's partner."

[Thong]

FRIDAY, JANUARY 14TH, 2005—LATE AFTERNOON

Gigi was at least partially correct in her assessment of Brian W. Stanfill, Esquire. He ran his practice out of a storefront in a strip mall on Sunrise Highway in Seaford. As to whether she was right about the lawyer being slimy, Serpe couldn't yet say. Cops, even disgraced ex-detectives, don't, as a rule, hold lawyers in high regard, but Stanfill had a pleasant enough phone voice and had been very courteous when Joe called to schedule the appointment. What he did know was that Stanfill wasn't a complete idiot. For while the strip mall had the classic Long Island lineup of stores—deli, dojo, pizzeria, Chinese take-out, bar, card store—it also contained a doc-in-the-box walk-in clinic and a real estate sales firm.

The lawyer's office was shouldered on one side by the dojo and by the walk-in clinic on the other. The real estate company was next to the clinic. So it was by no means coincidental that one of the two biggest signs in Stanfill's front window advertised a set fee for house closings. The other sign boasted of his success in medical malpractice and personal injury law suits. His mall neighbors must have just loved him. According to other window advertisements, Stanfill did criminal defense work—with a particular expertise in DUI and DWI—and flat fee divorce settlements. He also did mediation, prepared tax returns, pre-nups, and wills. The man had a bigger menu than Applebee's. Joe wondered if he did card tricks too.

Serpe pressed his face against the front window, cupping his gloved hands at the sides of his eyes, but couldn't see a thing through the maze of signs. The door glass was darkly tinted, but not quite to opacity. Stanfill's name—the "a" missing completely and the bottom of the "f" torn away—and his title were displayed at the top of the door with his office hours listed below. Hanging inside the door was one of those little *Out of the Office-Will Return At...* signs. The clockface on the sign indicated Stanfill would be back at 2 PM. Problem was that 2 PM had come and gone nearly three hours ago and that his appointment with Joe was in less than five minutes. Serpe didn't pay much attention to the window sign. People were always careless about stuff like that.

Serpe tugged hard on the door handle. It stubbornly refused to pull back. He rapped on the glass to no good end. This crap was hard enough to stomach when his oil customers blew him off, but to have wasted his time driving down to the South Shore after a twenty stop day, fully pissed him off. He thought about getting a few slices of pizza or a quart of pork chow fun for dinner. Angry as he was, Serpe realized he didn't have much of an appetite.

He got halfway to his car and about-faced. He stormed through the parking lot to the end of the mall building and went around back. Here was the real world, the back alley, no neon signs or fancy facades here. This was a cop's world, an oil driver's world; a place of loading docks and Dumpsters, of rotting refuse and kitchen steam, of little brown men in white aprons smoking cigarettes. Serpe counted backdoors and found Stanfill's. Unlike its front counterpart, the pitted metal backdoor pulled right open.

Before the door swung shut behind him, just enough light leaked in with him to let Serpe catch a glimpse of the storage room. He called out Stanfill's name and ran his right hand along the wall. He flicked up the toggle switch and a bare bulb mounted to the ceiling popped on.

The unpainted walls were unadorned, the tape and joint compound showing at the seams on the bare plasterboard. There was a bathroom to his left, shelves of office supplies on his right, and another door straight ahead. As he walked forward, checking to see if the bathroom was empty—it was—Serpe was treated to a muted serenade of grunts and screams, thuds and smacks coming through the walls from the dojo.

He pulled open the storage room door, once again calling out Stanfill's name. There was, as before, no reply, although the dojo chorus was even louder in here. He found the wall switch, but the light fixtures in this room were a few steps up from a bare bulb. There were a series of recessed halogen highhats buried in the drop ceiling. This too seemed to be a storage room of sorts, but for case records and files, not toilet paper and ink cartridges. The walls were lined with file cabinets. Serpe tugged on some of the cabinet drawers. Locked. The walls above the cabinets were painted an off white and the floors were covered in a cheap gray industrial carpet.

Unlike the two other doors, the door in the file room pushed out into the office. The office was dark, but not completely black. Stray light from the parking lot filtered in through small spaces between the front window signs and through the door. Even before Serpe stepped into the vacated door jamb, he knew something was wrong. He could feel it and he could smell it. There was a heavy masking odor of Chinese food in the air and beneath it, the cloying, unmistakable stink of shit. Joe Serpe stopped moving, stopped breathing. He listened for noises that didn't belong, but all he could hear was the whoosh and splash of passing cars riding through snow melt puddles in the parking lot and the ever present dojo soundtrack. Serpe stepped back, shut the lights, and pulled out Healy's Glock in one seamless motion. Generally, it would be bad form to rack a weapon at this point, but given that he had made no secret of his presence, the unmistakable click-click of a round being chambered wasn't such a terrible thing. It would certainly let any potential attacker know that Joe was more than an agrieved husband armed with more than complaints about an unfaithful wife.

"All right, motherfucker! When I step into that room, I want you face down on the ground, hands behind your head. I come in there and see you in any other position or holding anything that even looks like a weapon and I'm gonna blow your nuts off. Now, get the fuck down on the ground!"

Serpe listened closely, but couldn't hear anything more than what he heard before. He crouched low, scanning the office as best he could. Neither the view nor the lighting was what he would have wanted. None of this is what he would have wanted. Joe could make out Stanfill's desk tucked in the far corner close to the front window, a few chairs facing the desk, a leather couch on the wall opposite, and a little magazine table next to the couch. No body. The one problem was that because the door opened out into the office, it created a big blind spot.

Serpe stood slowly out of the crouch and took silent steps back into the file room. He took a few deep breaths to calm himself, checked the Glock, counted to three in his head. At three, he ran. When his foot got near the threshold of the office door, Joe shoulder-rolled. He hit hard, crashing into the chairs in front of Stanfill's desk, but at least he had the corner of the desk between him and the blindspot. Righting himself, pushing the Glock before him, Serpe peeked around the desk. There *was* someone hiding in the blind spot, but he was in no shape to do Joe Serpe or anyone else any harm, ever.

It was difficult to say much about the body other than it was a man's and that he was dressed in an expensive suit. He was cold to the touch and lay on his side, hands and feet tied behind him. Serpe didn't want to risk turning on a light to get a better look. Instead he went back into the rear store room and searched around for a flashlight. He found one in a box on a shelf along with a hand-crank radio, a first aid kit, candles, matches, and other emergency paraphenalia. Nice try, Serpe thought, but there were emergencies that you can't prepare for. He latched the backdoor, tested the flash, and went back into the office.

Serpe made sure not to aim the flashlight out toward the parking lot as he more carefully examined the body. It was a pretty gruesome scene. The smell of urine and feces was very intense close to the body. The man's face had been savagely beaten to a pulpy mess, his nose pushed back in to the skull, lips swollen and shredded. A bloody gag stuck to a strip of duct tape, one end of the tape still attached to the dead man's cheek, hung down to the carpet. Bits of the man's broken teeth were embedded in the gag. There was blood spray all over the corner of the office. When Joe checked more carefully behind the body, he saw that the man's fingers had been broken and that one had been cut off. The crudely amputated finger lay in a sticky pool of drying blood a foot or two from the wall. Serpe removed the stiff's wallet from his back pants pocket. It *was* Stanfill. It had been a very slow and painful death for the lawyer.

Joe didn't know how to feel about it. There was nothing he could see that tied the lawyer's murder to Rusty Monaco. The best lawyers on Earth made enemies, so Serpe had no doubt that a cheap storefront shyster like Brian W. Stanfill might collect them by the dozen. During his own divorce, Joe had been angry enough at his wife's scumbag lawyer to have ripped the asshole's heart out and fed it to him in small pieces. It wasn't difficult to imagine a hundred scenarios that could have resulted in Stanfill being tortured to death. Now wasn't the time to consider them. Serpe had his own worries.

He felt like an ass for making an appointment with Stanfill instead of just walking in off the street. Chances were the lawyer had a record of the appointment somewhere, either written in a day planner, on his Blackberry, or on his computer. Even if he hadn't written it down, there would be phone records. "Fuck!" he hissed to himself. He had to get out of there. If he could manage that, Serpe thought, he'd be okay. This was Nassau County, not Suffolk, and the NCPD would have no reason to tie him to Stanfill or Rusty Monaco or his sister. Joe would just be a guy who wanted to have a lawyer prepare a new will.

As carefully as he could, Serpe retraced his steps and tried to make sure he hadn't left anything behind that would tie him to having been in the office. He even replaced the flashlight before heading back out into the alley. It seemed empty in the back, no one out smoking a cigarette, no one making a delivery. Joe walked quickly back around to the lot and made his way to his car in the shadows at the fringes of the parking area. Inside the car, he called Stanfill's number.

"Sorry, Mr. Stanfill, this is Joe Serpe. I'm running a little late," he said when the machine picked up. "It's about five-fifteen now. I should be at your office in a few minutes."

Serpe then started his car, left the parking lot with his headlights off, drove around the block, and re-entered the lot a minute or two later. He made sure to swing into the lot too fast and blare his horn at a few cars. He parked as closely as he could to Stanfill's office, removed his gloves, walked over to the office and banged loudly on front window and locked door. He made sure to comment to a woman leaving the dojo with her kid about how a lawyer couldn't be trusted. He called Stanfill's number again and left a somewhat angry phone message about the lawyer not being in his office. Serpe bought a slice of pizza to go, making sure to ask the counterman if he knew when the lawyer a few doors down was scheduled to get back in.

"Guy's an asshole," the counterman said. "I don't got anything to do with him."

As Serpe left, he hoped those weren't the last words that would be spoken about Stanfill. He didn't know the lawyer and he wasn't sure why he should care, but after seeing the way the man had died, it just didn't seem like a fitting epitaph.

☆   ☆   ☆   ☆

Fiddle-Faddle's was a big pub on Greenwich Avenue in the Village. The old plank floor had as many swells and dips to it as the surface of the Hudson on a blustery day. Healy figured the place would be busy on a Friday night. He figured right. The music was loud beyond his tolerance. He was old, he thought. You get near fifty and everything you once loved starts to make you cranky. There were hockey and basketball games up on the TV screens. Horrible thing, the mixing of TV sets and bars. It was hard enough to pay attention to someone in a loud bar. Throw in TVs and… His crankiness was showing again. It was wall to wall people and he wasn't sure he would be able to find Blades in the crowd. She found him.

"What are you having?" she asked, pulling him by the arm over to the bar.

"Beer."

"I'm not sure that's generic enough."

"No wonder you get along with Skip. You're a wiseass."

Blades twisted her body and looked at her backside. "That's not most men's reaction."

Healy felt himself blush and was glad of the dim lighting. "Corona. I'll have a Corona."

"You gonna be daring and have a lime with that?"

"Sure, I like life on the edge."

She was still laughing when the bartender took the order. When she came back with their drinks, Blades directed Healy into a private room only a few feet from the bar.

The side room had an unstocked bar, an unused pool table, and bench seating. There was even less light in here than in the main bar. They sat down on one of the benches.

"Why this place and not Cloudy Dan's, huh?"

"One reason is I live around here," she said.

"You gay?"

"You are old school, aren't you? Woman cop's gotta be a dyke or a slut."

"Whoa. I didn't mean anything by it."

"I strike you as a lesbian, Healy?"

"Not really, but what the fuck do I know about lesbians? How am I supposed to know if your special friends at DOI are men or women?"

"Well, I'm not gay. Okay then?"

"What's the other reason we're here?" he asked, happy to change subjects.

"Too many eyes and ears at Cloudy Dan's."

"Maybe, but they'd all be IAB."

"Yeah, and maybe sometimes there's things to say that's even too hot for friendly ears to know about."

That got Healy's attention. There had been a few times during his own tenure at IAB that investigations were too hot to discuss with even your closest friends. This was particularly true with big media cases. The press didn't give a shit about long term, far-reaching investigations. They seemed much like the public they were supposed to serve in that they had a short attention span. But if a street crime squad guns down an African immigrant in a hallway or if a drunken cop plows into a crowd of people at a street fair, then the press is all over it. The weird thing here was that Healy couldn't see the sexy angle with Monaco.

"The only thing I can think of in Rusty Monaco's jacket that could spark all this cloak and dagger bullshit is that thing in the projects with the kid taking the leap off the roof," Healy said. "But that was almost four years ago and while we didn't exactly clear Monaco, there just wasn't enough evidence to go anywhere with it. The Brooklyn DA couldn't even get a grand jury indictment. And that's saying something."

"You *are* good. Skip was right."

"Fuck Skip and tell me what's going on."

"The Reverend James Burgess."

"What about Reverend Righteousness, Justice, and Hypocrisy?" Healy sneered, unable to hide his contempt. "All I know is that he made it nearly impossible for me to do my job when I was looking into the incident. He held rallies and marches and got his face in front of every TV camera and microphone in the free world after the kid took the dive. He talked a lot, but I couldn't get anybody in the projects to talk to me because of him. He sucked all the air out of things. It was like on the one hand he told people not to talk to us and on the other he bitched about us covering shit up."

"You don't blame African-Americans for distrusting cops, do you?"

"I'm not blind, Blades, and my parents didn't have stupid children, but I don't get that people would follow a guy like Burgess."

"He gets stuff done."

"For himself, yeah. The man espouses every crackpot idea and conspiracy theory like AIDS being a plot by white scientists against the black race."

"Oh, you mean like the Tuskegee Syphilis Experiments?"

"That was a long time ago."

"Not for us, Healy. For us, that was last week. That's like saying to Jews that the Holocaust was sixty years ago, get over it. I don't think much of Burgess myself, but I understand why he appeals to people. He's sharp and he knows what buttons to push."

"Yeah well, if he wanted to find out what really happened to that poor kid, he musta gotten his buttons all confused."

A broad *that-canary-was-delicious* grin broke out on Detective Hines' face.

"What are you smiling at?" Healy demanded.

"I thought you said your parents didn't have stupid children."

"They didn't."

"Maybe not, but it seems one of their boys can't do simple math."

"Holy shit!" Healy slapped his forehead.

"That's right, Detective Healy, guess what name came up when I had a long talk with my friend over there at DOI?"

"The Reverend James Burgess."

"You just upped your math grade from a D to a C-plus."

"But did this friend of yours give you anything more than Burgess's name?" Healy asked.

"It was hard enough getting that and that's all I'm gonna get. My friend made it pretty clear that I could offer him the whole candy store and that he wouldn't be able to help me anymore. And trust me, he's been wanting the key to the candy store for quite some time, if you hear what I'm saying."

"I hear. There's something I don't get, Blades."

"What?"

"The DOI aren't the police. From what I understand, they're only supposed to look into people and companies that either work for the city or are contracted to do work for the city. Burgess's a private citizen. He's got a church, but—"

"I thought that too, so I did some scratching around. Seems like the Reverend Mister Burgess does do work for the city, a lot of work."

"What's a lot of work?"

Detective Hines put her drink down on the bench, stood, reached into the back pocket of her jeans and pulled out a neatly folded sheet of paper. She handed it to Healy.

He put his drink down, unfolded the paper, read. His eyes got big and his jaw actually dropped.

"What's Amble Services, Inc.?" Healy wondered.

"It's a company that supplies transportation to and from hospitals, clinics, and other medical facilities. Its two biggest clients are the New York City Department of Social Services and New York City Department of Health. It's third and fourth biggest clients are other city departments too."

"TempMedico, Inc.?"

"Supplies visiting nurse and therapeutic services to homebound patients."

"Let me guess," said Healy. "Biggest client is the City of New York."

"That math grade is climbing ever higher. Your moms would be so proud."

"So would Sister O'Steen."

"Who was that?"

"My seventh grade math teacher."

"And I'm the wiseass, huh, Healy?"

"I have my moments. I take it that every one of these companies does major business with the city."

"That's right. And James Burgess is the part owner of every one of those firms. The Rev got some deep pockets, some mighty deep pockets these days."

"Still, I wonder what it is the DOI is looking into exactly."

"Me too, but like I said before, I got all the help on that front I'm gonna get."

"And what the hell could they be looking at Rusty Monaco for? Unless there's a connection with Burgess that goes beyond the kid's death."

"I suppose we got our work cut out for us," Blades said. "You up for a trip down memory lane?"

"The Nellie Bly Houses you mean? Shit, I guess so. Those files still available to you or did the DOI close the door on them too?"

"No, I got copies of those files. So, when do we start?"

"Tomorrow's out. Saturday's our busy day in the oil business," Healy said. "How about we get together Sunday and go over the files? I don't want to just walk back into the projects blind. If there's something to find out, I don't wanna scare anybody away."

"Sunday! I'm not a convenience store, you know."

"What's that mean?"

"I'm not open twenty-four/seven. I got a life outside the job, though you'd never know it by how Skip treats me."

"My bad. Sorry, Blades."

"Forget it. What time Sunday?" she asked.

"Hey, you tell me."

"Meals all on you?"

"All expenses are on me," he said.

"Good. I need a new car."

"Nice try."

"Figured it was worth a shot. How about you meet me out front of here at ten on Sunday. There's a nice place for breakfast near here and we can go over the files."

"It's a date."

"No it ain't neither," she said, winking at Healy. "Sunday at ten."

☆   ☆   ☆   ☆

Serpe drove around trying to make sense of things. The uneaten pizza on the seat next to him was now utterly cold, the oil from the slice having long ago seeped through the white bag that held it. He finally pulled over and threw the bag down a sewer. As he pulled away, Joe tried to ignore the symbolism and hoped that his life wouldn't follow suit. He'd seen the inside of the sewer before and wasn't anxious to climb back in again.

At first, he considered making another anonymous 9-1-1 call, but decided it was best to let things play out as they would have had he not stumbled across Stanfill's body. Although he couldn't quite yet figure out how, Serpe thought his knowing about the lawyer's murder before anyone else except the killer might turn out to be an advantage. He knew that was a reach. He tried calling Gigi Monaco to give her a heads up about Stanfill, but got her answering machine. He started to leave a message, then clicked the phone shut. He didn't want to scare her.

He'd driven halfway up to Kings Park before remembering that Healy had called to tell him he was meeting Detective Hines in the city. Even so, he thought he might drive there and wait. Last year, before the hose monkey was murdered, before he met Marla and he and Healy reconnected, Joe Serpe was used to being alone. After his brother died, nothing much happened in Joe's atrophied, empty life worth sharing. For him, the world consisted of three places: the cab of the tugboat, his basement apartment, and the anonymous beds of women as hungry for a little comfort as was he. His cat Mulligan, Frank Randazzo, and a changeable cast of vodka bottles were his only constant companions. Mulligan and Frank were dead, Marla was gone, the vodka and the women at Lugo's were no longer options. The fact was, Bob Healy was pretty much all he had.

That notion just pissed Joe off.

He turned around and drove over to Marla's parents' house. He parked in the shadows across the street. Maybe, he thought, she had lied to him—she lied to him a lot before she moved out—about leaving Long Island. But what would he say to her if she did step out? What good would it do him to catch a glimpse of her walking past a window? He had punished himself enough. He had punished her enough.

Serpe drove into Islip to Gigi's apartment. He felt like she should know about Stanfill and he felt like holding her again. He hadn't called because he didn't want to be disappointed. It was stupid, he knew, childish, but there it was. He parked, strolled up the driveway of the split-ranch, through the gate, around back to the short flight of concrete steps leading down to Gigi's door. It wasn't until he went to knock that Serpe noticed something was wrong. The door was ajar and the lights were off.

Joe didn't announce his arrival like he had at Stanfill's office. Instead, he slipped off his shoes, pulled his gun, and gently pushed open the door. He swung the Glock to the back of the door as he stepped silently inside the little apartment. Nothing. It was impossibly dark, much darker than in Stanfill's office, and Serpe realized that he had only seen two tiny windows when he was here before. He tried picturing the floorplan in his head as he fought to push down flashes of Gigi laying dead in a pool of her own blood somewhere. His mind was racing with a flurry of images, a jumble of Gigi, Stanfill, Marla, and Debbie Hanlon; of blood, bullet holes, and broken teeth; of bound hands and feet. His heart was pummeling his chest wall, sweat soaking through his shirt, but he held the panic back.

The only sound beside the rushing blood in his ears was the hum and muted rumble of the furnace and he noticed the faint smell of heating oil in the musty basement air. There was, he thought, no escape from that smell. As he moved toward the bedroom, his foot knocked into something hard on the floor. His mind raced. *The coffee table.* With his next step, something else, softer this time. *Foam from a chair.* With every step, something new: glass, pieces of wood, clothing. The apartment had been ransacked and any hope he had of stealth or surprise vanished when he stumbled over a fallen kitchen chair. Bracing himself against a wall, he reached for the light switch. As the lights came on, his went out.

☆   ☆   ☆   ☆

His head ached and felt like a water bucket stuck at the bottom of a well, but it wasn't as bad as when he'd been run off the road last year and smacked his car into a stand of trees. The concussion back then was a bad one and he had lost all memory of the incident itself. Even after he and Healy had pieced it all back together, Serpe could never actually recall the event itself.

"Jesus, Joe, don't try and get up."

It was Gigi Monaco and though she didn't have a particularly pleasant voice, Serpe was happy to hear it.

"What the..." he reached a hand up to wipe away the drip of icy water running down his cheek. Then he felt the ice and water-filled plastic bag stuck on the side of his neck.

"I know I'm a good fuck, but if you wanted a souvenir thong, you coulda just asked."

"I didn't do—"

"I know. I didn't think you turned my place inside out and then banged yourself on the head just to make it look good. Did you see who smacked you?"

"No. What time is it?"

"About one."

"Is anything missing?"

"Nah," she said, "but everything's fucked up. The motherfucker even cut up my chairs and mattress."

"He was looking for something."

"No kidding?"

"I'm not fucking around here, Gigi. Stanfill's dead. He was murdered. That's what I came over here for, to tell you."

Serpe removed the makeshift icebag and sat up, slowly. He was still half on the kitchen floor, half on the living room floor. That made sense. Gigi was powerfully built, but moving dead weight is challenging for anyone. He saw that Gigi was more nervous than her voice had indicated. She was pacing, smoking a cigarette, drinking a glass of some amber colored alcohol, a large glass. She swallowed the contents of the glass in a swig, tamped the cigarette out on the kitchen floor, and knelt down beside Joe.

"Are you okay?"

"It's not so bad. You got some aspirin or something?"

"In a second. What about Stanfill?"

Serpe explained about what he found.

"I told you he was slimy," she said, stepping into the bathroom. "Maybe his murder's got nothing to do with—"

"Stop it, Gigi! He wasn't just murdered. He was tortured to death. People are tortured for only two reasons I can think of: vengeance or information. Take a good look around. Somehow I don't think this is about vengeance. Someone thinks either you or Stanfill has what they want or know how to get it."

"The money?" She handed him three tablets and a glass of water.

"Maybe."

"Fuck!"

"Get some things together and put 'em in a suitcase or gym bag," he said. "You can't stay here."

She didn't argue the point. Gigi was a woman who could take care of herself, one, Joe was certain, who didn't scare easy, but she was street smart and knew she was overmatched.

"I'm ready. Here, I found these outside and this on the floor." She gave Joe his Glock and his shoes.

He was surprised the guy had left the gun. "Okay, you take your car and follow me."

"Can you drive?"

"I guess we're about to find out."

[The Unfortunate Truth]

SATURDAY, JANUARY 15TH, 2005

He was already pacing when Gigi opened her eyes. They were both up before the sun. His head was achy, but he'd survived much worse, certainly worse hangovers, and still managed a day's work. On the morning he'd discovered the hose monkey's body in the tank of the truck that now held Gigi's money, Joe was suffering from the aftermath of a two day vodka bender. On a scale of bad days, this one barely registered.

Gigi propped herself up on one elbow, her bare breasts doing fair battle with gravity. Neither she nor Joe had slept very deeply or for more than a few minutes at a clip. Sometime during the wee hours, they made a half-hearted stab at fucking. It ended without orgasms, tears or angry words. They spent most of the night just holding each other, which is all either one really wanted to begin with. There is a primal sort of comfort in the warmth and touch of bare skin against bare skin.

"We've gotta go in about a half hour," he said.

"Are you sure about this?"

"I'm not leaving you alone today or tomorrow. We'll see about Monday."

Like the night before, she didn't argue, but she was a little less willing to do as told now that she'd put a few hours and a few miles between herself and her trashed apartment. She hadn't seen Stanfill's body. Serpe could see it Gigi's eyes that he was only going to be able to go just so far to protect her. He was pretty sure she'd tow the line for the weekend. After that... Well, he'd worry about it when the time came. For now, he would concern himself with getting showered and dressed.

This time Gigi followed him into the shower and the sex was anything but half-hearted. It was rough and angry and it was a miracle neither of them slipped in or fell out of the shower. Just like that primal touching thing, there's something about danger that kicks sex up a few notches. Sex always energized Serpe, but he knew he'd be paying a big price for it sometime between noon and one, when he had ten or twelve stops under his belt and grabbed a bite to eat. Between his worries, the welt on his head, lack of sleep, and the sex, he was bound to be worn to the bone by day's end.

It was at times like these that he regretted his decision to not train Healy for his Commercial Class B license. Healy wanted to do it and was a smart guy. He would have passed the written endorsement tests for hazardous materials, air brakes, and tank with ease, but Joe didn't want to spend the time. Serpe, street savy, but no genius, had passed all the tests. He remembered that he was so intimidated by the idea of all those tests that he planned to take them one at a time. Then the woman at the counter of the Department of Motor Vehicles practically forced him to take all the tests at once.

"For chrissakes, son," she said, "have you taken a good look at who else drives trucks? You seen any Einsteins out there? Half of 'em can't even read English. Now get your ass back here and sign up for the other tests."

It was too late to worry over his bad decision about training Healy. In the scheme of things, it was a small mistake.

☆   ☆   ☆   ☆

Healy and Gigi had mostly grunted at each other since Joe had left on the tugboat to do his deliveries. Healy had other things on his mind and didn't exactly enjoy babysitting duty. His only consolation was Gigi enjoyed playing the role of the baby even less. It wasn't that he didn't like Gigi. He didn't know her and she didn't seem anxious to make friends. She was all right, he guessed; cute, if a little rough around the edges. The thing was, Healy wasn't pleased about how far Joe was sticking his neck out and, by extention, Bob's, for this woman.

He was beginning to think that maybe Joe was right the other day. That they were getting in too deep and off the point. What had started out as a debt of honor for Serpe was turning into something else, something very different and much more dangerous. It was pretty evident that Stanfill's murder and the ransacking of Gigi's apartment were not coincidental. Healy couldn't help thinking that maybe Joe was trying to protect Gigi out of guilt over Debbie Hanlon. Then he realized it might not be guilt over Debbie at all. Healy liked that idea even less. He didn't think Serpe had it in him to lose another person close to him.

"Anything on the news about Stanfill?" Gigi asked, pointing at the TV.

"Nothing yet."

"You knew my brother too."

"Yeah, I did."

"Sounds like you didn't like him very much."

"I didn't, no. He had no business being a cop."

"So why you doing this, helping Joe out?"

"Joe owed a debt to your brother."

"You didn't."

"We're partners."

"In business."

"It's complicated," Healy said.

"It always is. I got nowhere to go."

"Joe Serpe was the best detective NYPD Narcotics ever had and I was the cop who took him off the street."

"Doesn't sound like a good start to a partnership."

"I told you it was complicated."

"I still don't—"

"Okay, let's say this. Joe owed your brother a debt and I owe Joe a debt."

"Yeah, but my brother saved Joe's life. What did he do for you?"

"He saved my life."

"How?"

"There's a long answer to that, but the short one's better."

"What's that?"

"He forgave me."

Gigi Monaco didn't ask any more questions.

☆   ☆   ☆   ☆

When Serpe got back in, Healy asked Gigi to give them a few minutes together in private. She scowled, but didn't complain.

"Listen," Healy whispered, "I didn't want to bring this up in front of her this morning, but there's something important that Blades found out."

"What?"

"The freeze on Monaco's files is probably tied to another DOI investigation."

"Well, yeah, we both sort of figured Monaco couldn't have been the target. What would anyone want with a cop who's been two years retired?"

"But you're not gonna believe it when I tell you the name Blades uncovered."

"Tell me and we'll see."

"The Reverend James Burgess."

"Get the fuck outta here!"

"That was pretty much my reaction, but Blades swears by her source."

"Rusty Monaco hated—"

"No shit! I'm the one who investigated him every other year for kicking the crap out of some black kid."

"But Burgess of all people. I mean, even white folks who love their fellow man and go to church every Sunday hate that blowhard prick. Shit, Bob," Serpe whispered, "half the brothers I know hate Burgess."

"I hear you, but Blades knows what she's talking about."

"Did she say what the connection was between Monaco and Burgess?"

"All she got was the name. Apparently, this is too hot to handle. Anyone gets caught leaking this… You could see how that would be trouble."

Healy explained to Serpe about Burgess's business connections to the City of New York. Joe sat and took it in, only half-believing it.

"All that clown does is bitch about the city," he said when Healy was through. "The cops are racists. The sanitation department doesn't plow the Brownsville streets fast enough. City hospitals don't treat African-Americans with the best drugs. It's fucking endless with that guy."

"Must be nice to bite the hand that feeds you and to get more and more food."

"You'd think no one in city government had heard the term conflict of interest."

"I think maybe that's what the investigation is about."

"Yeah, but I don't get what Rusty Monaco's got to do with it."

"Maybe nothing. Maybe they put a clamp down on every possible link to the Reverend Burgess and we're the ones making something of it. But we'll find out soon enough. Tomorrow, Blades and me are going over to the Nellie Bly Houses in Brooklyn and see what we can see."

"I'm coming too."

"No you're not," Healy said. "First off, you look like crap and you need to rest. I was the one who came and got you last year with your brains all scrambled and took you to Stony Brook Hospital. That was pretty serious shit. You still don't remember calling me or what happened to you. After that knock on the head last night, we both know you shouldn't've been out there on the truck today."

"If you got your Class B, I wouldn't have been out there."

"I wanted to get one, remember?"

"No. Must be the concussion."

"Very funny. Plus you gotta watch Monaco's sister. You can't schlep her along with us into the projects. We'll look like the fucking Mod Squad."

"You're pushing too hard, Healy. What's really on your mind?"

"You really wanna know, huh?"

"I really wanna know."

"No one's gonna talk to you in the projects. They'll smell narc on you like I smell oil on you right now. The one place IAB's got an advantage is in a place like the projects and even then, it's only a small advantage. Don't forget, Joe, in their eyes, IAB's out to fuck other cops. They'll help with that."

"Things got better after I got—when I left. Crime's down even in the projects. There must be better cooperation than there used to be."

"Don't fool yourself, Joe. The lovefest ain't happened yet. Remember Abner Louima? People don't forget that kinda torture. And Amadou Dialou? Those shots are still echoing around the projects."

Serpe knew what his partner was saying was the unfortunate truth. He understood that the projects were worlds unto themselves with unique cultures and codes and means of survival. It had been nearly impossible for him to get cooperation working cases in the projects. Even when he partnered up with black detectives or after some warring drug factions got innocent kids caught in the line of fire, folks in the projects kept their mouths shut. Not that he blamed them. The NYPD hadn't exactly distinguished itself by making it a friend to the black man. It didn't matter, anyway. On balance, the dealers had more to hurt you with than the cops had to protect you. You help the cops and this week's kingpin pays some shorty to stick a cap in your ear.

"Okay, for now, I'll keep away," Serpe said. "Besides, I gotta get those Suffolk PD files on the first four homicides. But you get a lead or something, I'm in."

"We get something and you'll know it."

[In Any Language]

The Little Greek Café was on Hawkins Avenue in Ronkonkoma. For years before Joe Serpe had rebuilt his life, he'd eat dinner there a few times a week. When he was done, he would head across the street to Lugo's for an evening of Absolut and absolutely any woman who offered up her bed. The place was crowded, if not full. Maria, the waitress who had been at the café for so many years she was as much a part of the décor as the blue vinyl booths and the cheesy frescos of the Mediterranean, lit up at the sight of Joe.

"You abandoned me, no?" she said with a wink.

"You? Never."

"You sure you're not Greek? I think you Greek."

"Italian, Maria."

"I think your grandparents, they swim to Sicily."

"Could be."

"Is so. I feel it."

Things had changed. Maria was a little older, grayer. The booths had a few more tears repaired with duct tape, but Maria didn't skip a beat. Although Joe hadn't been in for more than a year, her routine about his family tree was the same.

"What·happened to your head?"

"Banged it into a wall."

She didn't believe him. "Sure. Sure. Take any seat you want, Joe."

"I'll take that two-top over there by the booth. Someone's meeting me in a few minutes."

"A woman? I was right. You breaking my heart."

"When you see who's meeting me, Maria, your heart will be all better. I promise."

"Men and their promises. Pfffff!" She waved her hand. "Worthless."

Serpe sat down, staring blindly at the menu. He was pretty spent from work and he was still suffering the after effects of the knock on his head. He was also very much on edge about Stanfill. There was nothing on the radio all day. Now he figured it would be at least Monday before someone else found the body. No lawyers, not even the strip mall variety, worked on Sundays. Once they found the body, it would be a few days until the Nassau cops worked their way through the dead lawyer's calendar and back to Joe. The added time was anything but a reprieve. On the job, there was this detective who had to retire because of panic attacks. "It's not the attacks themselves," he told Serpe. "I can deal with those. It's the waiting for them to happen that gets to me." If he hadn't fully understood then, Joe got it now.

Detective Timothy Hoskins fairly strolled into the café like he owned the place. Everything about him, from his sneer to his lumbering gait, a warning to the rest of the world: *I'm a badass motherfucker. Keep your distance.* Serpe knew better. Hoskins dumped himself into the seat across from Joe with a thud and purposefully scraped the chair legs along the blue and white tile floor as he pulled up to the table. He waited for Serpe to say the first word.

"Christ, Hoskins, give it a fucking rest. Don't you ever get tired of this tough guy bullshit? We're here to do business."

"Maybe that's why you're here. I'm here to eat."

Serpe waved for Maria to come take the order. She scowled at Hoskins as he ordered two cheeseburgers, double fries and extra raw onion. Joe ordered gyro meat over a salad and asked Maria to bring over a couple of Greek beers. She came back with the beers, some bread, and yogurt sauce. Neither Serpe nor Hoskins made a move to clink bottles.

"You eat that gyro shit? It's cat meat."

"Meow." Serpe ignored him, dipping his edge of pita into the yogurt sauce.

"Very funny. So, what's this business?"

"I want copies of the files on the first four murdered drivers."

Hoskins made a show of spitting out his beer. "That's almost as funny as the cat noise and that wasn't too funny."

"I'm not joking."

"Good thing you're paying for dinner or I'd be outta here."

"That's weird. I thought you were paying for dinner because me and Healy solved your case for you and you didn't look like the total incompetent piece of shit that you are in front of the press," Joe said, smiling the whole time. "But as long as I get those files, I'll spring for dinner."

"Fuck you!" Hoskins made to stand.

"Sit the fuck down or I'll tell the press about how you had nothing to do with closing the case on Albie Jimenez, Debbie Hanlon, and Hank Noonan. How do you think you'll look on the cover of *Newsday* giving back your medal and commendation?"

Hoskins snarled, but he sat down. "I ain't got 'em yet. Besides, you don't have the balls."

"Try me."

"Maybe you don't give a shit about yourself, but you wouldn't do it to Healy's brother, the ADA. Never mind how I would look. He wouldn't look too good neither."

"And how do you think the DA and the Commissioner will look, Hoskins? The two of them would look worst of all. Who do you think would catch the shit for that? Not me. What could they do to my rep that hasn't already been done? I'm a private citizen, a disgraced cop, remember? You keep playing chicken with me and you'll find out what that feels like, being a disgraced cop. You wouldn't last five minutes without having people to bully or a badge in your pocket to bully them with. You'd eat your gun before the ink was dry on your papers."

"Fuck you."

"Yeah, you said that. Listen, thanks to me and Healy, you've had a good streak, but it won't last. Another driver gets killed and people will start paying attention again. They'll also notice that you haven't picked up Burns yet for the Hanlon and Noonan murders. I'm sure *Newsday* will be only too glad to remind the good people of Suffolk County. I've lived here long enough to know they don't like murderers running around the county."

Hoskins leaned across the table. "What is it you really want?"

"That's simple. I want to find out who killed Rusty Monaco."

"The guy was a piece of shit. He probably deserved what he got, the cunt."

"Did I hear you right?"

"You heard me right. He was a worse cop than you. He probably had it coming."

"Even if he did, I want the files. So here's the deal. Get me copies of the case files. If Healy and me find the killer, we turn it over to you. You get the glory and I find out who killed Monaco. Tough deal to pass up when there's no downside for you."

Hoskins considered it, running his fingers along the stubble on his cheeks.

"Keep your fucking deal," he said, standing up. "And keep your food too."

"Too bad, Hoskins, because I won't be the only one going to the media."

"Who—"

Just then, Gigi Monaco slid out of the booth behind the table Hoskins and Serpe were seated at.

"I believe you know Georgine Monaco," Serpe said to the detective.

"So my big brother was a piece of shit and a cunt who had it coming to him? Mr. Serpe warned me about you. He was right, you're not even trying to solve my brother's murder," she said loudly enough so that the other diners were beginning to pay attention. Hoskins noticed them noticing.

"You heard wrong. That's not how it is."

"No?" Gigi held up a hand held digital recorder. "Should I play it back so everyone here can listen?"

"Forget it," Hoskins said, but didn't sit back down.

Maria delivered the food to the table.

"Sit down and eat," Serpe said.

"I got no appetite to eat with a rat."

"I wrap it for you to go," Maria said to Hoskins.

"I got a better idea. Stick it up his ass." Hoskins intentionally banged into the table as he left. All the food spilled onto the floor, the thick white dishes smashing when they hit the tile.

Maria was still screaming at him even as the door shut behind him. Joe Serpe didn't understand Greek, but he didn't have to. Tim Hoskins was a detestable man in any language. Maria refused Joe's help in cleaning up the mess. Serpe put two twenties and a ten on the table and left.

"So, I guess that didn't go how you wanted it," Gigi said, as Serpe opened the car door for her.

"Don't sweat it. He'll get me the files. If he wasn't going to get them, he'd've stayed and eaten to rub my face in it. That shit with the breaking dishes, that's just what bullies do."

"I know, my brother was one."

Joe Serpe didn't say a word as he closed the car door.

[Cloaking Device]

Sunday, January 16th, 2005

The Nellie Bly Houses were four depressing, twenty story beige brick towers, that jutted up into the Brooklyn skyline like a grouping of amputated middle fingers. Healy shook his head at the sight of them. You didn't have to be a philosophical sort to wonder about the thought processes of the men who had created this vertical ghetto. He told Blades as much.

"Ghetto," she said, snickering. "There's a word you don't hear much in the twenty-first century. Next you're gonna start talking slums and shit."

"I don't mean ghetto like that. I mean it like warehouse. It's just backwards."

"I guess I understand."

They parked Healy's car and walked around to the back of Building #4; the building from which fifteen year-old Bogarde DeFrees either fell or was pushed. Healy pointed at a thick hedge that marked out a border between Building #4 and a sad little playground of moot see-saw anchors, swingless swings, and holes in the black rubber mats where slide support poles used to sit.

"There used to be a wrought iron fence right here where he landed. They replaced it with these bushes, I guess. It was pretty fucking gruesome with the kid impaled on the fence. Blood was everywhere and the fence was all twisted from the force of the impact. And I only saw the crime scene photos."

"These?" Blades said, opening her copy of the file.

"Those."

"He fell pretty far away from the building."

"That's why the detectives who originally caught it, pretty much thought the kid was pushed or thrown from the roof. If he just fell, he would have landed closer to the footprint of the building."

"Mighta jumped."

"Yeah," Healy agreed, "that could account for it too. Now you see why we had a nightmare making a case. Without eyewitnesses or forensics to prove Monaco tossed the kid... And it wasn't like the young Mr. Defrees was an untroubled victim here. He was pretty well familiar with the arcane workings of the child welfare system and the juvee institutions this fine city has to offer. He'd spent a few overnights at the Kings County Psych unit too."

"Even if Defrees was a gangsta or a total head case, it doesn't justify murder."

"You're right, but I'm just trying to point out how hard it was to make a case."

They walked around to the central commons, a quadrangle of asphalt paths and green-painted concrete wedges meant to imply lawns. They were marked off with short poles and slouching runs of chain between them. There was a big patch of blank concrete fill in the middle of the quad where a full-size bronze likeness of Nellie Bly, the world famous 19th century journalist and adventurer, had once rested. Where the statue had got too was anybody's guess. She always did suffer from wanderlust, that Nellie Bly. The main entrances to the project buildings were set at the extremes of the paths.

"So what were Monaco and McCauley doing here in the first place?" Blades asked as they made the turn around Building #4 for the commons.

"Guy in the building tipped off the local precinct about a fence operating out of an apartment on the top floor. Of course the guy who ratted out the fence had bought a stolen credit card himself. Problem was, the card had been cancelled and the fence had a strict no money back policy. When McCauley and Monaco came to arrest the fence, a woman on the floor came screaming that there was some sort of commotion going on in the stairwell leading up to the roof. Monaco told McCauley to stay with the prisoner and went to check it out. What really happened from that moment until the time Bogarde DeFrees hit the wrought iron twenty stories down is still pretty much unknown."

"What was Monaco's story?"

"He found blood in the stairwell and a bayonette at the base of the steps. He made his way up to the roof access door, which had been pried open. When he came out onto the roof, he didn't see anyone. Eventually, he found Bogarde DeFrees hiding behind a vent shaft. Monaco said he told the kid not to move, but that DeFrees pulled a gun on him and ran. Monaco gave chase. He claimed the kid was running at a pretty good clip, stumbled, and went over the side."

"Too easy," Blades said. "All too pat."

"Hey, I'm with you, but the prints on the knife were DeFrees' as were the prints on the nine millimeter."

"The blood on the steps?"

"African-American male, type O, but not DeFrees'. Never identified. The assumption was the blood belonged to the other party who was mixing it up with DeFrees in the stairwell."

"So Bogarde DeFrees was armed with both a knife and a gun, but DeFrees ends up dead and this guy he was fighting with…what happened to him? Did he have like a *Star Trek* cloaking device or something? Because if the pictures and diagrams in the file are right, he would have had to have run past Monaco to escape."

"We never found the other guy," Healy admitted. "Monaco contended that they musta both gone up to the roof when they heard him approaching and that they split up once they got up there. The assumption is that after DeFrees went over the side, the other party slipped back down off the roof."

"Bullshit."

"Well," he said, "let's see if we can prove it now. We couldn't four years ago."

The cover story that Hines and Healy concocted was purposefully lacking in detail. Their pitch was that there was new information concerning the identity of the second party in the stairwell that day in September 2001 and that they were rechecking all the facts they had gathered back then. When people asked what that new information was, they just said they weren't at liberty to discuss it. Hines did most of the talking with Healy hanging back and observing. Although people did seem motivated to talk, they didn't have much to say that shed any new light on the day in question. Many simply recognized Healy and asked after him. Those who didn't feel like talking were four years more beligerent and resentful and took the opportunity to rage against the machine.

"Well, that didn't get us anywhere," Healy said.

"I tell you what, you surprise me."

"How's that?"

"Most of those people liked you."

"For a white cop, you mean. I musta had my moments, huh?"

"I guess."

"It's what, four? I'm beat."

"Me too. Let's go get a drink," she said. "We'll start on Building #3 when we get back."

⋆　⋆　⋆　⋆

Things were different when they got back. Word had spread all through the houses about the two of them nosing around and their brilliantly vague story that had gotten some folks to open up a little, suddenly seemed a whole lot less brilliant. No one was talking now and no one was very interested in asking after Healy. Actually, this is what thay had expected in the first place and, if they'd gotten it when they made their initial canvass, neither Detective Hines nor Healy would have given it much thought. But the cold shoulders, slamming doors, and sideway glances coming now as they did, were just pissing them off. It was like a veil of silence had descended on the Nellie Bly Houses and it hadn't happened by accident.

"Somebody put the clamp down tight," Blades said, as they walked out of Building #3 into the fully fallen night.

"You could see it in their eyes, somebody put the fear of God into 'em."

"Ain't God they're afraid of."

"Who then?"

"Shit, in these projects, could be any number of candidates. We'd have to know what gangs run outta here, who's dealing outta what building."

"You wanna call it quits for today?" he asked.

"Hell no! They ain't talking today, not gonna be any better tomorrow."

"Okay. Building One or Two?"

"You pick."

Healy started for Building #1 with Hines at his heels.

They made pretty quick work of the first several floors of Building #1, though it would be more accurate to say the building made quick work of them. If door slamming was an olympic sport, there were several gold medal prospects in the Nellie Bly Houses. But when they got to Apartment 5F, things changed. The door to 5F opened wide for Hines and Healy and there was anything but silence waiting for them inside.

Based purely on the look of her, Evelyn Marsden was a bit of a caricature. She was a very heavyset black woman of fifty with dark skin, a massive bosom, and a dead serious demeanor. Her hair was slicked and straightened; wore a too-tight print dress; carried a tattered bible in her hand. Her apartment was plainly furnished, neat as a pin, and smelled faintly of frying bacon. The walls were lined with religious-themed paintings and quilts that featured bible quotations. There were several renderings of Jesus, on and off the cross. Interspersed with the religious wall hangings were seemingly incongruous framed photos of the Brooklyn Bridge, the distant Manhattan skyline, fog over the Brooklyn skyline, shots of the concrete and asphalt quad taken from a high vantage point, black and white portraits of homeless men, fishing boats at Sheepshead Bay, the rides at Coney Island. But the thing that caught the attention of both Hines and Healy was the shrine.

Lit votives of all shapes, colors, and sizes filled the center portion of an old roll-top desk. Scattered among the candles were wooden, plaster, and metal crosses, rosary beads, prayer cards, handwritten notes, bible pages, and wallet-sized photos of a smiling little boy with missing teeth and a school uniform. He was a skinny kid, but you could see Evelyn's face in his. On the top ledge of the desk, resting against the wall, were two 8" x 11" ornate, gold picture frames. One frame held a pastel drawing of a beatific Jesus. The other was of the kid. He was older in this shot, maybe eighteen or nineteen, more serious. The school uniform had been replaced by a sweater and a reversed Kangol cap. A gold cross was nailed to the wall just above the pictures, centered between the frames.

"That's my boy Edgerin. These here are his pictures," she said, gesturing at the photos on the wall. "He woulda been the next Gordon Parks had the Lord not taken him for hisself."

Blades and Healy stared at each other, wondering who was going to ask the question. Healy took the plunge. "What happened to your son?"

"I know it ain't Christian of me to hold the anger and hate in my heart against you folks, but Lord, it's so hard sometimes."

"How do you mean?" Blades wondered.

"It's near four years and y'all still askin' round 'bout that DeFrees boy. Now he been called to the Lord, but he was such a bad child, getting in all kinds of things. Y'all will never let that go, what happened to him. My boy Edgerin, he was killed not a day later, gunned down right in the courtyard, and you folks ain't never done a thing 'bout it."

"Gunned down?"

"Someone walked right up to him and shot him in the head, robbed his camera and all his film, took everything he had, everything he was ever gonna have."

"I'm sorry, ma'am," Healy said. "Can you give me the name of the detectives that spoke with you? Maybe my partner here can check if there's been any progress in the case."

Blades shook her head yes. "I will do that for you, Mrs. Marsden. And even if there's nothing to report, I'll get back to you. I give you my word."

"I can't never get past that day. Edgerin was upset about something, but I didn't have no time to listen to him."

"Somebody dies. Somebody close feels guilty. It's the way of life." Healy explained about his wife's death and his own guilt. He may have been talking about Mary, but he was thinking about Debbie Hanlon.

"Edgerin was never no troubled boy," Evelyn was crying now, clutching her son's portrait to her chest. "He was blessed to always know what he wanted to be. Person knows what he wants, makes him peaceful. But that day…Lord, I just didn't have no patience to listen. I know Jesus has forgiven me. Somehow, I can't forgive myself."

When the grieving mother wasn't looking, Healy gave Detective Hines a nod that it was time to go. She winked back in agreement. They spent a few more minutes with Evelyn Marsden, taking her phone number, and reassuring her that someone would get back in touch with her about Edgerin's case.

They did a few more floors, but it was getting late and getting them nowhere. Healy suggested they quit for the night. Blades didn't take much convincing. They walked back to the car in silence. When they got there, all four tires had been slashed and pellets from the smashed front windshield adorned the top of the dashboard like careless diamonds.

"Looks like someone else besides Evelyn Marsden took exception to our being here," Blades said. "Too bad they took it out on your car."

"Yeah, too bad," Healy agreed, trying unsuccessfully to contain a smile.

"What you smilin' at?"

"We hit a nerve."

"That's what you're smilin' at?"

"Someone's trying to warn us off. That means somebody's scared."

"And that's a good thing?"

"Maybe not for my car, Blades, but for us, yeah."

☆　　☆　　☆　　☆

It was near midnight when they got to Blades' West Village apartment. Healy had AAA tow the car back to Long Island, to the body shop he'd had Serpe's wrecked car taken to after Joe'd been run off the road last year. The whole time the tow driver was hitching up his car, Healy was thinking about Noonan's Body Shop and about Debbie Hanlon. That got him thinking about Albie Jimenez and the weird paths down which crimes can take a man. Healy couldn't believe that Rusty Monaco's getting murdered on a dead end street in Wheatley Heights had led him back to the Nellie Bly Houses. He thought he'd left behind men like Monaco and places like the projects when he put in his papers, but if being around Serpe had taught Bob Healy anything, it was that you never really leave the job behind.

"Nice place."

"You want something to drink?" Blades asked.

"A beer."

"My apartment's probably the size of one of your closets out there on Long Island."

"Just about," he confessed.

He could have hitched a ride back to the island with the tow truck driver, but decided to pass up the lift. He would only have to come back tomorrow anyway, so Blades and him could finish canvassing and talk to the local precinct detectives about Edgerin Marsden. He felt terrible for the mother. So did Blades, but like they discussed as they waited for the tow, Edgerin Marsden's murder was, like so much else that happened at the time, swallowed up in the wake of 9/11. He couldn't really blame the detectives who caught the Marsden case for not doing a full court press on it. Those were strange days. Everybody was in shock and operating on autopilot.

"Here you go." She handed him a bottle of Corona. She had one of her own.

"Thanks."

"The couch looks pretty, but sleeping on it don't do much for your back."

"I'll live with it," he said. "What did you think about the kid's photographs?"

"Edgerin Marsden's? They were good, I guess. I ain't much for photography. Why you wanna know?"

"I'm not sure. There's just something about them that I can't get outta my head."

"Whatever. Let me go get you some bedding."

As he watched Blades walk away from him, he felt a pang of desire that made him as uncomfortable as anything he'd felt in years. It also felt pretty damned good.

[Hard Hard Days]

MONDAY, JANUARY 17TH, 2005—MORNING

Most mornings it was usually dark and hauntingly quiet when Joe Serpe got to the yard. Sometimes the quiet would be shattered by an early morning LIRR train pulling in or out of Ronkonkoma Station or, when the wind blew just right, by the whining of jet engines from the airport. Snow only added to eerie silence. And it was snowing intensely by the time he got out of his car to unlock the chain link gate. Gigi got out of the car to help. She wasn't the type of woman to sit on her hands and let other people do for her. Joe had to confess, if only to himself, he kind of liked having Gigi with him. She seemed to like it too. Gigi fit in Joe's world. Blue collars didn't frighten her.

"Keeps snowing like this," he said, looking up into the dawn sky, "and I won't send any trucks out."

"You'll lose alotta money, won't you?"

"Some, but it's not worth getting someone killed by a skidding truck or having a truck flip over and spilling three thousand gallons of home heating oil into a front yard."

"Makes sense."

"Besides," he said, wiping the snow off his face and turning to Gigi, "if it stays this bad, most guys won't put trucks out today and my customers will still be there tomorrow."

When he reached the key to the lock, Serpe froze.

"What is it?" she asked.

"The lock's cut. Get back in the car."

"But—"

"Get back in the car!" he barked, pocketing the keys and replacing them with his Glock. "I'm not waving to you in five minutes, call nine-one-one and drive the hell away from here."

She didn't argue. Serpe waited until he saw her get behind the driver's wheel and lock the doors. He undid the ruined lock and unraveled the chain that held the two sides of the fence gates together. He wiggled his gun hand into the opening and pushed the gate back so he cleared enough space to walk through sideways. He closed the gate behind him so that if something happened to him, Gigi would have time to get away. As Serpe walked slowly ahead, he realized he should have taken the flashlight out of his trunk. It was just light enough to render the flash useless, but there were spots in an oil yard that were dark even under a noonday sun. He didn't turn back.

First thing he did was to look at the snow for other footprints. There weren't any as far as he could see, but that didn't mean someone hadn't broken in before the snow started falling. He turned to his right and saw that the lock on the trailer door had also been cut. He was tempted to check the trailer first, but thought that might be a set up. He'd be very vulnerable climbing the stairs and turning his back. So Serpe walked away from the trailer and did as thorough a search through the rest of the yard as he could in the diffuse light and intensifying snow. He was glad Healy was stuck in the city. Not that Healy couldn't handle himself. Serpe'd seen him in action. It was just that he didn't know his way around the yard and the trucks the way Joe did and that was dangerous.

Serpe climbed on top of the tugboat's tank, which gave him a good perspective on the entire yard and adjoining lots. Nothing. At least nothing out of the ordinary. By the time he'd climbed down off the truck and checked under the chassis of all the trucks, his mouth was cotton dry and his heart was pounding. It was time for the trailer.

He nearly slipped climbing the snow slick wooden stairs, which were wobbly at the best of times. The lock clanked to the landing without much of a fight, but Serpe hesitated to go into the trailer. As open to attack as he had been before now, it was nothing compared to his vulnerability at this point. The trailer door opened out. If he stood behind it, the door would pin him against the landing rail. He'd have nowhere to go and no way to get there. If he stood on the steps and threw the door open, he would be as easy a target as a shooter was ever likely to find. Still, he chose to open the door from the steps.

He yanked the door open and dived off the steps. When he hit the ground, he rolled into shooting position. Nothing. No one. No sound. He leaned over, found a stone with his free hand, and tossed it through the open door. Again, nothing. He carefully climbed the stairs, came into the trailer, sweeping his gun at the blind spots in the room. He was alone, but when he turned on the office lights, he saw that Santa had delivered a late Christmas gift.

☆　☆　☆　☆

Blades was right, the couch was incredibly uncomfortable and Healy hadn't slept very well. Problem was, Healy couldn't blame it on the furniture. He had spent half the time dreading that Blades might come to him in the night. He spent the other half hoping she would. It was clear she had been flirting with him the other night at the bar and although she had conducted herself like a complete professional during their time at the Nellie Bly Houses, Healy had caught her glancing at him when she thought he wasn't looking. He may have been out of practice with women, but he wasn't so far gone that he didn't recognize the signs of attraction. He certainly was recognizing them in himself.

They'd taken the F train back into Brooklyn. Detective Hines had thought to stop at IAB and get a car, but the snow put the kibosh on that idea. In any case, the subway stop was located only a few blocks from the precinct in one direction and the Nellie Bly Houses in the other. Neither Healy nor Hines was much in the mood for a morning of door slamming, so they chose to go to the precinct first. If they had known about the lack of enthusiasm with which they were to be greeted at the local precinct, they might have chosen differently.

It wasn't that they were getting the usual bullshit because Hines was IAB. On the contrary, both Blades and Healy had been purposefully vague about their departmental association. Blades had introduced herself as Detective Hines and she had introduced Healy as a friend and retired detective. It was the Marsden case itself that had produced the reaction. Though the number of homicides in New York City had shrunken from an astounding two thousand plus per year to somewhere in the six hundred range, detectives didn't like open cases any better now than in the bad old days. When they persisted, one of the detectives whispered to them in confidence.

"Come on, guys. It's a four year old homicide of a…" he hesitated, reminding himself about the color of Blades' skin, "of a Nellie Bly kid. He probably got mixed up in some drugs or shit and somebody put a cap in his ass."

"The mother said he was a good kid," Healy said.

"So did Hitler's mother."

"Still…"

"Look, even if the kid was a saint, maybe he pissed off one of the local gangstas. It don't take much."

"Did he step on the wrong toes?" Blades wanted to know.

"We didn't find jack shit. You know how it is. No offense, Detective, but no one talked to us from the projects. And after that other kid took the dive off the roof…forget about it. Word was a cop shoved him. All we know is that someone in a dark hooded sweatshirt walked up to Edgerin Marsden, put a Sig to his head, and blew his brains out. Then he knelt down and took all the kid's possessions."

"No new leads?"

"The only thing we ever hear is from the mother."

"You might wanna give her a call every few months, even if it's to tell her you got nothing," Healy said in an unassuming voice.

"Yeah, I might. But fuck you! Who are you to come in here and tell me how to handle my fucking cases?"

Healy kept his mouth shut because he had no official standing and because he understood where the detective was coming from. Blades kept her mouth shut too, but reached into her pocket and pulled out a card. She handed it to the detective. She watched his eyes get big.

"You call the mother today. Now," she said, "or I'm gonna make fucking up your career my reason for living. Understand?"

He tried acting tough, but didn't pull it off. Blades picked up his phone and handed it to him.

"Start dialing. We're headed over there right now."

☆   ☆   ☆   ☆

Joe Serpe thumbed through the Suffolk County PD reports on the oil driver homicides that Hoskins had left in the office. What a dick Detective Hoskins was, Joe thought, that he couldn't just drop off the reports or have a subordinate do it. No, not Hoskins, he had to make it dramatic and destroy something in the process. Some people just can't get out of their own ways. It wasn't like Joe hadn't met Hoskins' type when he was on the job. Christ, Rusty Monaco was no better. Maybe he was even a little worse. Hoskins was a buffoon, but Rusty had some ability. He had all the makings of a good cop that Hoskins lacked.

As he took his first pass through the files, Serpe wondered if it was worth all the trouble he'd gone through to get them. Nothing jumped out and bit him in the ass. The only things that linked all the victims together were the things the whole world already knew about: They were all C.O.D. oil drivers who had been assaulted making night-time deliveries in high crime areas. They all had at least two thousand dollars in cash on their persons. They were all shot with the same 9mm weapon. They were all dead. Beyond that, it seemed Hoskins had actually handled the cases by the book. Sure he'd managed to piss people off, but he hadn't really made any big mistakes. The only one he fucked up was Alberto Jimenez and that one didn't count. But Joe knew that sometimes files had to be massaged like cramped muscles before they gave up their secrets. Police work would be easy if all the important details floated to the surface. Maybe he was missing something that Healy would see. He shut the file, stood up, and stretched.

He'd called up John and Anthony and told them to get back to bed and enjoy the extra sleep because he was going to work them to death for the next week. Neither driver complained about the extra sleep or extra work. Gigi had already called in to her work and took the week off with vacation time she had coming. She seemed to enjoy playing Bob Healy's role; answering the phones, giving price quotes, and writing delivery tickets.

"There any way to steal in this business?" Gigi asked when the phones died down a little.

"That's a strange question?"

"Not from where I come from. Angles. My old man was always figuring angles. Of course, the angles he figured got him lots of time at Rikers, the Tombs… So, you gonna answer my question?"

"It's pretty hard to make a dishonest buck in oil. This is one of the most regulated businesses you can imagine. We have to account for every gallon of oil that goes in and out of our trucks. Hell, we get audited every few years whether we do something wrong or not. I mean, yeah, there are a few scams, but they usually catch up to you."

"Like what? What scams?"

"Prepunching tickets."

"Huh?"

"Come outside to the trucks with me."

It was still snowing heavily, but the wind had quieted some and it wasn't all that cold to begin with. Joe started up Anthony's big blue Mack because it still had some leftover oil in the tank. He climbed up to the top of the tank and asked Gigi to hand him the hose. When he climbed down, he took some tickets out of the cab and showed Gigi how to set the meter and place a ticket in.

"Normally you pull the hose to a house and pump oil out of the tank," Serpe said. "But the meter's a machine. It doesn't know where the oil's going. All it knows is that you've set it to pump a certain number of gallons; a hundred, two hundred, or whatever. As the truck pumps, the meter clicks off the gallons. When you're done pumping, you clear the meter and it stamps or punches the number of gallons you've pumped at the top of the ticket. That's an official number because the county calibrates the meter on every truck in the county every year and seals it shut."

"Yeah, but where's the scam?"

"Let's say I come in early every morning, turn on my truck, and pull the hose up on top of the tank and put it back inside the tank like I just did. I've created a closed system, pumping oil out of the tank and right back in. Now let's say I put a ticket in the meter," he said, slipping a ticket in the meter. "I pump two hundred gallons back into my tank, and stamp the ticket." He cleared the meter and stamped the ticket. "Say I do that for five times for different gallon amounts. Now I've got officially stamped, prepumped tickets with no names on them."

"But—"

"I'm getting there. Now I go to Gigi Monaco's house. Miss Monaco's ordered two hundred gallons, but like ninety-nine percent of all oil customers, she doesn't come out of the house and stand by the meter to make sure she's getting what she ordered. So instead of pumping in the two hundred gallons she ordered, I pump in one-eighty."

"You're shorting me twenty gallons, but you've got a prepunched ticket that says you've pumped in two hundred," Gigi said as proudly as if she'd gotten straight A's in school. "You just write in my name and that's that."

"Very good. And twenty gallons isn't so much that a customer will notice the shortage unless you do it to the same customers all the time. Let's say oil's two bucks a gallon. I just made forty dollars above what I would have made on the delivery and I've still got that twenty gallons in my tank to resell. Do it five times a day and that's two hundred bucks. Do it six days a week and it's twelve hundred bucks. Do it on three trucks and that's thirty-six hundred. Do it fifty weeks a year and... That's big money in this business."

"So why don't people do it?"

"They do, but they get caught," Joe said. "Either you get some OCD customer who measures inches of oil in his tank instead of trusting the gauge and he reports you to the state or the feds. Or you get sloppy and greedy and you don't find ways to bury your oil surpluses. But it's usually more simple than that. It's one thing if you're an owner and you do it. You're not gonna turn yourself in, right? But let's say you have a driver doing it for you and he fucks up. He curses at a customer or doesn't show up for a shift and you fire him."

"He rats you out."

"Right. He either drops a dime on you or makes a deal with the authorities and gets immunity while you rot in prison. Okay, now that Oil Crime One-oh-one is done, let's get back inside."

When they stepped back inside, the smile ran away from Serpe's face. On the TV that they'd left on was a photograph of Brian W. Stanfill, Esquire. The still was followed by videotape of a body bag being removed through the front door of his strip mall office. The crawl at the bottom of the screen read, "Nassau lawyer found brutally murdered inside his Seaford offices...." For Serpe, the clock was now running.

☆　☆　☆　☆

They didn't have much in the way of reserves after their visit to the precinct and the door slamming bullshit got very old very fast. The fact was they had missed their chance, if there ever had been a chance, to get people to talk about Bogarde DeFrees' plunge. Once Detective Hines and Healy had taken their break yesterday, they were screwed. Yet even if everyone in the project had been loose-lipped, the odds were there wasn't anything for them to say. Some crimes, some incidents, are just like that; somebody winds up dead that maybe shouldn't have, but there's no evidence, no witnesses, no video. It's frustrating. All you can do is your best and just move on.

What they did have was enough energy to make it back to the Marsden apartment. Evelyn was an odd mix of downhearted and humble. She smiled when they first came into the apartment. Her smile was a living reminder of the resemblance between Evelyn and her son. She offered them coffee. Neither Detective Hines nor Healy had the heart to refuse.

"That detective called me this morning," Evelyn said, as she fussed with the coffee machine in her galley kitchen. "He said there wasn't nothing new on my boy's case. I guess I already knew as much, but it was just better to hear it from him. He apologized to me for not being more attentive. I s'ppose I have y'all to thank for that."

"All we did was remind the detective of his job," Healy said, as he paced around the living room. He was very taken by some of Edgerin Marsden's photography. "Cops get discouraged too and sometimes they'd just as soon forget their failures."

"Well, it did make me feel kinda ashamed for the way I spoke to you both yesterday and I'm sorry for that."

"No need, Mrs. Marsden," Blades said.

"Your son was very good at this. There's something about these shots I can't get outta my head," Healy said.

Evelyn Marsden stuck her head out of the kitchen and could see that Bob Healy wasn't just being nice. "Please take that one," she said, "the one of the Brooklyn skyline. I like it, but it kinda depresses me, you know? It's all that fog and such."

"I couldn't take it."

"Oh, yes you could!" Evelyn stepped out of the kitchen, took the frame off the wall, and handed it to Healy.

He took it. He wasn't a cop anymore and he really was quite taken by the late Edgerin Marsden's work. "Thank you very much, Mrs. Marsden. I'll treasure it."

"I know you will. You would have liked my boy."

"I'm sure I would have."

"These days are the hardest on me," Evelyn said, slipping the frame into a shopping bag. "I'm home from work 'cause of the snow and all the kids 'round too. These are hard hard days."

As pleasant and as giving as Evelyn Marsden had been, Blades and Healy were glad to be out of there. Grief can be more than oppressive. It can be communicable and they already had too much on their plate to get sidetracked. When they got downstairs and stepped out into the commons, the paths had been plowed, but the concrete lawns were piled high with snow. Kids were having snowball fights, building snowmen and igloos, doing what kids do in the snow.

"What's next?" Blades asked.

"I guess we can go talk to Finnbar McCauley and get his take on what happened the day DeFrees died. We were gonna have to talk to him eventually, anyway."

"Waste of time. We know what he's gonna say. You debriefed him right after it happened. He'll say he doesn't know anything now and he didn't know anything back then. And when we turn our backs on him, he'll whisper 'Fuck you' and laugh."

"Maybe,"

"Maybe? C'mon, Healy. Monaco was his partner."

"I knew Rusty Monaco. He wasn't exactly the kind of man who inspired loyalty. His own pets would have growled at him."

"Yeah, but they were partners."

"So were Ralphy Abruzzi and Joe Serpe."

[Dracula's Dog]

MONDAY, JANUARY 17TH, 2005—LATE AFTERNOON

The 61st Precinct was on Coney Island Avenue in the Gravesend, Brighton Beach section of Brooklyn, so Hines and Healy just got back on the F train and rode it toward the far reaches of the borough. Although they hadn't wanted to, they called ahead. Both of them knew it would be better to catch McCauly off guard, but they couldn't risk making the trip for nothing.

McCauly picked them up at the subway station in an unmarked Chevy. He was just as Bob Healy remembered him; a jolly motherfucker; Santa Claus without the white face hair. He was six foot tall and five foot wide. He had a beer barrel gut, a gin blossom nose, and whiskey red cheeks. He had twinkly eyes that smiled like little blue suns and a charming way about him, but he was old school trained. He liked kicking ass and getting simple answers, but unlike his late partner, McCauly had a knack for skating right up to where the thin ice started. He had to be close to sixty and had probably done time in every other precinct in the city.

"I thought you retired," he said to Healy, seated in the front next to him.

"I did. I own a business on Long Island." Healy thought it best not to get specific.

"For fuck's sake, a businessman."

"I never think of myself that way."

"And you didn't think of yourself as a traitorous cocksucker when you were in IAB. Funny how we see ourselves," McCauley said, the charm vanishing.

"Now wait a fucking sec—" Detective Hines started to jump up in McCauly's face.

Healy cut her off. "That's okay, Detective. McCauly's earned the right to call me some names. Haven't you, you fat incompetent fuck?"

McCauly laughed a hearty laugh. "That I have. That I have. So what's this about Rusty?"

"That business I own on Long Island, it's a home heating oil delivery business and my partner's Joe Serpe."

McCauly slammed on the brakes and turned the wheel so that the Chevy skidded into a snow berm along the curb.

"Now you're just fucking with me," McCauly growled, turning to face Healy.

"No. Joe and me are partners."

"What's the company's name, Two Rats Oil?"

Healy could see Blades getting worked up again, but waved at her to stay calm.

"The company already had a name when we bought it, but otherwise we might've gone with Two Rats."

"So what is it about Rusty?" McCauly asked, keeping his eyes on Blades in the rearview.

"It seems him and Joe and Ralpy Abruzzi worked together on a drug task force in the late eighties. They were doing a bust in the projects and it went bad. Rusty saved Joe Serpe's ass."

"Jesus, well that was a mistake."

"Listen, McCauly," Healy said, putting his face close to the fat man's, "I don't give a flying fuck about you or Rusty Monaco, but he saved my partner's life. Joe thinks he owes him for that, so we're trying to find out who killed him and the other oil drivers."

"Why not let the Suffolk cops handle it?"

"Cause the detective on the case makes you look like Eliot fucking Ness."

"And what's she got to do with it?" McCauly threw a thumb at the backseat.

"She's here to make sure you don't lie to me. That's all."

"Lie to you about what? I mean, some nig—some perp stuck a gun to Rusty's head and killed him and took his money. What the fuck would I know about that? I mean, it's not like me and Rusty were tight. We only partnered for six months."

"You were tight enough to be in his will," Blades said.

That hit a nerve. All the piss and vinegar, all the swagger in his demeanor vanished. It came back as fast as it disappeared, but there was no denying something had changed.

"We weren't close, but we went through hell with that DeFrees thing. You know, Healy. You put us through it."

"I was doing my job."

"So was Eichmann."

"Nice. What'd Rusty leave you?" Healy asked.

"It's none of your fucking business, but it was a letter. That's all. What's any of this shit got to do with somebody robbing and shooting Rusty?"

"Probably noth—" Healy said.

"James Burgess," Blades whispered.

"Huh?" McCauly said, acting as if he hadn't heard. But he had and the mention of the name took the red out of his nose and cheeks.

"Forget it," Healy said. "I don't think there's any connection between Rusty getting whacked and your days together, but I had to ask."

"Yeah, well, at least you're interested," McCauly said, trying to change the subject. "Rusty didn't exactly make a lot of friends."

McCauly, a man who never turned down the offer of food or drink, turned down Healy's offer of both. He couldn't get away from Healy and Blades fast enough. He was like the female cat in the Pepe LePew cartoons. Still, he couldn't resist asking Healy what was in the bag as he dropped them back off at subway.

"This?" Healy said, pulling the frame out of the shopping bag. "It's a photograph taken by a kid named Edgerin Marsden. He was murdered at the Nellie Bly Houses the day after the DeFrees kid took the plunge. You like it?"

"I hope the East River floods the tunnel as your fucking train goes through," McCauly said before Healy closed the car door.

"How the hell did that man last on the job this long?" Blades asked as they watched McCauly's car fishtail away.

"Charm," Healy said. "Charm."

They were both silent for a few moments. Although subway cars are never exactly quiet, the white street scenes outside the window seemed to dampen the clangs and squeals of the train as it snaked its way back toward Manhattan.

"I don't know," Blades said, breaking the silence.

"What don't you know?"

"I was watching McCauly's face in the rearview mirror the whole time and I noticed his reactions to your mentioning Monaco's will and to me whispering Burgess' name."

"That's a cute trick, the mirror thing."

"Whatever. That's not the thing. See, I understand why mentioning the will and Burgess got a rise outta him. Shit, mention Burgess to any white cop in this city and he'll break out in hives. And the will, us knowing about it made him nervous because he was surprised we knew about it."

"Is this going someplace?" Healy asked.

"Did you see the look on his face when you showed him Edgerin Marsden's photography?"

"No, I was too busy looking at the photo myself. What did I miss?"

"He kept steady, but he got them buggy eyes. He seemed even more nervous than when you brought up the will. Why should Edgerin Marsden mean a thing to McCauly?"

"He shouldn't."

"My point exactly," she said.

Healy shrugged his shoulders. Except for the time he'd spent with Blades, he was beginning to seriously regret his decision to help Serpe. This Monaco thing just kept getting bigger and bigger and less connected to the actual murder that started the chain of events. Maybe, it was time to try something out of character for him to see if they couldn't reel it back in. He stood up.

"What're you doing?" Blades asked.

"We're getting off."

"We are? Why?"

"Do you like old movie houses?"

"What?"

"Come on," he said. "You'll see."

★　★　★　★

All morning long, Joe and Gigi had watched the screen crawl and jumped from channel to channel in hopes of catching something else on Stanfill's murder. They got nothing new because there was nothing new to get. But by about 3 o'clock, the local cable news channel had set up shop at the strip mall. The first person to be interviewed was the dojo owner. He said he had noticed a foul odor when he opened up the studio that morning and called the gas company. The gas man came and tested for a leak. He didn't find one, but he had to confess he noticed the odor as well. Frustrated, the dojo owner said he tried to locate the source of the smell himself. He figured out it was coming from the lawyer's office and went next door to talk to Stanfill.

"I knew he was there, because his car was parked in the lot. But he didn't answer the door or the phone when I called. I figured he was sick in there or something, so I called nine-one-one."

Next up was video footage of a twenty-something female reporter standing in the snow out in front of a condo development called Pine Winds Estates.

"Susan Stanfill Palanco, Brian Stanfill's ex-wife, who lives in this development, became concerned about the lawyer when he didn't show up to pick up their young son on Friday evening for his scheduled visit. At first, say police, she was angry when her former husband did not return her phone calls. Not having heard from him all weekend, she decided to call notify the Nassau Police. We tried to get a comment from Mrs. Palanco, who has since remarried, but no one answered the doorbell. When we called the home, a man answered and said Mrs. Palanco was grieving and attending to her son."

But the person Serpe was really interested in was last to appear. An impatient, hatchet-faced man, in a tan trench coat, a shield clipped to his left lapel, stood in front of several hand-held microphones. He didn't like the attention, but gave a brief statement.

"My name is Detective J.W. Keyes of the Nassau County Police Department. While the exact cause of death is yet to be determined, it does appear that Mr. Stanfill's death was the result of foul play. We are in the process of collecting evidence and we will release details when they are forthcoming. Now, if you'll excuse me, I've got work to do."

He retreated behind the yellow tape without answering a single question being shouted at him by reporters.

Joe Serpe clicked off the TV, trying to ignore the sick feeling in his stomach. He didn't know Keyes, but he knew the type. This guy wouldn't be easy to bullshit.

"Come on," he said to Gigi, "let's get out of here."

☆   ☆   ☆   ☆

It was a risky thing to do and neither Bob Healy nor Raiza Hines was generally the risk taking type. Maybe that's why Healy had prospered in IAB and why Hines looked like she'd have a similar career ahead of her. Joe Serpe, on the other hand, had risk taking in his DNA, and it had gotten him pretty far before his fall. Even so, Healy wasn't sure Joe'd approve. Five more steps and his partner's disapproval wouldn't matter.

The First Revelation Baptist Church had once been a grand movie theater much in the style of its big brother, Radio City Music Hall, but by 1979 it had fallen on hard times. They'd first destroyed its beauty by chopping it up into a multiplex that featured Blacksploitation flicks and low rent movies like *Dracula's Dog*. Then there was a suspicious fire that didn't quite do the arsonist proud because only one old bathroom was destroyed. *Who starts a fire in a bathroom?* Eventually, it was purchased by a local church group and its new minister, Reverend James Burgess.

The marquee, the only classic feature of the original theater that had remained intact over the years, protected a wedge-shaped shadow of dry sidewalk even as the snow piled up on the rest of the street. On the brilliant, red, blue, and yellow neon bordered marquee were the times for Sunday worship. There were emergency numbers to call for help with your heating bills, with your landlord, with the City. But the star of the show, the man with top billing, was James Burgess.

"You sure you wanna do this?" Healy asked Blades as he grabbed the door pull.

"No, but hell, we're not getting anywhere the way we're going. Let's give the Rev a shake and see what falls from his tree."

Healy held the door for Blades and followed her in. Once through the second set of doors and in the lobby of the old theater, they were greated by a tall, muscular man in his mid twenties. His coffee colored skin was freckled and he wore his hair in braids and corn rows. He had a jumpy, uneasy air about him, as if his well-cut black suit was the last thing he wanted to wear and this church was the last place he wanted to be. Still, he was polite enough when Detective Hines showed him her shield and asked to speak to the Reverend James Burgess.

"Follow me, please."

They did as he asked and walked up a floor to what had once been the balcony level.

"This here is where our pipe organ is situated," the young man said. "You can have a look while I see if the Reverend is available for y'all."

Healy and Hines shrugged at each other. They thought they might as well do as the man said and have a look. The pipe organ wasn't quite as grand as St. Patrick's, but it wasn't shabby either. The multiplex partitions had been undone and the original configuration of the theater, if not the art deco embellishments, had been restored. Long, curved pews had replaced the old lean-back seats and there was an altar on the stage. There were a few big crosses here and there, but not a crucifix in sight. To a Catholic like Healy, it barely seemed a church at all and he told Blades so.

"Beats my church growing up," she said. "One my folks took me to was an old dry cleaners. No matter what they did to fancy it up, you could still smell those awful chemicals."

The young man reappeared. "The Reverend will see y'all now. Please follow me."

"I didn't catch your name," Healy said.

"Khouri." He left it at that. "Here we are. Just through that door there."

The Reverend James Burgess was a larger than life figure and a big man. He had a cool smile, an easy energetic manner, a rich voice, and a sharp tongue. He kept his head shaved, his moustache trim, and his clothes neat. The clothes didn't call attention to themselves, but they were well tailored with a high thread count. As he approached Hines and Healy, there was a flash of recognition in his eyes.

"Detective…Healy," he said, extending a hand. "I never forget a face, especially one that belongs to one of New York's Finest."

"I'm retired," Healy explained before the bullshit got higher than the snow. "This is Detective Hines."

"Anything but retired," she said.

"Pleasure to meet you, sister."

Blades let that go. Healy kept quiet too. Burgess was certainly more charming than Finn McCauly, even if he was just as full of shit.

"Please sit. The church office, I fear, is a little spartan. My office at our charity headquarters on Utica Avenue would be more comfortable," Burgess said. "Maybe you'd like to meet me there at a—"

"That's okay, Reverend. We're here unofficially, really," Hines said.

"How's that?"

"Well, the detective that you accused of covering up the murder of Bogarde DeFrees at the Nellie—"

"Monaco, Detective Monaco," Burgess said, a prideful smile on his face.

"Yes, him," Blades answered.

"What about him?" The smile vanished.

"He drove an oil truck on Long Island since his retirement two years ago. He was robbed and murdered while making a night delivery," Healy said. "Monaco was one of five men killed over the last few months while—"

"Yes, I do believe I read something about that, but I was unaware that Detective Monaco was among the victims. It's a pity for his family. Still, I am not sure why you are both here. Especially you, Mr. Healy, as you're retired."

"We hoped Detective Monaco's death might reignite the investigation, stir up people's memory," Hines said. "As you know, although there wasn't enough evidence to take disciplinery action against Monaco, that the case is still open. Since Mr. Healy was the lead detective back then, I've asked him to consult."

"That's very admirable, Detective Hines, but I haven't heard a whisper on the street. I am afraid that there are continuing threats to our community's young men in the guise of a uniform and badge. The death of one racist bully who had already done his damage and gone is like one drop of rain in a vast ocean."

"Then there's nothing you can tell us?" Hines said.

"I will keep my ears open, detective."

"Thank you for your time, Reverend. We'll let you get back to your good works."

Burgess shook Raiza Hines' hand and wished her well. But when he shook Bob Healy's, he held on tight. "Thank you, Mr. Healy," he said. "I recall that you did try to do the right thing by us when this happened."

"No thanks necessary. For me, the right thing is the right thing."

Hines and Healy found their way out on their own and made their way back to the subway. This time the silence between them lasted much longer than on the ride here. Maybe that was because the ride was underground and there was only black and grimy walls visible outside the train. Gone were the bucolic snow scenes to soften the subway's metal chatter. It was also that Healy was exhausted and still had a long ride back to Kings Park ahead of him.

"That got us nowhere, with Burgess I mean," Blades said, the train pulling out of the Broadway-Lafeyette station. "That man gives nothing away."

"I know. Still, it was worth a shot, huh?"

"But now he knows people are watching."

"Blades, that man knows people are always watching. That's how he can be so cool."

The train slowed.

"This is me," she said, standing up. "You sure you don't wanna stay over again and just go home in the morning?"

"I wish I could, but tomorrow will be really busy. I gotta get in early."

"You sure I can't tempt you?"

"No. I'm not sure of that at all."

She smiled, leaned over, kissed him softly on the mouth, their lips pulling apart slowly. Then, suddenly, before he could think, breathe or speak, she was out of the train. When the subway jolted forward, he looked up to see half the people in the car with him were staring. Not all of them were smiling.

[Last Laugh of the Day]

THURSDAY, JANUARY 20TH, 2005—AFTERNOON

Mayday Fuel had finally caught up with all the stops they didn't service during the snow storm. They had picked up several new customers from other companies that were still too backlogged. Healy even appreciated having Gigi around for help because the volume of calls was beyond anything he'd yet to deal with. Unfortunately, the Monaco thing was at a standstill. Healy's fresh set of eyes hadn't seen any red flags in the homicide files that his partner hadn't picked up on and days had gone by without any revelations or new information. Sometimes, as Serpe had said to Healy that morning, there's less there than meets the eye, sometimes a lot less. Any good detective knew the truth of that. They both had a long list of investigations that started off promising and led nowhere.

Serpe had yet to hear from the Nassau cops and he was beginning to hope, if not quite believe, that Brian W. Stanfill had neglected to make a note of their appointment. Even if the lawyer hadn't written it down, the cops would hear the phone messages and backtrack to him through phone records. Maybe the cops just didn't think he was worth talking to. It had been confirmed that Stanfill's death was a homicide.

Although the news reports didn't list all the damage, it was pretty clear that he had suffered a lot before succumbing. That came as no surprise to Joe.

Healy hadn't heard from Blades nor had he called her. He couldn't stop thinking about the kiss. That wasn't the only thing he couldn't get out of his head. He was ashamed to admit it, but the looks he got from the people on the subway car had stayed with him too. He tried convincing himself that their disdain was because he was twenty years Blades' senior. He knew better. The world never changes as fast as you want it to. Healy wondered if the world really did change where race was involved.

The phone rang and Healy waved at Gigi that he'd get it. He was glad for the distraction.

"Mayday Fuel, how can I help you?"

"That was a kiss goodbye, Healy, not the kiss of death." It was Blades.

Healy smiled so broadly that Gigi noticed and she wriggled her eyebrows at him. He spun his chair around.

"Hey, about that..." he said, not having a clue how to finish the sentence.

"Forget it. Wasn't the first dumb thing I ever done."

"Don't say that."

"That's not why I called, anyway."

Healy's heart sank. "Why did—"

"I'm outta IAB. Cleaned my desk out today. Got the bump to detective second. Gonna be working outta One PP as a liaison with the feds."

"One Police Plaza, huh? Congratulations," he said without meaning it.

"You just said congratulations like I'm sorry your dog died."

"Congratulations," he said it with a little more feeling.

"I guess the dog's only sick."

"I'm sorry, Blades. It's just suspicious timing. Were you up for a—"

"Fuck you, Healy! Fuck you!"

Click.

"What's the matter?" Gigi asked. "You look like your dog just died."

His laugh had nothing to do with humor. But what he had said to Blades was true: the timing of her promotion did seem strange. Healy could see she was good and she had integrity. The thing was, Skip wouldn't have thrown her to the wolves if she'd already proven herself and was ready for a bump. He didn't blame her for taking the promotion and transfer. He felt like shit for opening his big mouth without thinking how his doubts about the offer might come across as doubts about her.

"When you think Joe'll get back?" Gigi asked.

"Unless my ears are failing me," Healy said, "that's the tugboat now."

And sure enough, as Healy finished his sentence, the old green Mack pulled into the yard. It was still light out and the other trucks would be in soon. Even though there hadn't been a driver killed since Albie Jimenez, Joe was wary about keeping trucks on the street after dark, especially now that word was out that he was looking into the murders. He didn't want someone making an example of his drivers. The old Mack's brakes squealed as Serpe aligned the truck and backed it into its spot of honor right next to the trailer. Bob Healy may not have learned to love life in the yard, but he did find a strange comfort in the sounds of the place; the rumble of the Mack's engine at idle, the clicking of the meter during truck transfers, the quiet after the morning surge of phone calls.

★   ★   ★   ★

"Hey," Joe said, limping into the office. He tossed his map and ticket box on the desk, handed his cash to Healy, and smiled at Gigi. He found he wanted to stroke her cheek, but stopped himself. "I'm gonna wash up. I'll be out in a minute."

"Come over here," Healy said to Gigi. "Let me bore you with how to cash out a driver until he's ready."

"You're fifty-seven cents short," Gigi announced proudly when Serpe stepped out of the bathroom.

He threw three quarters on the table and told her to keep the change. They got a small laugh out of that. The last laugh of the day. There was a knock at the trailer door. Since Serpe was standing he got it. When he looked through the small, scratched pane of plexiglass in the door, his heart jumped into his throat. He recognized the hatchet faced detective from the TV, though he struggled to remember the name that went with it. Joe waved through the plexiglass for the detective to step back and pushed the door open.

"Can I help you? You lost or something?" Serpe asked.

The detective flipped out his shield. "Detective E.W. Keyes, Nassau County PD. Can I come in?"

"Nassau. I guess you *are* lost."

"I didn't realize you did standup, Mr. Serpe. Can I come in?"

Serpe hadn't figured on this. He thought that if the Nassau PD wanted to speak to him, they'd just call and invite him in. But Joe should have paid more careful attention to his own initial assessment of Keyes when he'd seen him on TV. Keyes was good and knew he'd catch Serpe by surprise by showing up this way. Serpe wouldn't make that mistake again.

"Come on in," he said, gesturing. "This is my partner Bob—"

"—Healy. Yeah, I know. Nice to meet you Detective Healy," Keyes said, shaking Healy's hand and making it clear he was thorough and not to be fucked with.

"Detective Healy's retired," Bob said. "I'm just Bob these days, half owner of Mayday Fuel."

"This is Gigi, our phone girl." Serpe omitted her last name. The name Monaco would have set off all kinds of alarm bells for the detective.

Keyes nodded. "Pleasure."

"Gigi, do me a favor, go run to the deli and get us a six pack of Blue Point and some coffees," Joe said, handing her a twenty and his car keys. "Take my car."

Gigi understood and was out of the office before anyone could protest. When she was gone, Keyes asked if they couldn't talk privately. Serpe said that they could talk in front of Healy, that he had nothing to hide from his partner. That was true. Healy wasn't the one Joe was about to lie to. But Joe wasn't stupid or someone to fuck with either. A good cop learns how to lie and the best lies are those closest to the truth. That's what he planned to do, stick as close to the truth as possible.

"Do you know what I'm here about?" Keyes asked.

"I can guess."

"Guess."

"That lawyer who was murdered, Stanfill. I had an appointment with him."

"Did you keep that I appointment?" Keyes asked.

"I did, a little late. He didn't. I knocked at the door, but he didn't come. I called him a few times."

"I know. I heard the messages. Why didn't you come forward when you heard he had been murdered?"

"Because I didn't really know the victim and I didn't know shit about the murder."

"But once you knew about the murder, you'd know we'd want to talk to anyone who had an appointment with Stanfill on the day he was murdered."

"I knew," Serpe admitted. "But all I was hoping was that Stanfill hadn't written my appointment down and that you guys would just leave me alone."

"Why?"

"Come on, Keyes. If you know who Healy is, you know about me. I've had all the dealings with the police I ever wanna have. That shit is behind me and I hope it stays there."

"Fair enough. But if you didn't know Stanfill, why go to him?"

"I think some customer recommended him to me once. Said he did good divorce and custody work. After that shit came down in the city, my wife divorced me and took my son to Florida. Lately I've been think-ing I might want him to come live with me. We haven't had the best relationship and I want to try and change that before it's too late."

"Very noble of you. Do you remember what customer recommend-ed him?"

"No. It might not even have been a customer. Might've been an-other driver or my old boss. Who knows?"

"But you must have access to a ton of lawyers. For chrissakes, Serpe, your partner's brother is a Suffolk ADA. And between your business lawyer and the lawyers who defended you in the city..."

"I was just making inquiries and I didn't want to tell anyone. Maybe if Stanfill said I had a chance, I might've gone for someone more high-powered."

"Have you gone to another lawyer?"

"Not yet. I was a little shaken by what happened to Stanfill and then the snow hit. We're still catching up."

"Have you ever been in Stanfill's office?"

Bang! Now Serpe knew why Keyes had come. The other stuff was just the prelims, now he was getting to the main event.

"Once, a few weeks ago. I walked in, looked around to see if this guy was a total dirtbag or not. I mean, he did have a practice in a strip mall, right? Used his bathroom, but he had too many people waiting, so I left and called him back for an appointment."

"People told me you were sharp, Serpe."

"Not sharp enough to save my fucking career or marriage."

"Happens. Just one or two more questions."

"Go ahead."

"On the night you had the appointment, did you enter the premises of Stanfill's office?"

"How could I, the office was locked?"

"That's funny, because we got a witness that says a man meeting your description walked around the back of the mall and entered through the backdoor of the victim's office."

"I went around back, but that door was locked too," Serpe said.

"Funny how you didn't mention that."

"Not so funny. I didn't see the point."

"The body was moved."

"What?"

"The body was moved post-mortem," Keyes said. "It was done carefully, but it was done. I'm just curious why someone would find the body, move it, and not report it?"

"Hope you find out," Serpe said.

"I was hoping to find out tonight," the detective said as one of the other trucks pulled into the yard.

"It's only five, you've still got plenty of time. I don't. I've gotta cash my drivers out. So, if you'll excuse me…"

Keyes removed two cards and gave one each to Serpe and Healy. "I'm pretty sharp too. I know you didn't kill Stanfill, but there's something going on here you're not telling me about. For your sake, Serpe, I hope it doesn't bear on the case. I like getting fucked as much as the next guy, but only with consent. I get pretty fucking ornery when it happens the other way around. Remember that. Goodnight, gentlemen."

[Lies and Favors]

FRIDAY, JANUARY 21ST, 2005

He was walking down one of the paths in the courtyard of the Nellie Bly Houses, only the green paint patches had been replaced by grass so green and thick it might well have been carpeting. But the over-whelming scent of cut grass put a lie to that notion. The sun was out everywhere except over the four towers, whose beige brick had turned blood red. A dense, gray layer of fog hung over the buildings and when he looked up at the fog, it descended slowly down to the ground. He could not move as the fog washed over him, settling at his feet. He could not see the grass through the veil, but when he looked back at the buildings he saw they were once again beige; the blood washed off in the fog.

He smiled. As he smiled, the fog rose. As it rose, it lifted him up. Oddly, there was no sense of movement, no noise, no wind. He did not look down, but he was more curious than terrified. Passing the fifth floor, his mouth watered at the smell of frying bacon. He saw Evelyn Marsden standing out on the terrace, flanked on her right by Edgerin the little boy and by Edgerin the teenager on her left. None of the apartments had terraces, yet there they were. Evelyn and young Edgerin were smiling and waving. Teenage Edgerin was angry, thrusting his right arm skyward. He waved back to the Marsdens and their eyes followed him up. When he looked back at the terrace, teenage Edgerin was gone as were the smiles from his mother and younger self. When the elevator of fog had risen to the rooftops, he finally looked down and noticed two graves in the new carpet of grass. He was too high to read the names on the headstones, but he knew them just the same. He stepped off the fog onto the roof of Building #4 and followed footprints that had been painted on the tar like dance steps. They led to the edge of the building that Bogarde DeFrees used as a launching pad or from which he was launched into a better world. He felt someone close behind him and he spun around from the ledge. It was the teenage Edgerin Marsden. He was furious, his eyes raging as he made stabbing gestures with his arm. "Look! Look! Look! Look! Look!" he screamed, "Look!" He could hear himself asking Marsden what it was he was supposed to look at, but got no reply.

Healy knew it was a dream, but didn't fight it and tried not to get in the way of it. Sick with worry, he hadn't slept at all last night. He wasn't so much worried about Joe Serpe. Serpe could handle himself. The lies Joe told Keyes were his alone and if there was a price to pay, Joe would pay it. No, he was more worried about Raiza Hines. She could handle herself too, but the bump and sudden transfer were wrong. He could feel it. Healy had seen what happened to cops whose careers were built on a convenient lie or a favor. The NYPD was enormous and there were a few hundred places to bury mistakes or potential stars who got too far too fast and whose rabbi had since fallen out of favor. Merit and performance were no guarantees either, but they didn't evaporate as fast as lies or favors.

He had a lot of coffee and got through the morning pretty well, but by noon he was finding it nearly impossible to keep his eyes open. At Gigi's suggestion, he'd gone into the spare office in the trailer and stretched out on the old couch they kept there for occasions such as this. It wasn't ten minutes before he was deep into sleep. When the dream had come to him, he could not say. It morphed into something else, something about his wife Mary, and then there was nothing but the womb of sleep itself.

At about four, Gigi came in and shook him awake. Joe had called and said he was headed back into the yard. Healy felt rested, if not better. He thanked Gigi and called Serpe on the truck.

"So nap time's over?" Joe said. "Gigi told me you were out like a light."

"She did, huh?"

"I'll be in in fifteen minutes. What is it that couldn't wait?"

"Can you cash everybody out tonight? There's something I gotta take care of."

"What?"

"I made a mistake that I think I've still got time to fix."

☆   ☆   ☆   ☆

Healy did it right. He called his brother and asked what kind of champagne he should buy. George knew about stuff like that. Bob didn't need any help with the flowers. He always had a good eye for flowers. Driving in, he kept finding little pieces of windshield stuck in the folds if his seat. He wasn't angry about it. He knew that no matter how thorough you were, there were always cracks and crevices and things just small enough to hide in them. It was like the dream he'd had that afternoon. Pieces of it came back to him as he made his way into the city. He still had no idea what the hell any of it meant beyond an expression of frustration and grief. As he pulled his car into a legal spot, he wasn't much concerned with grief or frustration. He was too busy feeling like a sixteen-year-old on a first date.

She looked stunned when she saw him standing in the hallway, an arrangement of two dozen white and yellow roses and a cold bottle of Mumm's in his hands.

"Congratulations, Detective Hines. These are for you," he said, handing her the flowers. "This is for us." He waved the bottle. "Do I get a second chance?"

She put the flowers down, reached out for his hand, and pulled him in.

[Torture Works]

When he woke up, he could feel Blades' body against his. And as outrageous as the sex had been, he thought he enjoyed the proximity and the warmth of her body almost as much. Almost. He pulled her closer, her back pressed hard to his chest and abdomen.

"You're up," she said.

"Gimme a few minutes. It takes us old white guys some time."

"Yeah, but when you get goin'..."

They laughed quietly.

"I didn't take it."

"You didn't take what?" he asked, not understanding.

"The bump, the transfer."

"Why?"

She spun around in his arms to face him. "Because after I came down from the high of it, I knew you were right. The timing *was* suspicious. So I did a little checking and found out that this was a rush job. Skip said he was happy for me, but that he wasn't the one who put me in for it. It wasn't easy and I know I pissed a whole lotta people off, but I sort of pieced together how..." she stopped, noticing that Healy seemed not to be listening. "Are you paying me any kind of attention?"

"What did you say?" he asked.

"That I knew you were right."

"Not that part," he said, jumping out of bed as if he were shot out of it.

"What part then?"

"Coming down."

"After I came down from the high of it, that part?"

"That's it! I know what the dream means now. Come on. Get dressed."

"Dream! You crazy? I gotta shower."

"Later, come on."

"Where we going?"

"Long Island."

There were only the vaguest hints of sunrise toward the East River. The sun hadn't quite reached over the tops of the buildings to throw its light this far west. As they stepped out of Blades' building, a bug buzzed by their ears and smacked into the door behind them. The glass broke, but didn't shatter. They both froze for a second, puzzling over insects in January. And when they turned to see the shape of the hole in the glass, they understood and hit the deck. Something buzzed overhead and pinged off the door handle. Both Blades and Healy went for their weapons. They both rolled for cover behind a tree and the minivan parked in front of it. When Blades then reached for her cell, Healy shook his head no.

"Not yet," he said. "If we get the cops involved now, there'll be time for people to cover their tracks."

Blades put the phone down. They waited for another shot that didn't come. Tires screeched. They combat crawled to Healy's car and sat with their backs to the passenger side doors, heads below window level.

"You okay?" Healy asked.

"Never been shot at before," she said, taking huge gulps of air.

"Always a first time."

"For alotta things."

★　★　★　★

The four of them stood around the desk looking at the photograph Edgerin Marsden had taken of the Brooklyn skyline.

"He took this picture from the roof of one of the other towers of the Nellie Bly Houses," Healy said. "And there was more than one taken from up there. Evelyn had them all over her walls. He was up there a lot. My bet is, we check around and we'll find he was up there taking pictures the day Bogarde DeFrees took his solo flight. It's why the kid was executed the next day."

"It's interesting, but pretty thin, Bob," Serpe said.

"Maybe not. Bla—Detective Hines, why don't you tell my partner and Detective Monaco's sister here the short version of what you uncovered about your promotion and transfer."

"I was promoted and transferred because Assistant Chief of Detectives Desmond Green signed off on it and told his subordinates to make it happen immediately."

"Desi Green is Assistant Chief of Detectives!" Serpe was incredulous. "I knew Desi from Brooklyn North Narcotics when he first made detective. Nice guy and an okay cop, but how the hell did he get—"

"In the wake of the DeFrees incident and because we needed to put on a unified face for the world after nine/eleven, one of the concessions the mayor and commissioner made in order to stop the constant protests was to appoint more African-Americans and Hispanics to positions of authority inside the department," Healy said. "Remember, I was still on the job then. Guess who was the leading citizen advisor to the commissioner on the appointments?"

"Burgess?"

"That's right, Joe, Reverend James Burgess."

"But how does it all fit together that winds up with Rusty Monaco and the other drivers getting murdered?"

Healy turned to face Georgine Monaco. "Look, Gigi, I'm gonna say some stuff about your brother that maybe you don't wanna hear. So, if you're not up for it—"

"No, that's okay," she said. "I got no fantasies about who my brother was. Go ahead."

"The way I see it is that McCauly and Monaco show up to make their arrest and then this woman comes and tells them about the disturbance in the accessway to the roof," Healy paused, taking a deep breath. "Rusty investigates and when he gets up on the roof, he witnesses Bogarde DeFrees being thrown off the roof by Burgess himself or one of his associates."

"This may sound stupid, guys," Gigi interrupted, "but why would an important man like Burgess throw some dumbass kid off a roof?"

"That's not a stupid question," Joe said. "The thing is, I don't know why. Maybe the kid stumbled onto Burgess making a dirty business deal. Maybe the kid worked for Burgess and fucked up bad. Like Healy says, maybe it wasn't Burgess, but one of his associates. For now, let's work backwards and hear Bob out."

Gigi agreed. "Okay."

Joe nodded for Healy to continue.

"So the kid gets tossed and let's assume it was by Burgess or someone associated with him. Meanwhile, Rusty spots Edgerin Marsden taking pictures from one of the adjoining rooftops. Rusty confronts Burgess. Burgess offers to bribe Rusty if he'll take some heat for the kid going off the roof. Monaco agrees to a price, but what Burgess doesn't know is that there's photo evidence of the the murder. Rusty sees that with pictures, he can squeeze Burgess like an orange that won't ever run out of juice. Rusty cuts McCauly in because he needs his partner's help in tracking down the photographer on the other roof. They find out it's Edgerin Marsden and they take the kid out and steal his photo bag. Maybe they did it themselves or had someone who owed them do it. I don't know."

"Okay, but why would Rusty drive an oil truck for two years and not just take the money and run?" Joe asked.

"Good question. My guess is that either Burgess convinced Monaco he couldn't raise a lot of money all at once and that he would have to be patient or Rusty, who was a thug but no idiot, understood that it wouldn't look good for a detective third who had just come out the other end of a scandal to retire to a life of luxury in Florida. Maybe it was a little bit of both."

"Why the protests?" Joe was curious. "Didn't they just bring more attention to Burgess?"

"Burgess is a smart man. It would have brought even more attention to him if he didn't protest. How suspicious would that look, the most vocal and effective black leader in the city not raising up his voice, huh? Besides, his ass was covered by the deal he made with Monaco."

"But why kill my brother and the other drivers if him and Burgess had this deal and Rusty was headed to Florida?"

"The DOI investigation. Look, if Burgess is so plugged into city politics and business that he has all these contracts and can get his cronies appointed to positions in the NYPD, he must have known about the DOI investigation. Maybe he knew about how they were looking into Rusty's background too. Put yourself in Burgess's shoes. You might be willing to cop a plea on corruption and do a few years in a country club prison. But there's no country club for murderers. Rusty would've flipped on him in a second to save his own neck. Burgess knew that, so your brother had to go. But you can't only target only Rusty. It might look suspicious to the DOI. On the other hand, if he's just one of a bunch of oil drivers who are robbed and murdered..."

"What about Stanfill?" Joe wanted to know. "Why torture him to death?"

"That's easy," Healy said. "He was Monaco's lawyer."

"So what?"

"McCauly killed him," Blades said. "We think it was him who shot at us this morning too."

"Holy shit! I get it," Joe said. "Gigi, you said that McCauly got an envelope at the reading of the will, right?"

"Yeah, a plain white envelope. He took it and left."

"Imagine the expression on old Finnbar's fat face when he opened it and found that the blackmail photos weren't in there like he thought they were supposed to be," Joe said. "He probably went apeshit and figured the lawyer fucked him and kept the pictures for himself to use. He went back to Stanfill and tried torturing him into telling where the photos were. Problem was, Stanfill didn't know where they were."

"How can you know that?" Blades asked.

"Because torture works," Serpe said. "And I saw how bad Stanfill was tortured. He would've talked…Shit, *I* would've talked a long time before it got to that point. And there's something else. Stanfill was killed sometime that afternoon, but Gigi's apartment was ransacked that night, sometime between when she went out and when she found me on her floor. If McCauly had gotten the pictures from Stanfill, he wouldn't have needed to check Gigi's apartment."

Almost unconsciously, all of them turned their gaze at Georgine Monaco.

"Don't look at me. I don't know where those fucking pictures are. I swear."

"Okay," Serpe said, putting his arm around her shoulders. "Is there anyplace you can think of where they might be, because without them, all we got is a nice fairy tale to tell that no one's gonna believe."

"Like I told you, Joe, me and Rusty weren't exactly close."

"He left you the money."

"I don't know, I'm his only real family left besides that cunt ex-wife and their kid."

"You think maybe he hid it in his police stuff that he left his son?"

"Nah, my brother always thought the kid was better off without him. I think that insurance policy money in the kid's name was all he would give and he never woulda left anything his ex could use for money."

"Can you think of any place he mighta hid the pictures at?" Blades asked.

"I guess we can check that storage place in Plainview again. I still got the key," Gigi said. "But there wasn't anything in there except the money."

"Bob," Joe said, "help me get the hatch cover off the International's tank."

It was an inspired idea, but the picture or pictures were nowhere to be found either in the grocery bags themselves or stuck between the bundles of money Rusty Monaco had left his sister. Serpe had to go out on the truck, so it fell to Gigi, Raiza Hines, and Healy to re-assemble the cash into neat, rubber-banded piles. Healy stacked the piles into blocks, which he then double-wrapped with heavy duty plas-

tic and duct tape. He put the wrapped blocks in more plastic before
putting all the money back into the International's tank and locking
the hatch.

[Go]

Gigi's apartment still had the tornado decor it had the night she found Serpe unconscious on her floor. They had been back once to get her some more clothes and her toiletries, but they hadn't bothered to stay and clean up. Now, as Gigi searched through the mess in her bedroom trying to find the key to the storage unit, Joe straightened things up a little in the dinette and living room. He might just as well have tried to glue an eggshell back together. The place was hopeless.

He laughed when he came upon a stash of erotic magazines, many of which he had copies of at home. It was a reminder to him that the week he had spent playing house with Gigi was just that, playing. He didn't doubt that once the circumstances that had brought them together evaporated, they would go back to their old lives. At their core, he knew, people were who they were. No one changes anybody. And for the first time in a while, he found himself thinking about where Marla had gone.

He put the magazines down and put things in stacks and piles as best he could. It was amazing, he thought, how much crap Gigi had managed to cram into such a small place. He flipped the couch right-side up and put the shredded cushions back in place. Didn't do much good. He did the same with the chairs, but it was a waste of time. Gigi was going to have to spend some of her newfound money at Ikea in Hicksville.

"Joe, Joe, come in here," Gigi called. "Hurry up!"

He didn't like the sound of her voice, but unless someone was hiding behind the baseboard, he didn't think there was reason to draw his gun. She handed him a bundled up garbage bag as he stepped into her bedroom.

"Christ, Gigi, I thought there was something wrong. If all you needed—"

"That's the bag."

"What bag?"

"The bag," she repeated. "*The* bag."

"Maybe I'm missing something here."

"Remember, I told you that inside the storage unit I only found a big garbage bag with—"

"—the two bags of money inside. Okay, but so what?"

"Jesus Christ, Joe, for a fucking cop, you're a little thick. You were right this morning, but you had the wrong bags. Feel it. Feel the bag."

He squeezed the bundled bag, moving it around in his hands. It didn't take more than few second before he felt the square edges. He unfurled the bag and turned it inside out. There, duct-taped to the bottom of the green plastic bag was a manila envelope with Gigi's name written across it in black marker.

"That's Rusty's handwritting," Gigi said, her hands shaking.

As carefully as he could, Serpe peeled the plastic away from the tape until he was holding only the envelope. There was a strip of the same gray tape across the flap.

"You got a sharp knife around here?" Joe asked.

"I'll get one. Might take me a minute under all the piles of crap."

As he listened to Gigi rummaging through her kitchen draws, he felt the envelope, held it up to the light. He knew it was stupid, that he'd have his answer soon enough. Then he realized that he had transferred the knife he carried with him when he was on the truck from his work clothes to the pants he was wearing. He reached around into his back pocket, removed the knife, snapped it open with a flick of his wrist—a skill he'd perfected on the streets of Brooklyn a long time ago—and slit open the envelope with one clean cut.

Inside the envelope was a second envelope; white, standard letter-sized. Serpe could feel the negatives through the paper. *Negatives!* Joe smiled sadly. *Who used film anymore?* Had the Marsden kid's camera been digital, he thought, a lot of dead men and a woman—some innocent, some not—might still be alive. If it had been a digital camera, the images of Burgess tossing the kid would have been up on the internet fifteen minutes after they were taken and on the cover of every major newspaper the following day. No secrets. No blackmail. No need to kill the blackmailer.

He snapped the knife shut, slipping it back into his pants, and stuffed the white envelope into his coat pocket. As he was about to take a look at the pictures themselves, Joe became accutely aware of the silence. He could no longer hear Gigi searching through the rubble. If something was wrong out there, it was probably too late to stop it. It wasn't to late to reach beneath his coat and pull out his gun, but it might just as well have been.

"Gigi," he called.

"Yeah. I'm coming."

Her answer did anything but reassure him. Joe heard the cracks in her voice, big cracks. Before he could take a step, there was another voice.

"Drop the fucking gun and kick it over here," McCauly said, a self-satisfied smile on his cheery red face. He had his right forearm tight around Gigi's neck and his left hand held a snub-nosed .38 to her temple. Gigi strained hard against his arm and shook her head no. Joe Serpe took her advice.

"I don't think so, Finn," he said, waving his Glock. "I drop this, I'm dead."

"You don't, she's dead."

"That's her problem…and yours."

Suddenly, McCauly's smile didn't seem so self-assured. "Mine? How you figure?"

"Because the second you squeeze that trigger," Serpe said, racking his weapon, "I'm gonna put a hole in your head where your right eye used to be. Then you'll be dead and these will still be mine anyway."

"But they ain't no use to you."

"You tell me about them and maybe we can talk. Maybe we can be partners."

"Why, so you can fuck me outta what I got comin' like this bitch's fucking brother?" McCauly tightened his grip around Gigi's throat and she was gasping for air. As she gasped, he moved the barrel of the gun into her mouth. She'd been pretty stoic until that point, now the panic in her eyes was profound.

Serpe lowered his weapon. "Calm down, Finn. I know you're not kidding, but neither am I. Talk to me."

"Rusty played me for two years. He threw me maybe thirty, forty thousand bucks, but I know he had the big money. He goes up to that roof and gets rich. Me, all I get is table scraps. We were supposed to split the money and if anything happened to him, I was supposed to get the pictures."

"Pictures of what, Reverend Burgess pushing the DeFrees kid off the roof?"

McCauly started laughing. "You're a dumbass, Serpe. You know that? What do you think, that Monaco caught the most powerful nigger in the city throwing some little pissant nigger off a roof? How fucking stupid is that? The guy is cold-hearted enough to do it, no doubt, but he ain't stupid like you."

"Then who'd Rusty catch up there?"

"Burgess' son, Khouri."

"I don't under—"

"I know you don't understand, fucko," Finn said, shaking his head and easing his grip on Gigi. "Burgess was doing this outreach thing in the projects, taking some kids who'd been in trouble with the law and making his own little Guardian Angels out of them. He was gonna show us that the projects didn't need cops and that the niggers could do for themselves. Problem was, he put his asshole son Khouri in charge of the troops at the Nellie Bly Houses. Let's just say that Khouri had his own kinda problems with anger management and was getting impatient with one of his new recruits."

"Bogarde DeFrees."

"Bogarde DeFrees," McCauly repeated. "Seems Bogarde was smoking a little reefer in the accessway to the roof instead of patrolling the upper floors of Building Four like he was supposed to. Khouri Burgess took exception to his boy's misbehaving and explained as much with a right cross. DeFrees pulled a blade. Burgess pulled a gun and it was off to the races from there. Rusty said that Khouri Burgess just like grabbed the little nigger and tossed him off the roof. Just like that. Like he was throwing away a balled up napkin or something."

"That's cold."

"Yeah, but he pissed his pants when Rusty cuffed him. When he told Monaco that he was James Burgess' son and begged him to let him get his daddy on his cell phone, Rusty saw an opportunity. Rusty was smart that way. The Rev parted with twenty grand that day and promised much more. Only he tried to fuck us once the investigation began and Rusty was taking the heat. He started a big protest that night saying that Rusty was guilty and the cops were gonna cover it up like they always did. He figured he had us by the balls because his kid wasn't in custody anymore and we'd fucked with the evidence. What he didn't know was that Rusty had seen the kid on the other roof taking pictures of the murder in progress."

"Who killed Edgerin Marsden?" Joe asked.

"Carter Blaylock, a gangsta snitch who we threatened to expose to his boys if he didn't do us this favor. We didn't have to ask him twice. He walked right up to Marsden and popped him. Stupid nigger. We gave him up anyway."

"No witnesses."

"No witnesses. His boys did a lot worse to him than throwing his ass off a roof."

"And Burgess?"

"Rusty said the Rev almost fuckin' died when he showed him the pictures. Gave him a full set of copies and told him to keep them for his album. But Burgess recovered pretty quick. Said he'd pay Rusty off, but that he couldn't risk big chunks of money out of his businesses and charities. So over the last four years, Rusty and me, we had a little supplemental income. Too bad Rusty supplemented himself better than me."

"Did Burgess ever try to buy the pictures back?"

"Nah. He knew better. Knew Rusty'd always keep the negatives for insurance."

"You killed Stanfill then."

"That was stupid," McCauly confessed, shaking his head. "I thought he knew about the pictures and kept them for himself. Instead Rusty lied to me and stashed them away for this bitch."

"And you came here looking for the pictures," Joe said. "That's when you sapped me."

"Yeah." '

"Why not kill me?"

"I guess maybe I shoulda, but there were already too many investigations going on with Rusty's murder and you sniffing around. Then there was Stanfill. If you went down too…"

"But—"

"Enough," Finn said. "Gimme the fucking envelope." He tightened his grip again and was lifting Gigi up off her feet. Her face was turning all colors as she kicked her feet wildly. She was struggling to breathe, the fear and pleading in her eyes was impossible to ignore.

"Alright, okay," Serpe said, his posture indicating surrender. "I'll put the gun down, but the second I do, you let her go."

McCauly squeezed harder. "I'm not in the mood for bargains." Gigi's eyes rolled up in her head and she was going limp.

Serpe tossed the gun, but kept the pictures.

"That's better," Finn said and let go of Gigi. She collapsed on the floor in a heap. It was difficult for Serpe to see if she was still breathing. "Now the photos. Flip 'em over here."

Joe flung the envelope at Finnbar McCauly's head to obscure the fat man's vision. Serpe charged at him. McCauly got off a shot, but it was high of the mark as Serpe came at him low. Joe dodged Gigi's limp body, digging his left shoulder into McCauly's gut. Finn's belly wasn't as soft as it looked, but Joe still managed to knock the cop backwards. Backwards was good, just not good enough. McCauly didn't go down and he still had the .38 firm in his hand. He brought the gun down on Serpe's back, just missing his right kidney. Joe understood the next thing to hit his back was probably going to be a bullet, so he threw a fierce uppercut into McCauly's groin. That took the wind out of Finn's sails, but instead of tumbling backwards, he sprawled on top of Serpe.

Joe struggled to get out from under McCauly's dead weight. Finn was making wounded animal noises; a mixture of barking coughs and furious growls. He was no weakling and he grabbed a fist full of Serpe's coat even as he fought to catch his breath and to not puke up his lunch. Serpe considered trying to find the hand that held the .38 or to find his own discarded gun, but thought it better just to get to his feet. Finally, he pulled himself out of McCauly's grasp and up. A little too easily, he thought. That meant McCauly was regaining control and was also struggling to get up himself.

He turned and swung his right leg at McCauly's head. The fat man, who had gotten to his hands and knees, tucked his head and threw out his left arm to block the kick. Joe's ankle smacked hard into Finn's forearm with a sharp crack that reverberated back up Serpe's leg. Finn groaned, but raised his .38. Joe ran for the front door. That's when his ears filled with fluid and the world shifted into a low grinding gear. He couldn't hear anything but his own exaggerated breaths and disconnected sounds that didn't seem to make any sense.

Joe pumped his legs as he made it through the bedroom door into the kitchenette, but the bottoms of his shoes seemed velcro-ed to the linoleum. He turned back to see McCauly scrambling to his feet, coming through the door behind him, the .38 in one hand, the envelope with the photos in the other. There was a burst of fire out of the tip of the .38, smoke, a roar. Something hot whistled past Serpe's chin. The world shifted gears again and it lurched forward. He whipped his head around and he lost his balance, falling forward. On the way down he

saw a silhouetted figure standing in the doorway. Something hard and
sharp smashed into the side of Serpe's head. The sun exploded behind
his eyes and then slipped into darkness. In the darkness, Joe thought
he heard voices and a more steady roar. Then he heard nothing at all.

☆   ☆   ☆   ☆

He didn't know how long he'd been out. He heard distant sirens
and guessed it hadn't been that long. When he opened his eyes, the
sun reprised its earlier explosion, only this time there was a side order
of pain with the flash. As his eyes refocused, he saw the apartment was
nearly as dark as his forced nap had been. Slowly, he got to his hands
and knees. He was a bit nauseous, but it wasn't too bad. This getting
knocked unconscious and waking up on Gigi's floor, he thought, was
getting to be a bad habit. He smiled at that. It was going to be his last
smile for the night.

Serpe found a wall and let his fingers crawl on it till they found a
light switch. No interior lights went on. And he remembered that all
the lamps had been smashed up by McCauly when he came looking
for the pictures the first time. But the outdoor entrance fixture came
on, throwing just enough ambient light inside the basement apartment for Serpe to see he'd been the lucky one.

When he turned around, he saw McCauly's lifeless body sprawled
out on the kitchenette floor. As he passed the dead cop to see about
Gigi, Serpe saw part of Finn's forehead had been blown off and there
was a hole three times the size in what used to be the back of his
head. He heard faint groaning coming from the bedroom and as he
stepped, his shoe slipped in an invisible puddle of blood, but he managed to use the wall and keep himself upright.

He reached into the bedroom and flicked on the switch. Here the
fixture worked. Gigi was on her back, an ugly red stain spread across
her upper body from her right shoulder down. Her eyes were open,
she was panting, shivering, in shock. Joe's Glock was still in her right
hand. Serpe found a few pair of Gigi's panties that were laying on the
floor and he pressed them hard against the hole in her shoulder.

"You're gonna be alright," he said. "Can you hear the sirens? They'll be here soon. You're gonna be alright."

"There was…" she gulped air. "There was someone else…here."

"Don't talk."

She didn't listen. "He was…tall, black…young. When…McCauly came after…you…I found your…gun. I went to…shoot…but the black guy—" Gigi's body clenched in pain. "He shot…McCauly. One of the…shots…hit me." She clenched again. "I squeezed…the…trigger. I think I hit…him."

"Shhh," he said. "I know it hurts, but I think it's just your shoulder." The sirens were louder now, maybe a block or two away. "Listen Gigi, I've gotta get outta here now, but if you—"

"Go!"

"But—"

"Go."

Joe took the Glock and moved it onto the patch of panties on her shoulder, and told her to press as hard on the wound as she could until the cops got there. He knelt over and kissed her.

"Go!" was what she said.

[All The Kings Horses]

Serpe changed out of his bloody clothes and into the fresh ones in the backseat of Bob Healy's car as they sped along the Grand Central Parkway in Queens towards the Jackie Robinson Parkway. As Joe changed, he explained to Healy and Blades about McCauly and Khouri Burgess.

"You were right about almost everything," Serpe said, pulling a sweater over his head. "When you think about it, we were kinda dumb to think the Reverend James Burgess would throw some kid off a roof himself or be there when one of his minions did."

"I guess," Healy agreed. "So you think it was Khouri who showed up at Gigi's apartment tonight, huh?"

"Yeah. I don't know who else it could be."

"And he got the pictures," Blades said. "Shit."

"He got the pictures, but he didn't get these," Joe said, reaching into his coat pocket and handing Detective Hines the white envelope. "He was in too much of a rush and I think Gigi might have wounded him. There was blood on the steps from her apartment."

"Holy shit!"

"That's right, partner. Holy shit."

Raiza Hines popped on the dome light, opened the envelope, and held the strips of negatives up to the light.

"These are the real goods," she said, carefulling replacing the negatives. "Edgerin Marsden caught the whole sequence of them tusseling and DeFrees going over the edge. It's kinda tough to see on the negatives, but it looks like you'd be able to make out the faces of the two of them when they're developed."

"I'm sure that's true, otherwise Burgess wouldn't have paid anything beyond the first twenty grand."

"Then what are we doing?" Blades asked, agitated. "We got the evidence right here about the DeFrees murder. You got McCauly to give up Edgerin Marsden's killer. Chances are we'll be able to track down who in his posse killed him. So, Joe, explain to me why are we breaking every rule in the book to go to Reverend Burgess' headquarters and get ourselves jammed up or worse?"

"Because I wanna know who killed Rusty Monaco."

"It was Khouri Burgess," Blades said. "That's pretty clear."

"Maybe to you. You're probably right that it was Khouri Burgess. Or maybe it was one of his daddy's less savory business partners or maybe someone who owed him a favor. I mean, it was the Reverend Burgess who was under DOI investigation, not the son. It was the Rev who had the most to lose. It could have even been Finn McCauly, though I doubt it. I just don't like getting half or most of the story."

"Is it *that* important to find out exactly which one of the three actually put the bullets into Monaco? You already know why."

"Blades, you and me, we don't know each other real well, so I understand," Joe said. "But I was never much for cutting corners on the job. You go back, you check my cases. None of the convictions built on my work were ever overturned on appeal. None. Never."

"Not until the end, you mean," Healy corrected. "Before your partner Ralphy started fucking up your cases and sabotaging your work to protect the scumbags who were paying him off and feeding his jones."

Serpe relented. "Okay, not until the end, but it was Ralphy doing it. You know I didn't do sloppy work. The one time in my career I cut corners and didn't see things through; the one time I looked the other way and hoped for the best, I lost everything."

"Ignoring what your partner was doing?" Blades asked.

"With Ralphy, yeah. I'm not gonna do that here. Not this time."

"But why not let the NYPD and the Suffolk cops sort this shit out?" she asked. "The Burgesses ain't going nowhere."

"You know why, Blades?" Healy said. "Because the second they're arrested, both father and son will lawyer up and shut up. The only murder that there's any real evidence of is the DeFrees murder. On the Marsden kid's homicide, all we got is McCauly's word and he's dead. Khouri Burgess, if that's who really was at Gigi's tonight, will claim that Finn McCauly fired at him first and it was self-defense. Hell, if Gigi really did wound him, he'll say he had no way of knowing who was shooting at him.

"And a lawyer might not be able to talk a jury into believing that the Marsden pictures don't show what they show, but he might. He'll say DeFrees and Khouri were fighting and DeFrees went off the roof by accident. Khouri will say he wanted to turn himself in, but that Rusty Monaco wouldn't let him because he knew he could blackmail his dad. There *is* proof of blackmail. Shit, Blades, I could half believe it and I know the truth."

"But—"

"No buts," Bob said. "At best, they'll get Khouri Burgess for manslaughter and obstruction of justice in Brooklyn. He might get off on McCauly too. Even in Suffolk County, dirty, blackmailing cops aren't real popular. The Reverend James Burgess will look like a sympathetic character here. Neither him or his kid is going to cop to four murder one counts on Long Island. They'll claim it was McCauly turning on his partner in extortion who killed Rusty and murdered the other drivers to cover it up. No, we've gotta get to them first."

Raiza Hines didn't say another word about it.

"Look, Blades," Serpe said. "The minute we get off on Pennsylvania Avenue, we'll pull over and you can get out of the car. My reputation's shot. Me and Healy here, our careers are over. You've got a big career ahead of you. You got the goods. When we pull over, you can walk away from this, no questions asked."

"No questions asked," Healy agreed.

"Both of you just keep quiet. Besides, without me, how you two old crackers gonna get anywhere near Burgess's headquarters?"

As they got off the Jackie Robinson Parkway and onto Pennsylvania Avenue, Blades stayed silent. When they were a block away from the converted brownstone on Utica Avenue that Burgess used as his headquarters, Serpe told Healy to park. They each pulled out their cell phones and made a call or two. No one on the other end of the lines seemed too terribly pleased, but the three of them had already plunged so far into the deep end of the shit that they were beyond caring. When they were done with the calls, Hines, Healy and Serpe got out of the car and walked.

Out front of the beautifully restored brownstone—footscrapers, wrought iron gate and fence, faux gas lamps, et al—stood two men, one at either side of the steps like the lions in front of the New York Public Library. They were escapees from the NFL, more mountains than men, really. Both had necks, arms, and legs like telephone poles and torsos like concrete bunkers. They had ear pieces and mics clipped to the collars of their black leather dusters. Although their matching overcoats were just loose enough to conceal a holster and sidearm, it was safe to assume they were carrying. But none of that was nearly as intimidating as their *don't-even-fuck-with-me-I-will-kill* you demeanor.

Blades and Healy already had their shields out as they approached. Serpe just acted the part. The twin mountains were unimpressed and unintimidated. The one on the left held up his right hand. It was as big as the rest of him. Good thing he didn't hold it up high enough to blot out the moon.

"Where y'all goin'?" he asked, in a calm, sweet voice.

Hines did the talking. "Up those stairs."

His partner reached up his hand and leaned his head over to talk into his mic.

"Don't do that!" Healy said.

He put his hand back down.

"You got an invitation or a warrant? 'Cause if you don't, y'all ain't goin' up them steps," said Sweet Voice.

"See this?" Hines flicked the shield clipped to her lapel. "This is my invitation."

"Nah, it ain't neither," the other mountain chimed in. "That there is a few ounces of gold plated metal and ceramics. That ain't no warrant neither. Come on back next Thanksgiving when the Reverend give out free turkeys. Maybe he'll talk to you then."

"Enough," Hines barked, putting her face up close to Mountain Number Two. "Did Khouri Burgess enter these premises this evening? 'Cause he murdered an NYPD detective earlier this evening. I don't need no fuckin' warrant."

The distant wail of approaching sirens could just be heard above the street noise. The timing couldn't have been better. The guards were unmoved.

"How we know—"

Hines had reached her limit. "Look, you motherfuckas, this ain't no bullshit. Now let us in there or I'm gonna arrest both of you. Where's Burgess at inside?"

"Probably in what he call his war room up on the top floor," said Sweet Voice, his voice less calm.

"When did the son get here?"

" 'Bout five minutes before y'all."

"Okay, come on. Show us. And keep your hands off those mic buttons."

They heard the shouting before they were fully inside the brownstone. And when they reached the top of the stairs, they heard the first shot. Now they all broke into a run, but not even Superman on his best day could've gotten there before the second and third shots. They did get there just in time to see Khouri Burgess put the muzzle of his hand cannon under his chin and blow off the top of his head.

James Burgess was still alive, barely. He had been hit once in the liver and once above the heart. The sirens were loud outside the window, so Sweet Voice put down the telephone. Calling 911 suddenly seemed beside the point. Blades and Healy pressed their hands against the reverend's wounds, but his eyes were glassy; the pupils wide and unseeing. The blood that had already poured out of his body made a huge wet stain in the cream-colored carpet.

"Fool…didn't…even…get the…neg..a..tives. That…boy…has always…been…a…dis…a…pointment to…me. Always…a…dis…" Such were the last words spoken on this earth by the once mighty Reverend James Burgess.

Joe Serpe attended to Khouri; what was left of him, anyway. When he opened the dead man's coat, Serpe saw that the younger Burgess had only expedited the inevitable. Either Gigi or McCauly had hit him. He'd been gut shot and had tried to stem the flow of blood with a bunch of sanitary napkins taped over the wound. He'd either scooped up the pads and tape from Gigi's apartment or picked them up at a convenience store on the way into Brooklyn. But like everything else about the dance between the Burgesses, Rusty Monaco, and Finnbar McCauly, the patch was futile and soaked with blood.

Serpe stood up and looked at the photos that lined the walls. They were pictures of the Reverend James Burgess with some of the most powerful men and women in New York City, New York State, the country, and the world. He was pictured with senators and congressmen, presidents and popes, prize fighters and a princess. Healy noticed Joe Serpe staring at the walls.

"Look at Burgess' desk," he told his partner.

Serpe walked over and saw the blackmail photos laid out in sequence across the desk, Khouri Burgess' freckled skin apparent in every picture.

"Amazing, huh?" Healy said.

"What?"

"All those pictures of the rich and famous and powerful."

"Big fucking deal," Serpe said. "In the end, all of his connections couldn't do a thing to save his ass. None of the pictures on the walls mean a fucking thing in the face of the pictures on his desk."

"All the kings horses and all the kings men…"

Serpe opened his mouth to answer, but half the uniforms in New York City came rushing through the door.

[Dead Cow]

FRIDAY, JANUARY 28TH, 2005

Serpe was waiting at Gigi's bedside when she opened her eyes. The ugly red marks around her neck from McCauly's choke hold had turned purple. In the end, they had a longer shelf-life than he did. The bullet had shattered her clavicle, punctured her lung, and broken a rib. She wouldn't be playing tennis or the violin any time soon.

Joe'd been by every day since Monday, when the NYPD released him and Healy from the Seven-seven Precinct. They hadn't been formally charged or even arrested, although there was plenty of evidence that they'd broken any number of laws. A lesson had to be taught and they were being taught it the only way police departments know how to teach them: with all the delicacy and nuance of a plummeting bowling ball. Joe and Bob actually felt pretty fortunate, because, as NYPD lessons went, the holding cell at the Seven-seven was dream vacation territory. If the NYPD or the Brooklyn DA had really wanted to fuck with them, they would have spent an all expense paid forty-eight hours at the Brooklyn Tombs on Atlantic Avenue or at Riker's Island. Besides, they knew what was really going on and didn't want any part of it.

When George Healy picked them up, he told them about how the negotiations had gone. From the sound of it, things had gotten pretty ugly. That's what happens when the police departments and the prosecutors from three counties do the high wire act of credit and blame. Between the blackmail and the fourteen bodies that had piled up since September 2001, there was precious little of the former and an abundance of the latter to go around. Most of the people who actually deserved credit weren't going to get any. Only Raiza Hines and Detective Keyes were going to get a bit of light shined on them. Hoskins was going to get some spotlight time too, but he hadn't earned a lick of it. As for Serpe and Healy, they were destined to be footnotes; grateful, silent, unprosecuted footnotes. They knew the negotiations were over when they heard they were getting kicked.

After the negotiations were done, the real work began. The cops from all the counties and the DA offices from Suffolk, Nassau, and Brooklyn, combed over all the financial documents, credit card receipts, phone records, travel records of all the principals involved. With the road map of the case laid out for them, it was in everyone's self-interest to confirm what Serpe and Healy believed; that all fourteen deaths sprang from the murder of Bogarde DeFrees by Khouri Burgess. And the sooner it was confirmed, the better. If even one of the principals had survived, there might have been some player willing to keep the case going for political gain. But as one newspaper hack told Serpe during Ralphy Abruzzi's trial, "You can beat a dead horse, but you can't milk a dead cow." Now Joe finally understood what he meant. This case was a dead cow and it was best for everyone to bury it and move on.

"Hey you," Gigi rasped, turning her head over to her left to where Serpe was sitting.

"Hey yourself. How you feeling?"

"Like shit."

"I don't know," he said. "You're the hottest looking gunshot victim I've seen in a long time."

"It's the diet."

"What diet?"

"Hell of a way to lose a few ounces, getting shot. I think I'll try Atkins next time."

"Bullets are low carb, aren't they?" He stood up, leaned over her, and stroked her cheek with the back of his hand. "You saved my life, Gigi."

"Bad habit I picked up from my brother."

"Only bad habit of his you did."

They were quiet for a moment.

"What day is it?"

"Friday. You've been pretty much out of it until today."

"It's the drugs and the pain."

"I know," Joe said. "Trust me, I know."

"That's right. Your leg."

"I spoke with your doctor before. He says you're lucky."

"No, he's lucky. He didn't get shot."

"My doctor said the same thing. He didn't get shot either. But your doctor did say that you could probably start rehab pretty soon."

"Great! More pain, less drugs."

Serpe checked his watch and the wall clock.

"What's the rush?" Gigi asked.

"The news conference is on in a few minutes."

"News conference?"

"Yeah, I told you, but you were probably so fucked up you don't remember."

"Tell me again," she said.

Serpe explained to her about what had happened after she'd been shot. "We could hear Burgess yelling at his kid the minute we got in. I think that he was calling him a stupid, incompetent fool. Probably hurt him almost as much as the bullet you put into him. He had probably heard it his whole life and maybe it was true, but… Khouri, the kid, shot him and then blew his own brains out."

"What's the news conference for?"

"To shut the door on any lingering questions."

Gigi seemed to understand.

Joe clicked on the TV that sat on a swiveling platform in the corner of the room and put on the local cable news channel. On screen was a very serious looking reporter speaking in hushed tones. He was saying something about how things were about to get underway. Behind him, a room full of people—photographers, other reporters, political types—were milling about in groups, whispering in each other's ears. There was a background buzz of low voices. Behind them, on a crowded stage, were lots of men in uniforms that featured some funny hats, lots of gold stripes and shiny brass buttons and stars. If there had been a Sousaphone up there, you might almost have mistaken them for a wayward marching band. Their middle age and sour expressions, however, were a dead giveaway. *Cops*! Up there as well, were several suits; George Healy among them. But it was the Brooklyn DA who stepped up to the array of microphones aligned in rows atop the rostrum. There was a flurry of activity in the auditorium and on stage. Then things got very quiet, all cameras focusing on the stage. Still cameras click, click, clicked away. The introductions alone took nearly eight minutes. Boredom began to show on the faces of the men on the stage and an impatient chatter came up from the crowd. Understanding he was losing the audience, the Brooklyn DA sped up the proceedings.

"On September twenty-fourth, two-thousand-one, while the city and the nation were still reeling from the tragic events of the terrorist attacks at the World Trade Center and the Pentagon, several nine-one-one calls were received by the NYPD. These calls, the transcripts of which are included in your press packets, were to report that someone had either jumped or was thrown from the roof of Building Four of the Nellie Bly Houses. A pair of New York City Police personnel, Detectives Russell Monaco and Finnbar McCauly, were already on scene..." His narrative went on like that for a few minutes, laying out events in the most linear and vague fashion possible. Then he came to the part where the lying began in earnest. You could tell he was lying because his narrative became far more detailed. "...and upon learning of the homicide of retired Detective Monaco on the fifth of January this year, and in receipt of a tip from a reliable and confidential source alerting her to past possible illegal financial transactions between Reverend James Burgess and the recently deceased Detective Monaco, NYPD

Detective Hines of the Internal Affairs Bureau, with the approval of her commanding officer, Captain Skip Rodriguez, began an exhaustive review of Detective Monaco's past cases..."

When the Brooklyn DA had finished his compelling fairy tale, several representatives from the various other law enforcement agencies took their turns at the podium to explain their parts of the puzzle, to tell their lies. Blades got a turn to stand before the cameras and explain that she was most gratified for Evelyn Marsden, who had, after all these years, finally found out why her precious son had been taken from her. She also got to explain that the NYPD had several suspects under arrest in the killing of Carter Blaylock, the man who had been forced to execute the Marsden boy.

Detective Keyes was his usual terse self and did less than two minutes in the spotlight. Not surprisingly, the longest part of the presentation was done by George Healy. Somehow that bothered Serpe the most. Joe didn't mind so much that he had been left out of the story. He hadn't gotten involved in this mess for glory or gain, but to pay a debt that was long overdue. It didn't even bother him that every clown who'd been at the mic had lied through his teeth. It was that George Healy was the biggest liar of the bunch. His brother had risked his life and deserved better than what George was giving him. Bob wouldn't see it that way, but brothers can be easily blinded.

The main thrust of George's song and dance was that the Suffolk PD had concluded, with a high degree of certainty, that Khouri Burgess had murdered the first three oil drivers in order to cover up the true target of his intentions; Rusty Monaco, the fourth victim. With credit card receipts, electronic toll records, they could place Khouri Burgess on Long Island on two of the dates of the murders. One of those dates was the night Rusty Monaco was murdered. Eyewitnesses said that Khouri often spent time playing ball at a community gym his father's foundation had built in Wyandanch, very near where Monaco's body was found. George also explained that no one could provide exculpatory alibis for the nights of the other two homicides. There was mention of the shooting at Gigi's apartment, but if you sneezed you would have missed it.

"What about that?" she asked Joe, pain and exhaustion creeping into her voice.

"It's a done deal. The cops will take your statement when you're feeling up to it. You shot in self-defense not knowing whether Khouri Burgess was shooting at you or McCauly."

"How did Khouri Burgess know to come to my apartment?"

"He was following McCauly. Finn wasn't the sharpest tool in the shed. Since it was always your brother who had dealt with the Reverend Burgess, Finn didn't know how to make contact without calling too much attention to himself. So the idiot tried to squeeze money out of the kid first by claiming he already had the pictures and negatives. The idiot led Khouri right to him and the blackmail material. Cops always say that if criminals had half a brain, they'd be in trouble. When cops become criminals, I guess some of them lose half their brains."

"And the money…"

"We haven't told anyone about it," Serpe said. "I don't think they give a shit. They assume that your brother used most of the money to buy the condo and that if there was any leftover cash, McCauly took it and hid it somewhere. Wouldn't be the first time money got stashed and the guy who hid it died without sharing the whereabouts. Word is that's what happened to the Lufthansa money that was stolen at JFK."

The rest of the news conference went pretty much as expected. The press seemed almost complicit. They asked very few incisive questions or ones that raised even the specter of doubt. The one or two probing questions that were asked were swatted away like one-winged flies. Really, the only surprising thing was Tim Hoskins' absence. George Healy made liberal mention of him and he would get credit for doing the leg work, but he was nowhere to be seen. Hoskins wasn't great with the press, so maybe the bosses didn't want him around.

Serpe clicked off the TV. He had spent the better part of his morning rehearsing what he wanted to say to Gigi. The first part was a speech about Rusty. That it was awful that he turned out to be exactly what everyone thought him to be. Joe meant to say that he never intended for things to work out the way they did and that all he ever wanted to do was to repay his debt to her brother. That he considered the debt paid in full, but that he wished the truth could have been less painful. The second part of his prepared talk was about the two of them. How he understood that they didn't have much of a future together as a couple. Still, he meant to say, that he'd like to see her when he could. That he liked being around her because he didn't have to pretend to be somebody he wasn't. When he put the clicker down on the bedside table and leaned over to talk to her, Serpe noticed she was sleeping. Whatever he had to say would keep.

[Dead Serious]

MONDAY, FEBRUARY 14TH, 2005—VALENTINE'S DAY

It was an anniversary both dark and light; exactly one year ago to the day that Serpe'd received the late day call to make an emergency delivery up in Kings Park to someone named Healy. Later that evening, the Russians caught the hose monkey hiding in the oil yard and beat him to death. The monsters left him to rot in the sludge at the bottom of the International's tank, the tank that still held Gigi's money. Frank had taken Joe to Lugo's that night for a drink before they headed their separate ways. Frank went home to his wife and kids and approaching destiny; Joe to his cat and a bottle of Absolut.

Joe sent John and Anthony home early so they could do what young men did on Valentine's Day. Bob Healy had the whole day off. He and Blades were up at some ski resort in Vermont and weren't scheduled back until later that night. Serpe suspected they weren't doing much skiing up in the Green Mountains. They were up there celebrating Valentine's Day, Blades' justly earned promotion, and her transfer from IAB to Brooklyn North Homicide. Shit, Joe thought, a month into a relationship, you really didn't need an excuse for celebrating.

He put in a call to Gigi to see how she was doing. She'd been trans-

ferred to a rehab facility in Connecticut about a week ago and Joe
called her every day just to bust her chops and make sure she did her
work. He remembered how much he hated that part of his recovery
and how much it helped to have Marla around to push him. Joe'd
even gotten in touch with Gigi's last girlfriend and urged her to call
and visit. But he wasn't acting out of guilt. This wasn't like what had
happened to Marla. In fact, the way Joe saw it, Gigi would probably be
dead if he hadn't gotten involved with her. Finn McCauly would have
come calling regardless. Given what he'd done to Stanfill in order to
get his hands on those pictures, there's no telling what he would have
done to Gigi. Hell, he nearly broke her neck anyway.

Joe shut the trailer lights, set the alarm, closed the door behind him,
and padlocked it. It was about five and the sun was still above the hori-
zon, if not by much. Only a month ago, he would have been standing
in fallen night. Spring was coming and, for no reason he could explain,
that made him really excited. He came down the steps in two strides,
checked the trucks to make sure their tank valves were closed, and
walked through the gates to chain them shut.

"Happy Valentine's Day." The voice was familiar, the words were
strange.

"Hoskins?" Serpe turned ready for battle.

"Calm down, shithead. I'm not here for a fight."

"Then what?"

"You ever get an itch on the bottom of your foot?"

"What?"

"An itch, you ever get one on the bottom of your foot?" Hoskins
repeated.

"Sure."

"You know when those are the worst? When you're driving. You like
struggle to move your foot inside your shoe and that don't work. Then
you're reaching down and sticking your finger inside your shoe and
you're trying to drive and that don't help."

"Is there a point to this?" Serpe asked, but not too impatiently.

"But you know what's really frustrating is when you manage to work
your way out of your shoe and you can like rub your foot on the car mat

or against the corner of the brake pedal and that still don't help."

"I know how that feels."

"Well, Serpe, I got an itch like that, but it ain't on the bottom of my foot."

"Sucks."

"I think you wanna hear about it."

"You do?"

"I do. You got a hot date with Monaco's sister?"

"She's rehabbing her shoulder."

"Then let me buy you a drink. Lugo's okay?"

"I'll meet you there in five minutes," Serpe heard himself say, but not quite believing it.

This was getting to be a weird tradition, Joe thought, as he pulled into the back lot of the bar. This was the second Valentine's Day in a row he'd be drinking with a man at Lugo's. At least he liked Frank. The same could not be said for Hoskins. But for him to approach Joe, never mind ask him for a drink, took a lot. Drinking with your buds was one thing. Drinking with your sworn enemy was something else entirely. As he walked through the parking lot entrance into Lugo's, Serpe remembered the last time he was there. He imagined he could smell the cloying scent of Kathleen Cummings' perfume, feel her arms around his neck. Men had sacrificed their left testicles to be with her, so she said. He wondered how much they were willing to sacrifice to get away?

"What are you smiling at?" Hoskins asked Joe as he walked up to the bar.

"The thought of drinking with you."

"Fuck you, Serpe."

"That's more like it."

"What are you having?"

"Blue Point lager."

"I got you a Bud. Come on over. I got us a booth in the back."

"How romantic."

Hoskins didn't say fuck you, but he thought it. Serpe could see it spelled out on Hoskins' jowly face. When they slid into the booth, neither even bothered to make a move to clink bottles.

Joe got to it. "About that itch…"

"I got leukemia," Hoskins said. "Some kind you need lessons for just to pronounce."

"Fuck!"

"Yeah, fuck is right."

"I'm sorry," Joe said reflexively.

"Bullshit, but thanks anyways. I started treatment and the doctors got that look on their faces like maybe I shouldn't invest in that condo in Myrtle Beach. I think that's why the itch is so bad. If I'm going, I'm not going with this bullshit case hung around my neck. My coffin's gonna be big enough without having to stuff a fucking albatross in there. I don't want it on my conscience."

"You'd need a conscience to worry about that," Joe said.

"I discovered mine late. About thirty seconds after the doctor told me I had leukemia. World would be a better place if everybody thought they were dying."

"Everybody *is* dying."

"Then if they realized it more," Hoskins said. "So like I said, the itch is bad. I don't think the Burgess kid killed those drivers."

"Is that why you weren't at the news conference?"

"Joe 'the Snake' Serpe noticed I wasn't there. I'm honored."

"Look, Hoskins, just because you're dying doesn't mean I like you any better. So let's—"

"Okay, you're right. This is business. No, I missed the press conference because that's the day the doctor gave me the good news. I thought they were gonna ask me to prepay my bills."

"Honesty. That's a start. So what is it about the case that you don't like?"

"How about everything? I mean, the stuff in the city, the stuff about Burgess and his son, okay, I buy that. I buy the blackmail. What I don't buy is that it was Khouri Burgess that killed those drivers."

"Why?"

"The Burgess kid, he strike you as a criminal fucking mastermind?"

"Not really," Serpe admitted.

"More like a frightened little kid, you ask me. Besides, the case is weak. It's all circumstantial," Hoskins said.

"They've executed people on less."

"Sometimes they executed the wrong man."

"I'm listening."

"We got no physical evidence tying Khouri Burgess to any of the crime scenes. I mean like zero. The piece he killed himself with was a three-fifty-seven. All the oil drivers were done with a nine, the same nine. The NYPD searched high and low and couldn't find a nine millimeter or anyone who says he ever knew Khouri Burgess to be in possession of one. Christ, Serpe, there's not even an African-American hair at any of the crime scenes except at the one where the nig—"

"—Cameron Wilkes was murdered."

"That one, yeah. I did a little canvassing on my own. Went back to Wyandanch, Hagerman, and the other neighborhoods where the murders took place and not one person could remember seeing anyone who looked like Khouri Burgess at all. It's not like you wouldn't remember him with that weird freckled fucking skin of his. Remember, the Mets had a player with skin like that a few years back. Butch something."

"Huskey, Butch Huskey."

"Right. Him. You remember someone like him walks by you or is hanging on your corner at night. Even nig—black folks remember a face like his and he wasn't exactly a shrimpy little guy."

"Okay, I agree with you there," Serpe said. "That *is* odd."

"And why make Monaco the fourth victim? That don't sit right with me. Killing him first or last just calls too much attention to itself."

"Even if I agreed with you—"

"You don't?"

"You make some good points. I'm not saying you don't make some good points, but what does it matter? What do you expect me to do about it?" Joe asked.

"Help me prove it."

"You're serious."

"Dead serious."

Serpe thought about it for a minute before answering. "Did you go to your bosses or George Healy with your suspicions?"

"Come on, Serpe. They're still orgasming over getting this shit wrapped up in a nice bundle. They don't wanna hear nothing that doesn't fit in with the story they told the world or the one they told themselves."

"You're right. But why come to me? You hate my guts. Last time I checked, you were coldcocking me in the parking lot of a funeral home."

Hoskins squirmed in his seat. "Look, I don't wanna marry you or nothing, but I'm not as blind as this lazy fucking eye makes me seem. I saw how you flushed out the Russians and found the retarded kid's killer. It was you and your partner that found out that the fifth oil murder was a bullshit copycat thing. Shit, if it wasn't for you and Healy, Burgess would still be preaching this Sunday. And even though I can't stomach what you did to Ralphy, he used to talk about you all the fucking time. He thought you were the best detective the NYPD had."

"Enough. Okay. What do you need?"

"Let's look over the files together," Hoskins said.

"Me and Healy have been over those files twenty times."

"Maybe, but it's been a couple of weeks. We could go to the actual crime scenes together. Maybe you'll see something I missed."

"Tomorrow, four pm, my office." Serpe stood up and took a final pull on his Bud.

Hoskins held out his hand. "Come on, it won't kill you."

Serpe shook it. He didn't melt like the Wicked Witch of the West, but he wasn't exactly filled with Christian love for the man either. Too much bad had passed between them to forgive. As he left Lugo's, he swore to himself that he was going to spend next Valentine's Day with a woman no matter what it took. Before he left the bar, he made sure Kathleen Cummings was nowhere in sight.

She wasn't around, but Serpe didn't quite make it out of the bar. Stan Brock grabbed Joe by the forearm, and when the ex-boxer grabbed you, you tended to stop in your tracks. They shook hands and Stan demanded Joe have a beer on him as payback for the last time. It wasn't like Joe had anywhere else to get to.

"What'll you have?"

"Blue Point lager."

"Hey, Pete. Blue Point and an O'Doule's here," Stan called to the barman.

"O'Doule's! You're drinking near beer? You quitting, Stan?"

"Nah. I got a date meeting me hear in a few minutes and I want to be straight when she gets here."

Serpe took a good look at Stan. The ex-pug was in nice black wool slacks and a gray wool sweater. It was the first time he'd ever seen the man out of his work clothes and boots. You could really see his boxer's build when he wasn't dressed in coveralls and hoodies. Hell, he even smelled like something other than #2 home heating oil. The barman put the drinks up. They clinked bottles.

"Looking sharp, Stan the Man. Looking sharp."

"Thanks, bro."

"So they found out who was killing us," Brock said, recalling the conversation they'd had the previous month.

"That they did." Given his bizarre evening to that juncture, Serpe didn't feel like discussing it further. Brock had other ideas.

"Murder, man. It's like a fucking virus. Once Cain done in his brother, it spread."

"You religious, Stan?"

"Me? Nah."

"A philospher?"

"Yeah, sure. Brock and Plato Home Heating Oil, Incorporated."

"Sounds good to me," Joe said.

"You hear?"

"Hear what?"

"Jimmy Mazzone's selling Baseline," Brock said. "Gastrol bought 'em out for big big bucks. Millions, I hear."

"Baseline Energy?"

"Never thought I'd see the day that Jimmy Mazzone would sell out to one of those full service motherfuckers. What's this business coming to?"

"It's rough."

"I guess. Maybe after Stevie got murdered... The wife and the daughter had probably had enough. I heard he was gonna marry the daughter."

"I heard the same thing."

"Life's too short."

"Watch it, Stan, or that philosophy thing is gonna get around."

They clinked bottles once more and had a laugh. Joe said his good-byes and shook Brock's hand again.

"Thanks for the beer, Stan." Serpe was about to ask his friend who the lucky woman was when Kathleen Cummings came in through the front door. Brock fairly twitched at the sight of her. "Watch your left nut, bro."

"What'd you say, Joe?"

"Have a great time. See ya."

[Twenty-two Gallons]

TUESDAY, FEBRUARY 15TH, 2005

Bob Healy nearly swallowed his tongue when Hoskins showed up the next day asking for Joe. Serpe hadn't warned Healy, hadn't discussed last night. He'd thought about letting his partner in on the news of his alliance with Hoskins, but realized he scarcely believed it himself. Serpe stepped out of the bathroom when he heard the trailer door shut. He checked his watch.

"Four on the nose. Good."

"I never saw you limp that heavy," Hoskins said as Healy sat in utterly stunned silence.

"After a full day on the truck… It'll be better when I'm off it for a little while. Give me and Healy about five."

"I'll be outside."

Healy stared at his partner in disbelief. His mouth moved, but every word he tried to put in it seemed not to fit.

"I'll explain it to you later, Bob, when I understand it. Is the money right?"

"Fifty cents over."

"Don't let the IRS find out. I'll call you about it later. Right now I gotta go.""

Serpe picked up the cardboard box in which the copies of the homicide files had sat dormant for the last few weeks and left. Healy sat, looked at the door, and shook his head.

Hoskins followed Serpe to his condo in Holbrook. The two of them walked from the parking lot, each with a cardboard box of his own.

"Nice digs," Hoskins said.

"It's too big for me, but... Fuck it!"

"I can find her, you know, Marla Stein. I know she split."

"You've been checking up on me?"

"Yeah, for a time there, you were my hobby," Hoskins confessed. "You gonna ruin a man's life, you gotta know about that man's life."

"Sick kinda logic to that, I guess."

"The offer stands. I can find her."

"Thanks, but no thanks. I've already done her too much harm. You want a drink?"

"JD on the rocks."

"Coming up."

Serpe spread the files out on the living room floor, while Hoskins did his work at the dining room table. Joe couldn't help but think about how empty the place had been since Gigi left. It wasn't so much that he hungered for Gigi's presence. It was more that some places are just meant for two. At that moment, there with his former enemy at his table, Serpe decided he'd put the townhouse on the market as soon as he could. Marla had long ago given him her power of attorney.

"This is bullshit!" Joe shouted, his eyes tired and sore. "There's nothing here."

"You're not seeing it."

"I'm not seeing it because there's nothing here to see."

Hoskins shrugged his shoulders in defeat.

That only pissed Serpe off. "Are your files any different than mine?" he snarled. "Is there anything in the originals that you left out when you made these copies?"

"My hand to God, what you got is an exact copy of what I got here." Hoskins swept his thick arm above the files. "Check for yourself. The only thing not here is the actual crime scene evidence and that we've got pictures of."

"Come on," Serpe said, already throwing on his leather jacket. "Let's go have a look."

"At what?"

"At what's not here."

*   *   *   *

They had the plastic bags laid out on a table, no one paying the two of them any mind. Most Suffolk cops gave Hoskins wide berth to begin with and none of them really knew Serpe. Hoskins was right; there wasn't much evidence. There were the recovered bullets, of course, swaths of bloody clothing, some papers, etc. There were contents from the cabs of all four trucks. Serpe imagined he could smell #2 oil even through the plastic bags.

"How the fuck can you stand that smell all day long?" Hoskins asked. "Christ, it stinks."

Serpe was glad he wasn't imagining it. "Like anything else, you get used to it."

"Does it ever go away?"

"Not really. It's almost impossible to wash outta your clothes and there's no getting it out of your head. Is it alright to handle the evidence out of the bags?"

"Here," Hoskins said, handing Serpe a pair of latex gloves. "Officially, these are still open cases for now. In a few months, when everyone's moved on and forgotten, they'll convene some sorta pow wow and declare them closed. My luck, I'll be dead already. When you wanna look at a different case, I'll give you new gloves."

It wasn't five minutes before Hoskins asked for Joe to come over by him and explain something about the business.

"Serpe, come over here," he said, a scratched and dented metal ticket box next to him on the table. On the box was a blue plastic label, the name STEVIE in raised white lettering.

"It's a ticket box. So what? I've got one for every truck."

"What do you keep in it?"

"My drivers have to keep a copy of the BOL—sorry, the bill of lading. That's how much oil is loaded on the truck at one time. They keep a manifest, which justifies the differences between what's newly loaded and what's already on the truck. They have their delivery tickets, trip/inventory card, and whatever non-cash payments they receive. Checks and money orders, that kinda thing."

"Okay," Hoskins said, flipping open the ticket box with a pencil in spite of the fact they were both wearing gloves. "So this here is the trip/inventory card."

"Right. See, the driver writes down after each stop where the delivery was made and how much oil he pumped. And there, next to each entry, he's marked the method of payment. You can keep a running inventory that way, so you know when you're running low on oil."

"Makes sense. And these two sheets are the BOL and the manifest?"

"Right."

"And these are the delivery tickets, right?" Hoskins fanned ten Baseline Energy tickets across on the table.

"Holy fucking shit!"

"What is it?"

"They were prestamping tickets. Look," Joe said, pulling out two of the tickets. "See, they're both for the same address: 108 Hilltop Avenue in Brentwood."

"So what?"

"See this ticket is dirty and the stamp at the top says one-hundred-seventy-eight gallons. That ticket's been handled by a driver who's been out working, who's got grime on his hands and gloves."

"I see that, yeah."

"But look, the rest of the ticket is blank; no per gallon price, no tax, no total, no nothing. And see here, the yellow customer copy is still attached beneath the merchant copy. Look carefully at its twin. It's pristine. It's all filled out. It's signed for and the customer copy has been torn out. This ticket was punched by a man with clean hands and fresh gloves. But most importantly, look at the gallons pumped stamp."

"Two hundred gallons." A light went on behind Hoskins' sled dog eyes. "I get it! He's charging for two hundred gallons, but he's pumping in twenty-two gallons less. It's like keeping two sets of books."

"Bingo! And see the trip/inventory card, the driver wrote down two hundred gallons."

Some of the steam went out of the cop. "But is it worth killing over? I mean, it's only twenty-two fucking gallons."

"It's more," Joe said, pulling out another pair of twin tickets. "That's thirty more gallons. Now we're up to fifty gallons. That's two phony tickets outta ten. Baseline's got eight trucks. They go out seven days a week in the winter. You do the math and tell me if it's worth killing over."

"I seen people kill for less, a lot less."

"Me too. And there's something else."

"What?"

"Last night after you split, a friend of mine, an old timer in the business bought me a beer. He told me that Jimmy Mazzone is selling Baseline to Gastrol."

"So what?"

"The sale price of an oil company is based upon the average gallons pumped over a two or three year period. You get like a buck a gallon, give or take. We're talking millions of dollars here, Hoskins. Shit, my little rinky-dink outfit is gonna pump a few hundred thousand gallons this year. So if Mazzone has been doing this for years, it's major fraud. He's been shorting customers on one end and inflating his pumping figures on the other. What if Steve Reggio got a guilty conscience and planned on going to the authorities or to Gastrol?"

"But this Stevie guy was engaged to Mazzone's daughter."

"Yeah," Joe said. "And Khouri Burgess just murdered his own father and blew his head off. Under normal circumstances, neither thing happens. But neither situation is normal."

"Okay, so he kills the kid, but you think he killed three innocent men just to cover it up?"

"Why not? It's the same theory everyone was working on for why Monaco was killed, right? Rusty was the real target and the other drivers were killed to obscure that fact. Maybe we were right, but about the wrong victim. Besides, once you've killed your son-in-law to be, I figure it's gotta get easier."

"Even if I buy this, and I'm not saying I do, why would Mazzone leave the tickets there for the world to see? Why not destroy the evidence?"

"Maybe he didn't have it planned out. Maybe he went to throw a scare into the kid, but Stevie wouldn't listen. They struggle. *Bang*! The kid is dead. Somehow, I don't think Mazzone's first thought is to clean out the ticket box with his daughter's fiance bleeding out at his feet. Besides, by making it look like a robbery, he must've figured the cops would focus on that, not on fraud."

"He was right. I didn't know what the double tickets meant."

"Come on, we got some photocopying to do."

[Vengeance and Forgiveness]

THURSDAY, FEBRUARY 17TH, 2005

The two of them sat in Hoskins' Crown Vic down the block from Baseline Energy, Inc. watching the fleet of trucks pull out of the yard and head toward the oil terminal for loading. Neither man was in a very good mood because neither man enjoyed the prospect of what they were about to set in motion, but they had been left no choice. The fact that they'd let Bob Healy in on their theories and that he was most miserable of all, gave them no comfort.

Serpe was wrecked, bleary-eyed and a bit disheveled. Hoskins, never the fittest looking specimen to begin with, was showing signs of the disease. He was swollen and bruised. They had kept Healy up late and he'd been the one to make the call to his brother. Joe didn't think he'd likely forget his partner's expression as he laid the phone back in its cradle.

"So, what'd he say?" Hoskins had asked. It was an unnecessary question. They both saw the answer in his face.

"He said to forget it. He won't take it to the DA. He said there aren't enough chickens in the world to lay the eggs to match how much egg on their faces him and the rest of the brass would be wearing. After the press conference, he said, there was no going back. It's a dead issue."

"How about another ADA?" Joe said. "Or we can take it to the DA ourselves."

"George says that's a non-starter. The DA won't see us and any ADA who even entertains the thought will be committing career suicide. He says we can try to do it through the cops."

"He knows that's bullshit. We got more at stake than the DA's office," Hoskins said. "I went to my commander after Serpe and me looked at the evidence. I laid it out for him and showed him the photocopies. I told him I'd reopen the investigation quietly, that I'd do it on my own and that unless it was an air tight lock, a hundred percent, I'd keep my mouth shut."

"And?" Healy was curious.

"He told me if I said another word about it, he'd bring me up on charges. Took a thick file outta his desk. A history of my past indiscretions, he called it. I'm sure you two understand that there was stuff in there he could make stick. Normally, I woulda told him to jam it up his ass, but I can't afford to lose my benefits, not now."

"What did your brother say when you said we'd take it to the press?" Joe asked.

"That shook him up, made him nervous."

"Good," Hoskins said.

"No, not so good. My brother said that if we went that route—the nuclear option, he called it—that we'd all better be prepared for all out war. That there were too many people in Suffolk, Nassau, and Brooklyn who had too much to lose. They'd ruin us and Gigi would be prosecuted to the full extent of the law. He also said some stuff I'm not gonna repeat. So forget the media."

"What about the truth?"

"That's a pretty funny question coming outta your mouth." Healy said.

"Ain't it, though? Just the same..."

"George said that the truth was only for us to know and that as far as all these victims were concerned, they'd already gotten all the justice they were ever going to get."

Serpe turned bright red. "Fuck him and fuck that!"

Bob Healy didn't disagree.

There was little need of discussion after that. The three of them pretty much understood the mechanics of what had to be done and how to do it. Each had his own reason for doing it. That was eight hours ago. Now the justice clock was about to start ticking.

"Okay," Serpe said. "The trucks are all gone."

Hoskins put the Ford in drive and he purposely skidded to a loud stop inside the yard just outside the office door. Hoskins went in first. With his hulking build and lazy, pale eyes, he was an intimidating presence. The puffy face and bruised skin only heightened the effect. Both Marie and Toni Mazzone sat back in their seats at the sight of him blocking up the doorway. It took them a second to notice his shield and for them to remember who he was. Serpe stepped in behind and then around him. To Marie and her daughter, Joe Serpe seemed like salvation. You could see it in their eyes. Good. That's what they wanted.

"You heard we got the guy that killed Stevie," Hoskins said, not waiting for an answer. "We just got some details to clear up before we close the files. Serpe's here cause he knows the oil business, so don't mind him."

The women were both too stunned to talk right away. They looked at each other then turned to Serpe, a plea for help on their faces.

"Congratulations," Joe said, flashing a broad smile. "I know it's still tough about Stevie, but I heard Jimmy sold to Gastrol."

"Where'd you hear that?" Marie said, confused.

"Around. Big money. Good for you."

"Thanks."

"Serpe, you talk to the daughter in here. I'll talk to the mother in the office."

Hoskins spoke about the women as if they weren't there.

Half an hour later Serpe and Hoskins were back in the front seat of the Crown Vic still parked in Baseline's yard. As planned, Hoskins waited a minute before going back in.

"I almost forgot," he said, handing a white envelope to Marie Mazzone. "This is for your husband, for Jimmy. He really needs to get in touch with me to explain this stuff to me before we can finally put an end to things. Make sure he gets it. I know he'll wanna do the right thing."

"What are you talking about?"

"Just make sure he gets the envelope."

☆   ☆   ☆   ☆

Hoskins parked the car where it had been before, far enough away from the yard not to be noticed, but close enough for Serpe and him to keep an eye on things.

"The daughter's still a mess," Joe said. "She said the fiancé had been acting strange for about a month before he was killed. He was going to church a lot. She even found him crying a few times in the morning, but he wouldn't say what was wrong. The most she said he would say was that he needed to think about big things. I think she just assumed he was getting cold feet."

"Maybe he was."

"Maybe. What did Marie say?"

"She's suspicious, you know."

"About us showing up?"

"That too, yeah," Hoskins said. "But it's more than that. I think she's a smart cookie and she don't like the timing of how everything worked out. Plus the old man's been drinking a lot since the fiancé was killed. Temper's been a little short too. I think maybe he's smacked her around a little."

"You think she knows about the double stamping?"

"She knows. You see her face when you congratulated her on the sale? The woman almost had a fucking canary."

"Drop me back at my car," Serpe said.

"Why?"

"It's been too long since my last confession."

☆   ☆   ☆   ☆

The priest was a hearty man in his early thirties. He had clear blue eyes, thick crooked lips, and peasant teeth. He had the hands of a farmer and a straightforward, friendly manner. His Polish accent matched his Polish name. His hand swallowed Serpe's before giving it back.

"I am Father Dudek. You asked to see me."

"I did."

"How can I help you, my son?"

"I don't think you can."

"Please, we are here to help. I know is sometimes difficult what you have to say, but God's Holy church is love."

Father Dudek wasn't trained by the priests and nuns at Joe's old school and church in Brooklyn. Those folks had a very different concept of God's Holy church.

"Do you remember Stevie Reggio, Father?"

Dudek withered. "I remember the young man, may the Lord Jesus Christ have mercy on his soul." He crossed himself. "What is this about?"

"I own Mayday Fuel, Father, so I knew Stevie a little bit. He seemed like a good kid, but I know he was troubled at the end of his life." Dudek's face showed the truth of Joe's words. "Toni Mazzone told me he had been coming to you for advice and you were his confessor."

The priest's blue eyes were wary and rightfully so. "This is true what you say, but I—"

"Let me finish, Father. I'm Catholic…at least I used to be. So I know you can't talk to me about what you and Stevie discussed, but could you listen to a story I have to tell?"

"A story?"

"Do you like the movies, Father Dudek?"

"Yes, very much. It was one of the reasons I was so happy to come to America, to see the truth behind the movies. But I don't underst—"

"You said the word yourself, Father: truth. The story I have to tell you is like one of those movies when in the beginning it says that the movie is based on the truth."

The confusion went out of the priest. "I will listen. Come sit with me."

Dudek genuflected and crossed himself as he entered the church from the rectory. Serpe refused. There was only so far he was willing to go. After his brother's death, he and the Almighty weren't on speaking or genuflecting terms. They sat in a pew close to the altar, Christ's eyes involved with his own pain.

"Please, my son, begin."

"The story goes like this, Father. When I first started working in the oil business, I was hired by a man I respected and grew to love. He took me in, made me part of his extended family. He placed faith and trust in me, so when he asked me to do certain things that I didn't understand, I did them out of a sense of love and honor. Over the course of the years, I fell in love with this man's daughter and we were engaged to be married.

"I was offered a partnership in the business after the marriage, but by then I had come to understand that the things I had been asked to do by this man I so loved and honored, were both illegal and immoral. They placed everyone I loved in danger from the law and placed my soul in peril. I was terribly conflicted because if I went to the police with what I knew, I would lose not only my job, but the woman I loved and her father would no doubt go to prison.

"So I went back to the one place where I knew I could find solace and advice, I came to the Church. After weeks of soul searching and guidance from a priest I had come to trust, I decided to do the right thing under the law and under God. I decided that nothing was worth the price of my soul and that I had to tell the authorities. If my fiancée loved me, she would stand by me. I made peace with my decision. But most cruelly, just after coming to the decision, I was robbed and murdered. Eventually, the police found the man they believed had killed me."

"Yes, it is a sad story." The priest's eyes were rimmed in red. He fought to hold back his tears. "But I still don't see what you want from me. I don't—"

"Maybe, Father, that's because the story's not over."

"There is more?"

"I'm afraid so. You see, a man and his partner who both used to be detectives and who own an oil company, they kept looking at the murders of the oil drivers. What they discovered was that the man blamed for the murders, though guilty of many crimes, was innocent of these murders. That the person who actually murdered me was my father-in-law to be. That he also killed three other innocent men to cover his tracks. And now not only is the man free of the murders, but he is on the verge of making windfall profits from the fruits of his sins."

Father Dudek's face went from sadness to rage, pure and unadulterated. This was more like it, Serpe thought, a face he recognized from his days in school. Priests were human too.

"This story is true?"

"My part is," Joe said. "But I can't—"

"Excuse me, my son. I must go pray."

"For what, Father Dudek? What will you pray for?"

"For vengeance and forgiveness."

☆   ☆   ☆   ☆

Serpe, Hoskins, and Healy sat waiting for the Baseline truck to pull up to Hoskins' house. Serpe and Healy had already done this ritual at Bob's house a few hours earlier. Now as they waited, Serpe recounted the story of his visit with Father Dudek.

"Vengeance and forgiveness, those were his exact words?" Healy asked.

"His words. But I can't do justice to the look on his face. I had the story cold."

Healy shook his head in disbelief. Then got up to break the spell. "I'm having more coffee. You guys?"

"I'm in," Hoskins said. "It's on the counter next to the stove."

"So how long did it take Jimmy Mazzone to show up at his office after you dropped me off?" Joe asked.

"His truck pulled in almost at the same time I got back there. He was moving at a pretty good clip too."

"And you parked your Crown Vic across the street?"

"Right where the prick could see me," Hoskins said. "The wife and daughter too. When he pulled the truck back out of the yard, I stayed behind him, right in the center of his sideview mirrors like you showed me. Every time he looked back, I was there. He sped up or slowed down, I kept the same distance. When he made stops, I parked down the street just ahead or behind him. At the last stop I followed him to, he tried walking up to the car. I let the fuck get within about ten feet, then I pulled away. You shoulda seen the look on his puss."

There was a knock at the door. "Baseline Energy."

Joe laughed. It had been a long time since he was on this side of an oil delivery, and now he'd gone through it twice in one day. Too bad for the driver, he was about to deliver something other than oil.

Hoskins got up and went to the door. Opened it. Driver showed Hoskins a delivery ticket. Hoskins showed him his shield. The driver took his coffee light and sweet. Both Serpe and Healy recognized him from Lugo's. His name was Dan Litzki.

Litzki was forty, stocky, and currently scared shitless. Perfect.

While Litzki sat down at the table, Serpe retrieved the ticket box from the cab of Litzki's truck. There were three sets of twin tickets. There was a fourth matching set. One, the blank one he'd showed Hoskins at the door. The other a perfectly pre-stamped, two hundred gallon ticket. Both had Hoskins' address filled in at the top.

"How much time you figure you'll do behind these pre-stamped tickets?" Hoskins asked, not bothering to wait for an answer. "You know you'll do more time for tax fraud than the other charges? That's federal time, dickface. No plea bargains. No parole. The IRS doesn't like getting fucked."

"You know what the worst part is, Hoskins?" Joe said. "It's that Danny boy here didn't even make much money from the scam. Mazzone made the money, but Danny's the one gonna take it up the ass in federal prison."

"It's a mistake," Dan Litzki said, puffing out his chest with false bravado. "The girl in the office fucked up. Never happened before."

Healy took the photocopies of the twin tickets from Steve Reggio's box and slid them across the table. "Take plenty of vasoline with you, asshole. Sorry, poor choice of words."

"What's the matter now, Litzki?" Hoskins growled, poking his meaty index finger into the driver's chest. "What was that about a mistake?" Hoskins cupped a hand around his ear. "I'm not hearing nothing."

"Here's the deal," Joe said. "The Suffolk PD don't want you. They want Jimmy Mazzone. Hoskins here wants to know every fucking detail about how he does this, who does what. Everything. You leave out one fucking detail and Hoskins is gonna drop the hammer on you so hard, you won't know what hit you."

"But—"

"But nothing!" Healy screamed. "If you don't flip, there are six other Baseline drivers we can call. In fact, how do you know you're the first driver we've talked to? You don't think one of them is smart enough to trade Mazzone for themselves. Maybe one already did."

"Okay, just let me call in with truck trouble," Litzki said. "This is gonna take awhile."

Hoskins let Litzki get his cell phone, but pressed the muzzle of his weapon to Litzki's neck as a friendly reminder not to warn Mazzone.

"Marie, listen, I'm heading into Lake Grove," Litzki said. "The truck's giving me a little trouble. I'm gonna check it out, so call the stops after the Lake Grove one and tell them I'll be running thirty minutes behind. No, I don't need road service. I can handle it."

Healy copied down everything Dan Litzki said, had him read it, and sign it.

"You mention this to Jimmy or anyone else at Baseline and you're fucked. Understand?" Hoskins asked, but it wasn't a question. "Remember, you have no way of knowing whether we've talked to the other drivers already. This gets back to Jimmy in any—"

"I'm not gonna say a word. You think I'm gonna cut my own throat for Jimmy Mazzone?"

"Get outta here."

"Wait a second," Serpe said, interrupting Hoskins' send off. "Just two more questions."

Litzki blanched. "What?"

"You worked for Jimmy a long time, right?"

"About fifteen years. Why?"

"Any of the other drivers that were killed ever work for Baseline?" Serpe asked.

"The nigger."

"Cameron Wilkes?"

"Uh huh, about eight years ago, but he worked for everybody at one time or another."

"Okay, get the fuck outta here."

When the door closed behind Litzki, he had taken all remaining doubts with him.

"Tomorrow?" Joe said.

"Tomorrow. Healy?"

"Tomorrow."

[Pennysaver]

Thursday's tomorrow was now two yesterdays ago. The world had twice turned and they had gotten what they wanted or what they thought they had wanted; a jagged shard of it anyway. Jimmy Mazzone was dead. But that taste in their mouths with their morning coffees wasn't victory. It wasn't justice and, ultimately, it wasn't even the truth. Those things were sweet and right and warm. For Joe Serpe, Bob Healy, and Tim Hoskins, this was as far from any of that as you could get without teleportation. It was brooding, bitter, empty.

The headline proclaiming the death and the inches of vague half-truths that ran down the column beneath it were hard to take. It was meant to look like suicide. That was their intention all along and suicide is what the cops were calling it, what the press were calling it; a second family tragedy for the Mazzones. It had been an execution, the tragedy of it extending far beyond the boundaries of any one family. What the three men now realized was that even had Jimmy Mazzone acted as they had hoped, like a man instead of a selfish coward, it would still have been an execution. What does it matter who actually pulls the trigger?

Some kid from the reservation spotted Jimmy Mazzone's body caught on the reeds in Poospatuck Creek. It was only a few hundred yards from where Albie Jimenez's truck had been found six weeks earlier. Even from the shore, the kid could see the hole in the top of the dead man's head. The .38, one bullet missing from its cylinder, was found on the opposite shore, where, the cops theorized, Mazzone had knelt down before pulling the trigger and toppling into the water. Jimmy's car was found close by. His wallet, watch, rings, and keys were neatly piled on the driver's seat. There was no note, not in the car, anyway.

It had all come together perfectly. They had him cold, painted into a corner from which he could not retrace his steps nor build out. Jimmy Mazzone called Hoskins early on Friday morning to set up a meet. That part was easy enough. With Joe Serpe and Tim Hoskins' visit to his office to question his wife and daughter; with the photocopies of the pre-stamped tickets from Stevie Reggio's truck left behind in an envelope; with Hoskins' less than subtle shadow in his sideview mirrors, it was understandable that Mazzone had figured he was being set up for blackmail. That's just how Hoskins' played it too. This wasn't about jail time or justice. This would be just another business transaction. Jimmy Mazzone had to believe the bloodletting was done. His mistake.

It didn't take Jimmy long to figure out that he had figured it wrong. Too late to do him any immediate good and he knew it. He saw it in their eyes. They saw it in his. He went along quietly, fooling himself, making the most human of mistakes. He let himself hope. Hope put the bullet in him. Hope was the cruelest thing humans did to themselves. Serpe wondered if Stevie let himself hope before Jimmy put a cap into the back of his head.

"What do you guys want?" Mazzone kept asking Serpe and Hoskins as they drove toward Mastic. Healy followed in Jimmy's car. When they didn't answer him, Jimmy gave them options. "Look, the Gastrol deal is worth millions. I'll split it with you, if that's what you want or I'll just give my business to you. I'll sign it over to you right now and you can take it all. Just let me walk away."

"You wanna walk, huh?" Hoskins said. "Four murders is a lot of blood to walk away from."

At first, Jimmy tried denying it. *He didn't know what they were talking about. They had it all wrong. They were confused.* He could see he was playing to the wrong crowd and shifted from denials to excuses. *It was all an accident. It was a mistake. It was Stevie's fault. Once one was dead, he had to keep killing. He had no choice. If he could undo it, he would.*

"Sign this," Serpe said.

"What is it?"

"It's a full typed confession."

Mazzone balked. "No way."

"You don't sign it, you're fucking dead," Hoskins said.

"He's right, Jimmy. You sign this, we got you by the balls. Whatever we want from you, we know we'll get it because we got this."

"No. You're gonna kill me anyway."

"You just guaranteed it. Pull over, Hoskins," Serpe said, shoving Hoskins' drop piece .38 into Mazzone's ribs. "This place is as good as any for this piece of shit to die."

Mazzone signed the confession. Joe checked the signature to make sure Jimmy hadn't gotten cute. Serpe folded the confession, placed it in an envelope, and flipped it over the seat to Hoskins. They rode in silence for a little while, then Jimmy got talkative.

"It really was Stevie's fault. He just couldn't let it be. Just another two months. Two lousy freakin' months until the lawyers firmed it all up with Gastrol. Toni and him woulda had half a mil as a wedding gift, but no. Outta all the guys in this business my daughter's gotta fall in love with, she had to find St. Stevie. Asshole."

"But how'd you find out about what he was thinking of doing?" Joe asked.

"Show you what a schmuck the kid was, he came to me himself. Told me he'd gotten the phone numbers of the IRS, of Suffolk Weights and Measures, of the DA's office. He said his priest advised him to come to me and ask that I do the right thing, that it was only fair to give me a chance to set things straight. Teach you to listen to a priest.

Priest cut the kid's throat for him."

Now Serpe understood Father Dudek's reaction. The words vengeance and forgiveness rang in Joe's head like untuned bells.

"Good thing it wasn't your daughter that came to you," Hoskins said.

Mazzone looked nauseous after that and didn't seem so talkative anymore, but Joe wasn't quite finished.

"How'd you pick the other drivers?"

"Just tell me how much you want and let me go home."

This time Serpe clicked the hammer back when he stuck the .38 in Mazzone's ribs.

"I picked Wilkes because he was a soft target. One man operation with nobody watching his back. I put in a call from a payphone in a 7/Eleven parking lot. Then all I had to do was wait. Besides, he knew that I'd been double stamping on and off for years. He was one less potential witness. The other two..." he drifted off.

"What about the other two?"

"The Pennysaver."

"What?"

"I looked in the Pennysaver to get numbers," Mazzone said. "You know, the oil page. You run an ad in there every week too. I couldn't kill off everyone who used to work for me. I realized Wilkes was a mistake, that a sharp cop might trace back his work history and connect him to me."

Serpe could see Hoskins screw up his face in the rearview mirror. Tracing work histories wasn't something he'd bothered to do.

"So when you killed Monaco and the other guy you were murdering strangers?"

"Not exactly strangers. I mean, I knew them from the terminal and Lugo's. I recognized their faces, but I didn't know them. That's just who showed up. Luck of the draw, I guess."

"They wouldn't see it that way."

"Big mistake, killing Monaco," Joe said. "That got me interested."

"Maybe, yeah...I guess. He was gonna be my last. My fucking luck!"

That was the end of the conversation until they dragged him out of the car at Poospatuck Creek. Serpe handed the .38 back to Hoskins and Hoskins handed it to Jimmy.

"Go do the right thing," Hoskins said.

That's when the hope went out of Mazzone's eyes. Healy laid it out for him.

"Here's the deal. We got two of your drivers' sworn statements explaining how you pre-stamped tickets for years and how you paid them an extra ten bucks a stop when they used those tickets. With time, they'll all flip. We got your signed confession. Go in there and do yourself," Healy said, pointing at the hard, brown reeds. "The Gastrol sale goes through. Your wife and daughter grieve, but come out rich on the other side and with loving memories of you. You don't go in there and it's gonna get ugly, Jimmy, very fucking ugly.

"First person we show the confession to is gonna be your daughter. How do you think she'll react when she hears her dad murdered her fiancé and three innocent men? I wouldn't count on any Father's Day cards coming to your cell block. Okay, so maybe you are a cold-hearted bastard and you're willing to lose your kid and live the rest of your life in a concrete cell. But we know your wife helped you with the pre-stamps, so she'll do federal time. The IRS doesn't like being cheated. They're funny that way."

Jimmy Mazzone swooned. His legs got rubbery, his eyes rolled up into his head, and he flopped down in a pile. An invisible hand had reached into him and snatched out his skeleton. Worse, when he came to, he was crying. The perfection was gone. Jimmy Mazzone needed killing and he wasn't going to do it himself.

"Get outta here!" Hoskins barked at Healy and Serpe. "Take my car."

"But—"

"No. Out!" He tossed his keys to Serpe. "This is my thing. If I had done my job right to begin with, we wouldn't be here. I can handle this better on my own. Go!"

They drove far enough away to get out of Hoskins' line of sight,

but no further. Having come this far, they could not escape the
fallout by running. The shot echoed through the night, but the
splash of Mazzone's body did not. The weight of a man's sins adds
nothing to the sound of his fall. No porch lights popped on. No
sirens interrupted the background rush of the wind. Gunshots in
the night were not unique on the banks of the Poospatuck.

When Hoskins came back from the creek bank, Serpe picked him
up. If he was looking for a thank you in the cop's expression, he didn't
find it. Killing, even for the right reasons, came at a bigger price than
any of them expected. There was no talk on the ride home. A line
had been crossed from which there was no going back.

[Confessional]

REQUIEM

Hoskins died in June. Healy read it in the Sunday paper and called Serpe about it. The three of them hadn't spoken since just prior to the moment Hoskins walked Mazzone down to the creek that night in late February. What was there to say, really? Murder made for many things, but not for lasting friendships. Hoskins' funeral was sparsely attended and Joe couldn't help but remember the night he'd gone to the funeral home for Rusty Monaco. This was much the same; most of the people present were there out of a sense of obligation. Seemingly few beyond the requisite police honor guard felt obliged. There were no tears.

On their way out, Serpe and Healy ran into Hoskins' former partner, Detective Kramer. Kramer had worked the hose monkey case with Hoskins and they'd parted ways shortly thereafter.

"Tim didn't bring out the best in people. He didn't inspire love. I'm surprised anyone showed up, especially you two," he said, shaking their hands. "I never had anything against you, Serpe, but Christ, Tim just hated you."

"I got my reasons for being here."

"Stupid stubborn prick," Kramer said, shaking his head as the coffin was wheeled toward the hearse. "He just stopped his treatments. The asshole just gave up."

"He must've had his reasons."

Kramer opened his mouth. Nothing came out. He shrugged his shoulders and left.

They found William Burns' body, what was left of it, anyway, in a sand pit out in Rocky Point. When Serpe and Healy first heard about it, they thought that maybe Hoskins had taken his new role as the avenging angel too much to heart. But when the autopsy results were published a few days later, they were relieved to know that it hadn't been Hoskins at all. Burns' broken femur and ankle had never knitted. Apparently his drug running biker buddies liked the color of his money, but not his baggage. The medical examiner said that because there was a lot of sand in his lungs and because his hands were badly mangled that Burns had probably been buried alive. There was a time when that might have made Serpe and Healy feel better. That time had passed. Debbie Hanlon and Hank Noonan were still dead.

The Sunday following Hoskins' funeral, Joe went to church service for the first time since his brother died. He'd only gone then because the FDNY had made the arrangements. He waited around until the church had emptied and the priest was done saying his goodbyes on the front steps.

"Do you remember me, Father Dudek?"

It took the priest a second, but the light of recognition eventually came on.

"The friend of Steven's," he said, unsmiling.

"Something like that, yeah, I was wondering, Father, could you hear my confession?"

Dudek began to make excuses, but he could see in Serpe's eyes that none of the excuses would do. And he had to confess to being curious himself.

"Come with me."

They took their places in the box. Joe felt as comfortable as if he were trying on his coffin for size, but he knew he had to get through it.

"It's been a long time, Father."

"Do you remember the words, my son?"

"As if I could forget. But there's something I wanna talk about first before you hear my confession."

"Certainly."

"These are the names I want to say to you. Khouri and James Burgess, Albie Jimenez, Debbie Hanlon, Hank Noonan, Bogarde Defrees, Edgerin Marsden, Carter Blaylock, Cameron Wilkes, Brian Stanfill, Rusty Monaco, Finnbar McCauly, Stevie Reggio, William Burns, Dave…I forget his last name."

"Many names, my son."

"Names of the dead, Father. All murdered. All sewn from the seeds of one mindless act. I can't understand that."

"It is not important for you to understand it, my son. Have faith that there are reasons beyond our ability or need to understand. It is why we must put our full trust in the Lord Jesus Christ."

"I was a detective for a long time, Father. I have seen many things that would make you physically ill. I arrested a grandmother who sold her thirteen-year-old granddaughter for twenty dollars worth of crack. She stood there and smoked it and watched the dealer and his friends gang rape the girl. I had a little trouble believing there was a higher purpose in that."

The priest was silent.

"I'm ready to confess my sins now, Father."

"Please, my son, go on." Dudek's voice cracked.

"Forgive me, Father, for I have sinned," Serpe rammed ahead, not willing to wait for the priest's mumbled blessing. "It has been too long since my last confession. A few months ago, I helped kill the man who murdered Steve Reggio."

"I don't understand. What do you mean you—"

"You don't need to understand, Father. I just wanted you to know that I helped answer your prayers."

Joe Serpe walked out of the confessional and never looked back.

The next day, the first Monday of summer, envelopes arrived at the offices of the *New York Times, Newsday,* the *Daily News,* and the *Post.* Similar envelopes arrived on the desks of all the local, county, and state prosecutors. There were two letters inside each envelope, both confessions. One was signed by Detective Timothy Hoskins. The other was signed by James Mazzone.

TONY SPINOSA is the pseudonym of Edgar-nominated Reed Farrel Coleman. *The Fourth Victim* is the follow-up to Tony's 2006 novel *Hose Monkey*. Learn more about Reed and Tony at www.reedcoleman.com.